Hall of the Rainbow Mage

Written by:
Patrick Lawinger

Pathfinder Conversion:
Michael Mars Russell

Editors:
W. Kenower, Jeff Harkness

D20 Content Editor:
Scott Greene

Art Director:
Casey Christofferson

Layout
Suzy Moseby

Interior Art:
Santa Norvaisaite, Quentin Soubrouillard, Michael Syrigos

Front Cover Art:
Michael Syrigos

Cartography:
Robert Altbaur

Playtesters:
Nathan White, Andy and Amy White, Jenny "Notdatone" Jones, Scott Wall, Brian Shack, David Cane, Beth and Michael Park, and "Gant Burnedtoes."

Special Thanks:
Thanks to Bill Webb, Clark Peterson, and the entire Necromancer Games staff for making both gaming and writing so much fun. Ryan Dancey for creating the D20 license, enabling such wonderful publishers to exist. Melanie for putting up with my addiction and my boys, Anthony and Alexander for helping me see the wonder of the world through children's eyes.

Necromancer Games
ISBN: 978-1-62283-911-7
PF PoD

Table of Contents

Hall of the Rainbow Mage

By Patrick Lawinger

An adventure for 4 to 6 characters of 7th to 9th level.

Chapter 1: Introduction

The Hall of the Rainbow Mage is a challenging mid-level site-based adventure designed for four to six PCs of 7th to 9th level. Ideal beginning parties should have a total of 28 to 36 levels and be balanced with respect to magic and combat.

While investigating the disappearance of Londar Brightrain, also known as the Rainbow Mage, the party comes across dark, twisted plans and deadly secrets before locating his famous treasures. Treasures found include several new spells along with a few magic items. Unfortunately, the traps and creatures left behind by Londar hamper the party's investigation and other adventurers compete for his famous secrets and treasures.

Londar Brightrain's modest mansion can be placed on a small hill near any village or small town. Hampton Hill, the small town provided, can be replaced with any town or city, but there should be a town relatively close to Londar's home to give the PCs an opportunity to rest and recover during the adventure. Some NPCs described in the chapter detailing Hampton Hill are provided to entice the PCs into investigating Londar's disappearance. If the GM uses different character hooks, these NPCs can be eliminated or used in other ways.

During their investigation, the PCs learn that Londar was killed due to his illicit dealings with the thieves' guild and a rogue baron. His death is related to his discovery of a powerful magical artifact, *Horgrim's Pyramid*, as well as *Korik's Ruby* and *The White Eye*, items required for the pyramid to function. To prevent all the parts from falling into the wrong hands, the PCs must trek to a forgotten temple dedicated to Horgrim, the god of war and magic.

Adventure Background

Londar Brightrain, a powerful wizard known to most as the "Rainbow Mage," is known for his beautiful displays of magical fireworks and complex multicolored illusions during his regular attendance at carnivals and celebrations. What is not commonly known is that his research into newer and more powerful spells led him to tap darker powers by delving into mysterious shadow magic and communicating regularly with demons. Regular communication with these dark powers made him greedy for more wealth and power, leading to the development of plans to conquer a small kingdom for himself. At first, Londar performed patient experiments aimed at somehow generating an army in the laboratory and library he hid deep beneath his modest home amid a network of natural caverns.

While many experiments ended in failure, his constant scrying on the surrounding area helped him locate a forgotten library. One of the books in that library held a key to gaining power, a description of powerful relic known as *Horgrim's Pyramid* and a description of the various items needed to make it function. Londar recognized several of the items instantly, including the pyramid itself, and a massive ruby owned and displayed by a wealthy merchant in distant Bard's Gate. Knowing he could not acquire these items alone, he sought the assistance of a nearby baron just as greedy for power. Using the completed pyramid, Londar and Baron Kurell could conquer the surrounding area with an army of undead shielded from sunlight.

Londar agreed to arrange the "acquisition" of the known items and research the location of the final piece of the pyramid. Baron Kurell agreed to finance the acquisitions. Londar hired a thief named Alfguir K'Eliek to acquire the pyramid and *Korik's Ruby* as well as some additional items he needed for spell components. Londar, though wealthy, needed money from the baron to help fund these efforts. He depended on his reputation and credit to extend payment deadlines until Baron Kurell provided him with the needed money. Unfortunately for Londar, Alfguir and other members of the thieves' guild are not known for their patience. When several members of the guild (sent by Alfguir) cornered him while he was traveling, a short, deadly battle ensued. Londar, though victorious, was poisoned. He teleported into his deepest laboratories but was unable to find an antidote for the poison before it killed him. Londar did not show up for his beloved niece Learah's wedding celebration, something so far out of the ordinary that everyone believes something horrible happened to him.

Before his death, Londar discovered texts and maps that allowed him to identify the location of a relic known as *The White Eye*, the final piece for *Horgrim's Pyramid*. While the ancient texts did not make clear its many functions, Londar determined that it is located in an ancient temple dedicated to Horgrim, the god of war and magic, and is hidden in a hollow mountain less than a week's travel from Hampton Hill. This knowledge, along with the new spells he created, are hidden in his mansion and library. Natural caverns and a number of strange creatures create a series of powerful defenses and deterrents to prevent the discovery of his dark secrets.

Londar's disappearance was immediately noticed when he did not show up for his niece's wedding. His niece, Baron Kurell, members of the thieves' guild, and a number of wizards are very curious about what happened to him, and, more importantly, what happened to his knowledge, spellbooks, and treasure.

Module Organization

The module is organized into several chapters. This chapter provides background information and character hooks designed to get the PCs involved in the adventure. The second chapter provides information about Hampton Hill and NPCs found there — including their motivations and actions. It is imperative for the successful running of this module that GMs spend their time familiarizing themselves with the NPCs and their motivations as detailed in the chapter on Hampton Hill.

Information the PCs gather in Hampton Hill should lead them on a short trek through the wilderness, detailed in **Chapter 3**, on the way to Londar's Mansion, detailed in **Chapter 4**. Information covering an ambush on the return to Hampton Hill, and further information acquired in Hampton Hill after locating Londar's corpse and the evidence he left behind, is found in **Chapter 5**. This information is designed to lead the PCs on a trek to Arn's Mountains and Horgrim's Temple, which are detailed in **Chapters 8** through **11**. Finally, the module closes with a concluding chapter and appendices covering NPCs, monsters, items, and spells discovered throughout the adventure. Monsters and NPCs used a single time have a full statistics block at that location. New creatures and the monsters used in random encounters are listed in **Appendix B: New Monsters**.

Character Hooks

It is presumed that GMs provide their own campaign reasons for the PCs' arrival in Hampton Hill. Perhaps they are just passing through on their way to other locales and simply wish a room for the night. Perhaps they have heard stories of the famous Rainbow Mage and have come to consult him or learn from him. Or perhaps they are friends of Learah Relight or her new husband and have come to offer their congratulations to the new couple. In any event, once the PCs arrive in the village, they can become involved in investigating Londar's disappearance through several different means:

- **Learah Relight**, Londar's young niece and sole relative, is worried about his disappearance and could hire the PCs to investigate. Perhaps the PCs were friends of Learah's (or her husband Trevor) and attended her wedding. The PCs might volunteer to investigate after they see how upset she gets when her uncle doesn't appear.
- **Alfguir K'Eliek**, a wealthy merchant, claims Londar owes him a great deal of money and could hire the PCs to help recover some of the money he is owed.
- **Ander Fierk**, a man claiming to be a simple wizard, offers money for some of Londar's "lost" spells.
- Alternatively, the PCs might become interested in Londar based on rumors of his treasure, magical items, and spells. The GM should plant such rumors about Londar before running this adventure.

GM Notes

Though primarily a site-based dungeon setting, this adventure covers several different types of terrain, so the GM should monitor ropes, light sources, and spells used to overcome various obstacles. The adventure incudes two large dungeons with a majority of the treasure at the end of each dungeon. GMs that include more random encounters might want to adjust rewards appropriately. Some of the treasure provided includes new spells that might not fit into the GM's game world. Other spells the GM considers more appropriate to his or her game world should be substituted.

GMs can adjust the adventure for lower-level parties by removing some of the more difficult encounters and cutting down on random encounters. The adventure can be adjusted for higher-level parties by adding additional encounters, or by adding random encounters with other adventuring parties to prevent easy rest and recovery.

Running the Adventure

Once the PCs arrive in Hampton Hill, the party finds that almost everyone in town is discussing Londar's mysterious disappearance. They should hear many conflicting rumors. Soon after their arrival, the party finds that several different people are looking for someone to investigate Londar's disappearance. It is likely that Alfguir K'Eliek and Learah Relight appeal for the party's assistance, and Ander Fierk makes his own requests whether or not the party hires on with one of them.

Whether or not they hire on with one of those interested individuals, the party realizes they must study the site of Londar's disappearance as well as his mansion in a search for clues. While investigating his mansion and tower — as friends or interested parties, not as looting explorers — they come across a secret entrance to caverns deep underground, caverns that conceal Londar's real laboratories, treasure, and Londar's corpse. Reaching his hidden laboratories requires successfully navigating the creatures and traps Londar left behind to guard his secrets. Careful exploration reveals Londar's dark plans aimed at conquering a small kingdom for himself and uncovers that he had a collaborator. After the adventurers discover Londar's corpse and find some of his hidden treasures, they return to town with their new knowledge only to find another dark deed has been performed.

The party learns that Baron Kurell tortured and left for dead an elven historian named Xanthaque. This cements their conclusion that the baron and Londar planned to conquer the surrounding area together but leads to another mystery. Xanthaque tells the PCs that the baron seeks a powerful relic known as *The White Eye*. Using Londar's books, notes, and maps, she gives the PCs an exact location for Arn's Mountain, a hollow mountain home to a temple that is reportedly the last resting place for *The White Eye*. She begs the PCs to locate the eye and destroy it before her torturers can locate it.

The PCs discover a hollow mountain filled with bright sunlight and the last guardians over an ancient, evil temple that an army was unable to breach thousands of years before. They must work their way through the various traps and treacherous creatures left behind to guard the temple's treasures before obtaining the relic and destroying its evil power.

Chapter 2: Hampton Hill

The town nearest Londar Brightrain's home is Hampton Hill. Hampton Hill is located in an area of rolling hills and light forests beside a deep ravine cut by a swift river. While fairly small, the merchants and nobles who keep vacation homes in and around the town help support the many shops and craftsmen.

HAMPTON HILL
NG Small town

Corruption +0; **Crime** +0; **Economy** +1; **Law** +0; **Lore** +1; **Society** +1
Qualities tourist attraction
Danger +0

DEMOGRAPHICS
Government Autocracy
Population 1,153 (human 89%, halfling 5%, elf 3%, dwarf 1%, gnome 1%, half-elf 1%)

NOTABLE NPCs
Mayor Strybyorn Arthand (male human Aristocrat 3/Expert 7)
Sheriff Hamra Ranthas (female human Fighter 7)
Deputies Anya, Ria, Mik, and Dane (male and female human Fighter 2)
Healer Mara Lighthand (female halfling Cleric of Arn 5)
Innkeeper of The White Boar Inn Baeris Blackoak (female half-elf Bard 1)
Innkeeper of The Red House Viarik Kite (male human Expert 3)
Blacksmith Ebbon Goldaxe (male dwarf Expert 5)
Merchant Kyrean Lane (female human Rogue 11)
Alchemist Maroof Sandwalker (male half-elf Alchemist 8)
Others male and female human Warrior 1 x15 (town and personal guards); male and female human Aristocrat 1-3 (x17); male and female human Rogue 1-4 x15 (thieves' guild)

MARKETPLACE
Base Value 1,200 gp; **Purchase Limit** 5,000 gp; **Spellcasting** 4th
Minor Items 3d4; **Medium Items** 1d6; **Major Items** None

DESCRIPTION
Thanks to Londar Brightrain's spectacular displays of magic, Hampton Hill is known for the fall festival it holds every year. People travel from surrounding areas simply to visit the festival and view Londar's fireworks. Due to the tranquil location, many nobles and wealthy merchants keep vacation homes in and around the area.

RUNNING THE ADVENTURE IN HAMPTON HILL

Much of the adventure centers on this town, its NPCs, and their various motivations. In order to run this adventure, it is imperative that the GM become familiar with the NPCs detailed below, their motivations, and the information they have in their possession. The following basic information is summarized here and then expanded upon in the NPC descriptions below.

THE CURRENT SITUATION REGARDING LONDAR'S DISAPPEARANCE

Preliminary investigations located Londar's overturned carriage on a road outside town with the corpse of his driver and the corpses of several unidentified people in dark clothing. There was no sign of Londar in the wreckage or at his home and there have been no ransom demands or other signs he might be alive.

One week later, Learah visited the mansion with her bodyguards, Sheriff Hamra Ranthas and several town guards. When they arrived, they found that looters already took anything transportable, though in reality these "looters" were members of the thieves' guild hired by Alfguir. A near-fatal encounter with the golems in Londar's Office (See **Londar's Mansion, Area 9**) and a trap on a door into Londar's tower led the sheriff to bring everyone back to town. Despite Learah's pleas for assistance, the sheriff refuses to expend more manpower searching for her uncle.

Such is the current situation as the PCs arrive in Hampton Hill.

The following list summarizes the initial actions of the major NPCs in Hampton Hill regarding adventurers. This list is simply a summary for the GM. Consult **Appendix A: NPCs** for a full description of each NPC's true motivations, information, desires, goals, and future actions.

Learah Relight: Londar, the Rainbow Mage, was Learah's uncle. Learah is disappointed with the sheriff and the town guards and is actively seeking adventurers willing to help search for her uncle. Learah and her guards have a suite at The Red House, and she can be found at The White Boar Inn every evening. When she hears of adventurers in town, she sends a message to them asking for a meeting at one of those locations.

Baron Kurell: The baron was collaborating with Londar and badly desires some of the items hidden somewhere in the mansion. He plays the role of a "family friend" supporting Learah and her efforts to hire adventurers while already having hired some of his own to search the mansion. The baron also has a suite at The Red House and is often found dining in The White Boar Inn or talking to merchants in the square.

Alfguir K'Eliek: Alfguir is not only a senior member of the thieves' guild, he is the specific thief Londar hired to obtain a number of special items. Londar never paid him for his work, using his reputation and promises of new magic items to obtain "credit." Alfguir wants his money and has decided to turn to hiring adventurers to do his dirty work. Alfguir is staying at The White Boar Inn and is found dining there every day. He is willing to contact and meet the adventurers any place in town, and at any time. He plays the role of a wounded merchant who has lost a huge amount of money and is searching for someone to help him recover at least some of his losses.

Ander Fierk: Ander is a wizard interested in Londar's new discoveries regarding golems. Ander wants the spells he knows Londar created, as well as the methods to create his own army of golems. When Ander discovers the PCs are investigating Londar's disappearance, he approaches them and offers great deal of money for the chance to copy some of Londar's spells. He presents himself as a simple wizard in pursuit of knowledge and offers a few potions as a sign of goodwill. Ander has rented a small, private cottage to allow him to watch the PCs through scrying and spying to determine whether or not they find Londar's spellbooks and papers.

Mayor Strybyorn Arthand: Strybyorn (male human **noble**) was once a very successful merchant and businessman and is now mayor of Hampton Hill. He can be found at the Village Hall (**Area 2**) or at his home (**Area 10**).

Sheriff Hamra Ranthas: Hamra (female human **veteran**) and her deputies (male and female human **guards**) can be found at the Village Hall (**Area 2**). She and her deputies discovered Londar's overturned carriage and the body of his driver shortly after his disappearance. She is able to tell the PCs many details (see her description below).

Londar was very important to the town and his recent disappearance has been big news leading to the creation of many rumors, some of them conflicting. The PCs can gather various bits of information either through roleplaying conversations in the local taverns or with the NPCs listed below, or the GM may decide to use Diplomacy checks to determine which rumors the PCs come across. Use the following rumors to provide information to the PCs:

DC	Information
10	A bunch of rather dangerous looking people have come to town, probably to steal the Rainbow Mage's treasure. (True, several groups of adventurers are interested in Londar's spells and treasures)
10	Londar's niece and her new husband are after his fortune. They killed him to inherit his gold. (False)
10	Londar got so busy with his spells that he blew himself up. (False, but a popular rumor)
14	People have been to the Rainbow Mage's house and taken everything out of it already. (Partly true, looters did make it into some of his rooms and have stolen a number of items)
15	Someone or something attacked and killed Londar and his driver along the Horrik Trade Path. (True, but Londar's corpse has not been located)
15	The Rainbow Mage has been toying with demons, one of his spells went wrong, and he fell into the Abyss. (Partly true, he has contacted and summoned demons but didn't fall into the Abyss)
15	Wizards jealous of his power assassinated the Rainbow Mage. (False)
15	Good luck getting anything Londar left behind. His house is full of traps and golems and things. (Partly true, Londar put deadly traps and creatures in his most important rooms but most of the house is unguarded)
18	Londar ran away from town because he owed the thieves' guild a huge amount of money. (Mostly false, Londar did owe the guild a great deal of money but didn't run away)

Aside from the rumors listed above, the PCs can easily learn the location of Londar's mansion as well as directions to the stores and merchants selling any materials they might need to investigate Londar's disappearance. They also hear rumors about "monsters" in the light forest in and around Hampton Hill but a check with any town guard quickly ascertains there have been no attacks in or near the town by creatures of any type for many years.

CONTENTS OF NOBLE AND MERCHANT HOUSES

If the home of a merchant or noble is entered and searched, roll 1d8 on the following table to determine any contents or treasure:

1d8	Result
1–4	A small, locked jewelry chest (the lock can be picked with a successful DC 15 Disable Device check) hidden in a dresser (can be found with a successful DC 20 Perception check) contains jewelry, gems, and coins worth a total of 1d4 x 100 gp.
5–6	A hidden safe (can be found with a successful DC 25 Perception check; lock can be picked with a successful DC 25 Disable Device check) holds a number of papers as well as gold and gems with a total value of 2d4 x 100 gp.
7	A small chest hidden in the bottom of a drawer (can be found with a successful DC 20 Perception check: the lock can be picked with a successful DC 15 Disable Device check) contains a jar of *restorative ointment*.
8	A thick chest (the lock can be picked with a DC 20 successful Disable Device check) holds scrolls with 1d4 1st-level wizard spells and coins with a total value of 5d6 x 10 gp.

Adding works of art or other items to different homes can also give them added flavor. Generally, PCs should be discouraged from robbing villagers. In addition, local law enforcement will pursue the PCs, and the thieves' guild will target them. The guild extorts protection money from the merchants and nobles, and PCs violating that protection is bad for business.

General Locations in Hampton Hill

Common Homes and Cottages

Most of the homes and cottages belong to commoners working for the various merchants and craftsmen in town. Hampton Hill is a relatively wealthy village due to the constant influx of vacationing nobles and merchants so even commoners maintain the appearance of their homes. Some commoners work outside the town on farms or in the surrounding forests. Larger cottages often hold several generations, with beds being bunked along the walls and in lofts of the main room. Commoners have very little hidden money and PCs should be discouraged from stealing what little they might have. Any homes not specifically marked should be considered commoners' homes.

Noble and Merchant Homes

Hampton Hill is a peaceful, relatively safe part of the world surrounded by beautiful forests and peaceful rivers. Nobles and wealthy merchants maintain vacation homes in Hampton Hill and come to relax, hunt, or simply enjoy the scenery. These houses are almost always occupied in summer and during festivals. Whether occupied or not, there is a 50% chance a hired **guard** is present, and an additional 20% chance that a **mastiff**, or other guard animal, is present. While the local thieves' guild isn't large, many merchants and nobles have chosen to pay "protection money." Theft from these homes makes the PCs a target for the local thieves' guild.

While most parties probably refrain from outright theft in town, some PCs might decide to search some of these homes. The GM can create a basic layout with several rooms and use treasure generated on the accompanying table to give the homes more life.

Guard CR 1
XP 400
hp 16 (Pathfinder Roleplaying Game GameMastery Guide, "Caravan Guard")

Mastiff CR 1
XP 400
hp 13 (Pathfinder Roleplaying Game Bestiary, "Dog, Riding")

Keyed Locations in Hampton Hill

1. The Town Square

Various merchants sell their wares during daylight hours at booths placed around the square. Fruit and food items are easy to find here, as are ropes, lanterns, weapons, and other equipment valued less than 100 gp. Two town **guards** are always stationed here during the day and other guards and deputies often wander through to talk to the merchants and ensure everything is going well. While evenings are usually quiet here, sometimes traveling carnivals or bards put on shows during the early evening hours.

Guard (2) CR 1
XP 400
hp 16 (Pathfinder Roleplaying Game GameMastery Guide, "Caravan Guard")

2. The Village Hall

This broad stone building contains offices for Mayor Strybyorn Arthand as well as offices for Sheriff Hamra Ranthas and her deputies. A large courtroom fills the center of the building and small jail cells fill the dungeon below the building. Strybyorn does his best to get all his work done in the morning so he can spend his afternoon talking with the merchants and wandering through town. Hamra or one of her deputies can be found here anytime during the day or night. In addition to guards patrolling through town, as least 4 town **guards** patrol the building at all times. The oak doors leading into the building are virtually always open, even in bad weather.

Guard (4) CR 1
XP 400
hp 16 (Pathfinder Roleplaying Game GameMastery Guide, "Caravan Guard")

3. The Hampton Hill Stables

The large, plain barn has 40 individual stalls that run along the sides of the building with a large open area outside the barn to tether additional animals and store wagons. Pegs and hooks in each stall hold saddles, saddle-bags, and other personal items. The large loft above is stocked with hay and oats and other grains are stored in barrels beside the door. While some pay local people to care for their animals, the stables are well stocked and Sasha Blaine (female human Expert 2) has a reputation as a fine caretaker for animals. Sasha employs two addition stable hands, Radik and Danae (human Commoner 1) and has enough work to keep all three very busy. Between the constant care Sasha and her hands give the animals, and the regular visits by the local militia, personal items left in the stables are generally considered safe. Horse theft is punished by hanging and is extremely rare.

4. Ebbon's Forge

Ebbon Goldaxe (male dwarf Expert 5) works in this large stone building. One of the few stone buildings in the village, it stands out against the backdrop of the small cottages that surround it. Ebbon lives in a small cottage behind the forge. The building itself has a single room that is dominated by the huge forge in the center. Barrels containing oil, water, and salt water are lined up beside an anvil that stands in front of the hot fire while bins containing raw ore and coal line the walls. Ebbon is a very elderly dwarf that refuses to make less than masterwork quality weapons and armor because the nobles and merchants coming through town keep business strong. He is happy to repair armor and sharpen weapons but often tries to convince people to simply purchase something new. Ebbon's last apprentice left to become a blacksmith in another town and he hasn't obtained another. Business is so steady that he hasn't kept up on the gossip about Londar's disappearance.

Children are often found sitting on some of the tables near the front of the building watching Ebbon work, and there is a 30% chance someone has come by to make a purchase. Ebbon closes up at night, boarding windows from the inside and locking the massive oak doors (DC 15 Disable Device check) that lead into the building. He stores 2 suits of chainmail, a set of plate, 2 war axes, 2 longswords, a shortsword, and a bastard sword in a heavy oak chest (DC 15 Disable Device check). All of Goldaxe's work is of the highest quality and although not magical, if well cared for will not break or dull even if roughly used.

N
N
N
Trade Route
N
8
9
N
N
7
2
1
Town
Square
6
3
10
5
4
Horrik
Trade Path
N
N
N
12
11
N
W
E
S
Map 1: Hampton Hill
1 Square =
20 Feet
Trade
Route

5. Kyrean's

A portion of her sign came down in a storm years ago, and Kyrean never felt the need to repair it. Everyone knows **Kyrean Lane** and that she sells a variety of fine goods, but very few people know that she is also the leader of the local thieves' guild. Kyrean sells everything from bolts of silk to fine weapons and leather armor. While she does have a great deal of money, she generally avoids buying anything very expensive from anyone outside a recognized thieves' guild. Although her life as a thief makes her a fence as well, she is smart enough to avoid trying to sell items that were stolen in or near the village. She makes an effort to maintain a stock of rare wines and expensive foods to cater to the tastes of the merchants and nobles that vacation here. Kyrean, a light sleeper, lives in a small room above the store.

A hidden trapdoor behind the counter (found with a DC 20 Perception check) leads down to a small cellar where a variety of items are stored. The various items stored in the cellar and in the store above have a total value over 3000 gp but Kyrean's position in the guild makes any theft a very risky proposition.

6. The White Boar Inn

The White Boar Inn is known for its fine food, excellent wine, wonderful music, and clean rooms. The lower floor of the massive, wood-frame building is filled with a large tavern and a fine restaurant. **Baeris Blackoak** (female half-elf bard 1) runs the inn with the help of her wife **Ivellia** (female human expert 4) and their 3 daughters, **Irena, Karia,** and **Sindria** (female half-elf commoner 1). Baeris has an agreement with the local thieves' guild that provides bouncers and guarantees the safety of her patrons in exchange for regular payments. At least 2 **cutpurses** are in the tavern during working hours. A human troubadour using the name Khenden Bright Sun performs in the tavern every night.

Cutpurse CR ½
XP 200
hp 10 (Pathfinder Roleplaying Game NPC Codex, "Cutpurse")

The restaurant area has subdued lighting and collections of tables and booths that are kept private through the use of carefully-positioned curtains. Despite the thick walls, music, laughter, and loud voices echo in from the tavern area, making the restaurant nearly as loud as the tavern. A long walnut bar lines one wall of the tavern with a stage positioned against the wall opposite it. Wood chairs surround heavy walnut tables throughout the room. The tavern closes in the wee hours and opens again before lunch the following day. As a popular place for gossip and discussion, Knowledge (local) checks to gather information in the tavern receive a +2 circumstance bonus. The restaurant serves breakfast, lunch, and dinner, with dinner being the most popular and crowded meal. It is not unusual to wait hours for a table in the restaurant on busy nights.

Rooms are located on the second floor. Each room is cleaned and checked before and after a customer moves into it to ensure proper maintenance. Doors for each room can be barred from the inside, but there are no other locks to protect valuables left in the room. The walls and floors are very thick, cutting down on most of the sounds from the tavern, but rooms near the stairs still get a great deal of noise.

NPC Notes: Learah Relight and her guards can be found here every evening. When she hears of adventurers in town, she sends a message to them asking for a meeting at one of those locations. **Alfguir K'Eliek** is staying at the inn as well and can be found dining here every day.

7. Ander's Cottage

Ander Fierk rented this cottage mere days after Londar's disappearance became known. Though small and poorly cared for, the cottage is close to the Town Square and the other places Ander frequents in search of rumors about Londar. Ander keeps most of his belongings with him but a small chest (found with a successful DC 15 Perception check, the lock can be picked with a successful DC 20 Disable Device check) hidden beneath the bed contains 200 gp, 38 sp, and 43 cp. Ander is found here only late at night or early in the morning. He spends his day in the Town Square talking to people and simply listening to rumors, while his evenings are spent at The White Boar Inn.

8. Xanthaque's Home

Xanthaque (female elf wizard 7 / loremaster 5), an elderly elven sage, lives in this small home (see **Appendix A: NPCs** for her full statistics). Xanthaque is a historian who spends her time researching a variety of different things, but mostly focuses on events of long ago. Considered a bit "off" by many of the townspeople, she is rarely visited by ordinary travelers. Books line sagging shelves that cling precariously to walls. Windows are boarded over to make more room for more bookcases. The only furniture in the room consists of an old oak desk, a leather chair, and a sofa with sagging cushions. She sleeps on her sofa, when she sleeps at all, and pays one of her neighbors to deliver food to her. Although her power as a witch is often discussed, few people have seen her cast even the tiniest of spells, so she is rarely beset by young wizards searching for new spells or apprenticeship.

9. The Path of Shrines

A small footpath circles through a collection of shrines that look out over the vast ravine and river west of town. These shrines provide the only location for worship because there is no formal temple in town. Each shrine is essentially a statue standing over a small altar where worshippers may put their offerings. Many gods are represented, and GMs are encouraged to include deities from their own campaign world. Two additional shrines — clearly much older than the rest — have been chiseled and broken, leaving little more than a base. While Mara Lighthand (female halfling cleric of Arn 5) worships Arn (see sidebar), she maintains all of the shrines for the gods of good. An elderly priest known only as "Father Rim" (male human cleric of Arn 6 / druid 3) visits town twice a month to perform services at the shrine to Arn and assists Mara with healing while he is in town.

Mara performs services at the shrine to Arn every morning and performs her caretaking duties immediately afterward. During her morning service, 3d6 villagers, mostly women, are usually in attendance. If the shrines are visited in the afternoon, 1d10–1 worshippers might be present performing their own prayers and vigils. While Hampton Hill is a fairly large town, few people in town actively worship the gods, aside from passing worship of Arn. Traveling clerics do come through fairly often, but Mara is the only cleric presently living in Hampton Hill full-time and she considers it her duty to minister to the health of all townspeople as well as any travelers or adventurers.

Arn, Lesser God of the Sun

Alignment: Neutral Good
Domains: Good, Healing, Sun
Favored Weapon: Sickle
Symbol: A radiant half circle of bronze, representing the rising sun
Worshippers: Simple townsfolk, farmers

Arn is commonly depicted as a male figure in glowing yellow and white robes carrying a bronze sun-tipped staff. His priests mimic these garments. Arn has a simple, practical, and undemanding theology and is therefore relatively popular among the common people. His followers shroud the symbol of their god at sunset and celebrate the rise of the sun by removal of that shroud in a short ritual with little formal ceremony, uttering only a prayer of thanks to their god. Unlike other clerics, followers of Arn's spells are renewed once the sun is fully risen at the conclusion of the unshrouding ritual. Arn's clerics must actually witness the sunrise and participate in the unshrouding ritual to regain their spells. Some followers of Arn are druids and it is not uncommon for priests of Arn to have a level or more in that class in addition to cleric levels. Such druid priests may be Chaotic Neutral. His priests are bound to heal anyone who presents themselves for such aid following the rising of the sun. Those in greatest need are treated first. It is believed among Arn's followers that the first rays of the sun ("the fingers of Arn") carry healing qualities. Scholars believe that Arn is a debased and simplified version of the greater sun god, Ra, though worshippers of Arn vehemently disagree.

10. Strybyorn's Home

Mayor Strybyorn Arthand (male human Aristocrat 6) maintains a beautiful, large wood frame home with the help of his servants Miri (female human commoner 2) and Leaf (male half-elf commoner 1). Strybyorn's wife died several years ago and both of his daughters are married and living in distant towns. His servants live in rooms at the back of the home. He is found at home only at night; during the day, he is either wandering the town or in his office in the Village Hall. Walls in his main living room are decorated with rapiers made by different artisans, several worn shields, and tapestries depicting great, glorious battles. The rapiers include 3 rapiers whose ornate designs give them a value of 600 gp but those decorations make them easy to recognize and difficult to fence. He keeps a small chest (found with a DC 12 Perception check, the lock can be picked with a successful DC 10 Disable Device check) in his bedroom that contains jewelry owned by his deceased wife (a diamond pendant worth 1000 gp, a pair of ruby earrings worth 600 gp, and a gold bracelet studded with tiny rubies worth 350 gp).

11. The Red House

Its bright color and prominent location near the center of town easily identify the finest inn in town. Viarik Kite (male human Expert 3) carefully maintains the inn and ensures it is the cleanest in town. Despite the size of the wood frame building, the inn has only 7 rooms, but each room has three bedrooms connecting to a large sitting area. The inn caters specifically to wealthy merchants and nobles visiting Hampton Hill on short vacations. While Viarik usually has one or two suites free, he refuses to lower his prices for fear it might hurt his reputation. Ornate wool rugs lining the oak floors and thick plaster walls cut down on sound, making all the rooms here quiet, peaceful, and very private. The Red House does not serve food, but servants willing to go obtain food from a local restaurant are always available. At any one time, Viarik has at least two people cleaning rooms and responding to customers' needs (male and female human commoner 1) and is always willing to hire more if the need arises.

NPC Notes: Learah Relight and her guards have a suite at The Red House. When she hears of adventurers in town, she sends a message to them asking for a meeting at one of those locations. **Baron Kurell** and his people also have a suite here.

12. Maroof's Elixirs

Maroof Sandwalker (male half-elf alchemist 8) lives in this small, quaint home, along with all the pottery and glassware he uses to make his products. Maroof is an odd half-elf who has taken a vow of silence. He communicates through simple signs and written messages. The small cottage is packed with shabby furniture, and various clay vases and glass vials line the shelves that cling precariously to the walls. A large cauldron stands over a fire in the center of the room. Maroof sells *potions of cure light wounds, cure moderate wounds, bull's strength, cat's grace, and remove curse*. While the carious clay jars and vials along the shelves at the back of his home clearly contain potions, only he knows what each potion is. Persistent rumors that his poisons are mixed in among the potions have kept away thieves. A small clay box hidden beneath the fire (found with a DC 25 Perception check) holds 500 gp in gold and gems.

13. Additional Shops and Information

Hampton Hill's economy is based mostly on trade, travel, and vacationers, along with minor dependence on grain farming and nearby orchards. It is a convenient stop for trade caravans and a pleasant vacation location. A number of additional smaller stores and merchants not listed here can provide any of the standard goods, services, and weapons.

CHAPTER 3: WILDERNESS

TRADE PATH ENCOUNTERS

Roll 1d20 for every 30 minutes:

1d20	Encounter
1	Medium-size merchant caravan with 3 wagons, 6 **guards**, and 1 **merchant**.
2–4	Small guard patrol, 4 **guards** and 1 **veteran** on warhorses.
5	Large caravan, 6 wagons, 10 **guards**, 1 **veteran**, and 3 **merchants**.
6	Heavily armed guard patrol consisting of 4 **guards**, 2 **veterans**, and 1 **captain** on warhorses.
7–20	No encounter.

Captain CR 6
XP 2,400
hp 57 (Pathfinder Roleplaying Game GameMastery Guide, "Watch Captain")

Guard CR 1
XP 400
hp 16 (Pathfinder Roleplaying Game GameMastery Guide, "Caravan Guard")

Merchant CR 5
XP 1,600
hp 31 (Pathfinder Roleplaying Game GameMastery Guide, "Traveling Merchant")

Veteran CR 3
XP 800
hp 34 (Pathfinder Roleplaying Game GameMastery Guide, "Guard Officer")

Warhorse CR 2
XP 600
hp 19 (Pathfinder Roleplaying Game Bestiary, "Horse, Heavy (combat trained)")

TRAVEL TO LONDAR'S MANSION

Londar's mansion is a little way northeast of Hampton Hill and is surrounded by the Horrik Forest, a light forest dotted with rocky ravines and gullies that is relatively easy to travel through. The easiest and safest route to the mansion heads east along the Horrik Trade Path until it reaches the dirt road leading to the mansion. Heavily used by merchant caravans and travelers, the wide cobblestone Horrik Trade Path is constantly patrolled and is generally free of bandits and other dangerous creatures. The dirt road leading to the mansion is wide enough for a single wagon or cart and has no patrols or guards to speak of. Looters who have already been to the mansion avoid the trade path due to its patrols and because there are shorter routes to Hampton Hill through the forest. Horrik Forest is home to creatures and people who avoid the patrols along the trade path as well as the "civilized" realm of Hampton Hill. Most of these creatures do their best to protect their own territories without becoming known by the guards that patrol the trade path and nearby town.

If the PCs travel along the trade path, it is likely they meet a merchant caravan or a patrol of guards but nothing particularly hazardous. The dirt road to the mansion is generally safe as well.

The first time the PCs are approached by a guard patrol, they are asked their business. The looting of Londar's mansion is appalling to many of the guards, and they do their best to prevent more damage without shirking their other duties. If the PCs are investigating Londar's disappearance for **Learah Relight** or **Alfguir K'Eliek**, the guards question them briefly and then leave them about their business.

Once guards know the PCs are on "official business," further encounters with patrols involve waving hands or nodding heads as the patrol rides past. If the PCs do not have a clear reason for traveling along the path or if they are in possession of goods taken from the mansion, they are questioned more closely, and eyed with suspicion each time they meet a patrol.

No random encounters occur along the dirt road to Londar's mansion, but the GM might choose to use a few encounters from the Horrik Forest encounters.

A. THE CRASH SITE

Bent branches and several crushed saplings mark the site where Londar's carriage was discovered. Hamra Ranthas and her deputies removed the carriage, bodies, and any other evidence they found and took it back to Hampton Hill. Wheel depressions in the soft earth off the cobblestone road suggest the wagon was moving very fast when it crashed. With a successful DC 13 Perception check, anyone can notice scorch marks on the stone road approximately 600 feet away. When thieves tried to halt the carriage, Londar set off a spell to scare them away. The flash of fire he created spooked the horses and caused them to run out of control. Once the carriage crashed, the thieves set upon Londar and his driver. The battle was brief but Londar was injured enough to trigger a contingency that *teleported* him back into his private laboratories (**Area 29**).

Searching with a successful DC 20 Perception check turns up several empty poison vials and 7 crossbow bolts that Hamra and her deputies missed. While the exact poison left in the vials is impossible to identify, the empty vials are marked with a skull and crossbones that clearly indicate what they once contained. The crossbow bolts are the work of Ebbon Goldaxe, as can be determined by anyone who makes a DC 15 Knowledge (local) check.

WILDERNESS ENCOUNTERS

Once the party is a mile or more away from the trade path, roll 1d20 for every additional 30 minutes of travel through the forest. Each encounter should be used once, if at all. A roll indicating a previously defeated encounter results in a result of "No encounter."

1d20	Encounter
1–2	A group of 6 **kobolds** attempts to ambush the party but flee when they realize the party's strength. They can be tracked back to their small lair with a successful DC 11 Survival check, where an additional 12 **kobolds** reside. They have standard treasure, to be determined by the GM.
3	**Byorik** comes from behind a group of trees and attempts to speak with the party (see **Area B**).
4–5	The party notices several humanoid figures in dark clothing fleeing farther into the forest.
6	A **griffin** drops from the sky to attack any horses or pack animals the party might have with them. If no such animals are present, the party notices the griffin flying over the forest in a hunting pattern.
7	**Ilariak** stands in the party's path (see **Area C**).
8	Two **trolls** attempt to ambush the party.
9–20	No encounter.

Griffon CR 4
XP 1,200
hp 42 (Pathfinder Roleplaying Game Bestiary, "Griffon")

Kobold CR ¼
XP 100
hp 5 (Pathfinder Roleplaying Game Bestiary, "Kobold")

Troll CR 5
XP 1,600
hp 63 (Pathfinder Roleplaying Game Bestiary, "Troll")

Map 2: Wilderness Map

B. Byorik's Cave (CR 7)

Byorik lives in a small cave set into the side of a hill surrounded by tall oak trees. Stone benches in the cave circle a small table, and a fire toward the back of the cave heats a large cauldron. While most trolls would have strange, bloody trophies throughout their lairs, Byorik's home is decorated with weavings made of different grasses and branches found throughout the forest. The art, while rough and abstract, is very easy on the eye and makes the cave feel warm and peaceful. Stone shelves hold clay pots containing various herbs and spices that Byorik uses for his potions and cooking. A successful DC 15 Perception check turns up a few potions stored on the shelves, including a *potion of speak with animal*, a *potion of cure moderate wounds*, and a *potion of water breathing*.

Description and Personality: Byorik, though a troll, met a druid in his youth, a druid that taught him many things and helped alter his outlook on life. Byorik knows that few creatures could understand or believe his fresh outlook on nature. He stays away from the trade path but the increased traffic through the forest by looters disturbs him greatly. He tries to stay away from people moving through the forest unless they are disturbing the forest or invading his home.

Byorik　　CR 7
XP 3,200
Troll druid 4
CN Large humanoid (giant)
Init +1; **Senses** darkvision 60 ft., low-light vision, scent; Perception +25
AC 15, touch 10, flat-footed 14 (+1 Dex, +5 natural, -1 size)
hp 105 (10d8+60); regeneration 5 (acid or fire)
Fort +15, **Ref** +4, **Will** +10; +4 vs. fey and plant-targeted effects
Speed 30 ft.
Melee bite +12 (1d8+6), 2 claws +12 (1d6+6)
Space 10 ft.; **Reach** 10 ft.
Special Attacks rend (2 claws, 1d6+9), wild shape 1/day
Druid Spells Prepared (CL 4th; concentration +6)
　2nd—barkskin, fog cloud[D], resist energy, summon nature's ally II
　1st—calm animals (DC 13), entangle (DC 13), faerie fire, goodberry[D], obscuring mist
　0 (at will)—detect magic, detect poison, know direction, purify food and drink (DC 12)
　D Domain spell; Domain Weather (Seasons domain subdomain)
Str 23, **Dex** 12, **Con** 23, **Int** 10, **Wis** 14, **Cha** 8
Base Atk +7; **CMB** +14; **CMD** 25
Feats Alertness, Brew Potion, Intimidating Prowess, Iron Will, Skill Focus (Perception)
Skills Acrobatics +1 (+6 to make high or long jumps), Handle Animal +11, Intimidate +11, Knowledge (nature) +15, Perception +25, Sense Motive +4, Survival +4
Languages Common, Druidic, Giant
SQ nature bond (Seasons domain), nature sense, trackless step, untouched by the seasons, wild empathy +3, woodland stride
Combat Gear potion of haste; **Other Gear** ring of jumping
Special Abilities
Untouched by the Seasons (4 hours, 5/day) (Su) As per Endure Elements

Combat Tactics: Byorik prefers talking to fighting, but when he does fight, he uses all his natural abilities. Byorik casts *barkskin* on himself before openly greeting anyone in the forest. If PCs willingly to talk to such a creature, he directs them to Ilariak and to the mansion. He also lets them know that a number of "people" have been going through the forest lately, many of them carrying things. He knows nothing about Londar or what happened to him. If the PCs attack Byorik, they find themselves facing a powerful, spell-casting troll with fire resistance. He uses his *entangle* spell to slow down PCs and casts *faerie fire* to keep them in view. Overly aggressive or dangerous PCs trigger Byorik's chaotic nature and he does his best to kill them all.

C. Small Field (CR 8)

A **lammasu** named **Ilariak** makes her home in this small grassy field. Now covered with dirt and grass, this area was once home to a small temple. While the temple may be forgotten by most, the area here is still *hallowed* and provides a comfortable home for Ilariak who sleeps out in the open. Ilariak noticed looters passing through the forest and increased her patrols through the forest. She is usually gone during the day.

Description and Personality: Ilariak has a light tan humanoid face with a large, flat nose surrounded by a leonine mane. Long scars acquired in a battle with a young dragon mar the left side of her pale golden body. Ilariak admires Byorik's ability to overcome his trollish heritage but doesn't openly admit it. She attacks evil heritage and punishes evil actions with single-minded ferocity. She does regular patrols through the forest but has increased them lately after noticing looters moving through the forest. -

Ilariak　　CR 8
XP 4,800
Lammasu
LG Large magical beast
Init +5; **Senses** darkvision 60 ft., low-light vision; Perception +15
Aura magic circle against evil (20 ft.)
AC 21, touch 10, flat-footed 20 (+1 Dex, +11 natural, -1 size)
hp 94 (9d10+45)
Fort +11, **Ref** +9, **Will** +8
Speed 30 ft., fly 60 ft. (average)
Melee 2 claws +14 (1d8+6), 2 wings +9 (1d6+3)
Space 10 ft.; **Reach** 5 ft.
Special Attacks pounce, rake (2 claws +14, 1d8+6)
Spell-Like Abilities (CL 9th; concentration +11)
　3/day—greater invisibility
　1/day—dimension door
Oracle Spells Known (CL 7th; concentration +9)
　3rd (4/day)—cure serious wounds, invisibility purge
　2nd (7/day)—bull's strength, cure moderate wounds, hold person (DC 14)
　1st (7/day)— bless water (DC 13), cure light wounds, detect evil, divine favor, shield of faith
　0 (at will)—create water, detect magic, mending, purify food and drink (DC 12), read magic, resistance, stabilize
Str 23, **Dex** 12, **Con** 21, **Int** 16, **Wis** 17, **Cha** 14
Base Atk +9; **CMB** +16; **CMD** 27 (31 vs. trip)
Feats Blind-fight, Eschew Materials[B], Improved Initiative, Iron Will, Lightning Reflexes, Power Attack
Skills Diplomacy +11, Fly +11, Knowledge (arcana) +12, Perception +15, Sense Motive +12
Languages Celestial, Common, Giant

Combat Tactics: Ilariak casts *detect evil* before boldly approaching anyone she notices wandering the forest. She attacks evil creatures as soon as they are identified but is willing to speak with good or neutral characters. She uses *greater invisibility* and enters into melee combat, saving her other spells and abilities for use if the battle goes against her. If forced to, Ilariak flies above her opponents and casts spells down at them. As a last resort, Ilariak uses *dimension door* to escape. Ilariak recruits Byorik (**Area B**) to assist her if a party is too powerful for her alone.

D. Londar's Mansion

The tip of the tower of Londar's Mansion is visible through the light forest from quite a distance, though the mansion is visible only when the party is several hundred feet from the door. Londar built his modest home and adjoining tower on a low hill somewhat outside town. It is slightly more than half a day's travel by foot and several hours on horseback, so it is easy to scout the home and return to town the same evening. See the following chapters for more details on Londar's Mansion, tower, and the caves beneath.

Traveling to Arn's Mountain

Later in the adventure, once the characters learn information from exploring Londar's Mansion and their investigation into his death, they need to travel to Arn's Mountain. Though such travel will not occur in the adventure until after the PCs visit the areas detailed in the following chapters, the wilderness areas regarding Arn's Mountain are detailed in this chapter for completeness.

The journey to Arn's Mountain is far more arduous and dangerous than the short trip to Londar's Mansion. Once the PCs travel over the small river west of Hampton Hill, they find themselves in a rough, wild area consisting of thick forest broken by large rocky hills. Vast armies once fought great battles here, and the release of powerful spells broke open the very ground and left behind scars that still exist today. A rare woodsman might be encountered here.

Wilderness Encounters West of the River

Once the party is a mile or more from the river, roll 1d20 for every additional hour of travel. Each encounter should be used once, if used at all. A roll indicating a previously defeated encounter results in a result of "No encounter."

1d20	Encounter
1–2	The party notices an orcish war party (10 **orcs**) studying them from a distant hill.
3	Three **trolls** attack the party.
4–5	The party notices a dragon circling above a distant hill (not a combat encounter).
6	A **roc** swoops down on the party and attempts to grab a horse, with or without its rider.
7	A **young green dragon** attacks the party.
8	The party notices a cave. As they near it, a **behir** protecting its lair attacks them. The behir has standard treasure to be generated by the GM.
9–10	Two **night hags** ambush the party.
11–12	Two **hill giants** ambush the party in a narrow pass. They can be tracked back to their lair with a successful DC 14 Survival check. The lair contains standard treasure for such creatures to be generated by the GM.
13–20	No encounter.

Behir CR 8
XP 4,800
hp 105 (Pathfinder Roleplaying Game Bestiary, "Behir")

Green Dragon (Young) CR 8
XP 4,800
hp 85 (Pathfinder Roleplaying Game Bestiary, "Dragon, Green (Young)")

Hill Giant CR 7
XP 3,200
hp 85 (Pathfinder Roleplaying Game Bestiary, "Giant, Hill")

Night Hag CR 9
XP 6,400
hp 92 (Pathfinder Roleplaying Game Bestiary, "Hag, Night")

Orc CR 1/3
XP 135
hp 6 (Pathfinder Roleplaying Game Bestiary, "Orc, Common")

Roc CR 9
XP 6,400
hp 120 (Pathfinder Roleplaying Game Bestiary, "Roc")

Troll CR 5
XP 1,600
hp 63 (Pathfinder Roleplaying Game Bestiary, "Troll")

E. Uvear's Camp (CR 8)

A peaceful **stone giant** outcast from his clan camps here. Uvear has untapped, untrained sorcerous powers that lead to the release of great waves of magical energy when he gets very emotional, even in his dreams. After several disasters, he was asked to leave the clan. He camps here in hopes of coming to terms with his strange powers and odd dreams. Uvear's camp is at the base of Arn's Mountain, and he has investigated several caves leading to the brightly-lit cavern inside. He is afraid to enter the mountain because he isn't entirely sure it isn't simply a vision brought on by his special "madness."

Description and Personality: Uvear is a surprisingly gentle, friendly stone giant. His hairless head and thin features make him appear quite a bit older than he actually is. For a stone giant, Uvear is barely into puberty. He is extremely shy and wary, warning strangers away because he is cursed. More frightened of hurting someone else than of being hurt, he stands a safe distance away from visitors and maintains a stony calm. He forces calmness upon himself in an effort to keep things from bursting into flames or exploding around him. Things have gotten so bad lately that he is afraid of sleeping; nightmares sometimes result in catastrophe. These strange powers and occurrences weigh heavily on his mind, making bad dreams all the more likely when he does sleep. Uvear's loneliness generally overcomes his fear of hurting people. He hasn't spoken to anyone for several weeks, during which his strange powers have begun to torture him.

If the PCs speak calmly to Uvear, they stand a good chance of recognizing the changes he is going through with a successful DC 13 Knowledge (Arcana) check. Once recognized, any PC wizard or sorcerer can give Uvear hints on how to grasp and control his powers. Uvear is immensely relieved to discover his powers can be controlled and that the gods didn't curse him. If the PCs help Uvear in this manner, he tells them about several caves that lead into a "sun cave" and offers to guard their pack animals for them. He is still afraid to travel with, or stay close to, other people until he has control of his abilities.

Uvear CR 8
XP 4,800
Unique Stone giant
N Large humanoid (giant)
Init +2; **Senses** darkvision 60 ft., low-light vision; Perception +12
AC 27, touch 11, flat-footed 25 (+4 armor, +2 Dex, +12 natural, -1 size)
hp 102 (12d8+48)
Fort +12, **Ref** +6 (+4 to catch a thrown rock), **Will** +7
Defensive Abilities improved rock catching
Speed 40 ft. (30 ft. in armor)
Melee +1 stone greatclub +17/+12 (2d8+13) or 2 slams +11 (1d8+4)
Ranged rock +6/+1 (1d8+12)
Space 10 ft.; **Reach** 10 ft.
Special Attacks rock throwing (180 ft.)
Str 27, **Dex** 15, **Con** 19, **Int** 10, **Wis** 12, **Cha** 10
Base Atk +9; **CMB** +18; **CMD** 30
Feats Iron Will, Martial Weapon Proficiency (greatclub), Point-Blank Shot, Power Attack, Precise Shot, Quick Draw
Skills Climb +9, Intimidate +12, Perception +12, Stealth +1 (+9 in rocky terrain); Racial Modifiers +8 Stealth in rocky terrain
Languages Common, Giant
SQ uncontrolled sorcerous powers
Other Gear hide armor, stone greatclub, amulet of natural armor +1
Special Abilities
Uncontrolled Sorcerous Powers (Su) Uvear has sorcerous powers he does not understand. Presently, his powers manifest in two ways. First, any weapon he holds glows and is treated as a magic weapon and gains a +1 bonus to hit and damage. Second, if under stress, a random object or creature bursts into flames for 1d6 fire damage.

Tactics: Uvear's powers caused enough catastrophes that he was outcast from his own home. If attacked, he simply flees into the mountains as fast as he can; he has no desire for combat or further destruction. If cornered, he fights to clear a path to escape and does so at the first opportunity.

F. Arn's Mountain

This mountain has not been identified as "Arn's Mountain" for generations. Only the books, notes, and knowledge from Xanthaque allow an easy identification of the gray, jagged-tipped mountain as "Arn's Mountain." A great cleft runs down the center of the peak of the mountain. Those who camp on the west side of the mountain first see the sun through the cleft; those who camp on the east side notice that their last view of the sun as it sets is through the cleft. Numerous caves lead into the mountain's hollow interior; it takes a very short amount of scouting to discover several different routes inside. The mountain is detailed further in **Chapter 7: Arn's Mountain**.

Chapter 4: Londar's Mansion and Tower

One would expect a wizard with Londar's reputation to have a home quite a bit larger, or, at the very least, more colorful than Londar's relatively simple mansion. The house itself has only one floor, though each room has a 20-foot ceiling. The tower at the back of his mansion rises to a peak more than 90 feet above the foundation and can be seen above the trees from over a mile away on a clear day. Londar chose this site for his simple home due to its position above a series of natural caverns.

Walls of the mansion are made of gray granite obtained from a local quarry and are fairly unremarkable. Dwarves consider the stonework solid, but unimaginative and unskilled.

Stained-Glass Windows: All the main rooms on the bottom floor (**Areas 2–8**) had beautiful stained-glass windows that looters broke to provide easy access to the building. Fragments of the stained-glass windows that once colored the gray stone walls remain in many of the window frames, but it appears that almost every window has been broken. Destruction of the windows provides a hint of the looting that has gone on since Londar's disappearance, as well as another sign that something terrible must have happened to him. Only the windows to area **9**, which have been magically enchanted, remain unbroken.

Lighting in the Mansion: Balls of glass with *continual flame* spells provide steady illumination throughout all the main rooms (**Areas 2–9**).

Entering the Mansion: The PCs can enter the home through the front door or by walking through one of the broken windows.

The Corpse on the Porch: A dark-robed thief attempted to pick the lock on the front door (**Area 1**). The corpse lies in a heap on the low steps before the front door. Decay makes the exact cause of death impossible to determine. Looters going through the mansion also picked clean the unfortunate thief's corpse. A search of the decaying body turns up nothing. A successful DC 11 Knowledge (Nature) or Heal check determines the corpse is about 6 days old, meaning the thief died several weeks after Londar disappeared.

1. The Front Door (CR variable)

The massive front door is made of solid oak boards surrounding an iron core. It has a delicate, well-constructed lock that is magically warded. The front door is the only entrance to the mansion that remains unbroken. The oak door can be unlocked with one of several specifically warded silver keys that Londar created. One of these keys can be obtained from **Learah Relight**.

Trap: The door inflicts a powerful electrical shock on anyone attempting to open the lock without the proper key. The trap does not come into play if the PCs obtained the key from **Learah Relight** or enter through a broken window.

Heavy Oak Door: 5 in. thick; Hardness 8; hp 80; Break DC 27; Disable Device DC 30

Electricity Arc Trap CR 4
XP 1,200
Type magical; **Perception** DC 25; **Disable Device** DC 20
EFFECTS
Trigger touch; **Reset** automatic
Effect electricity arc (4d6 electricity damage, DC 20 Reflex save for half damage); multiple targets (all targets in a 30-ft. line)

2. A Large Entry Hall

Fragments of the windows that once flanked the front door intermingle with pieces of a porcelain vase that someone dropped. The only items remaining in the entry hall, or the coat closet in the southern wall, are large pieces of furniture that couldn't be easily carried away. Blank spots on the walls indicate that even the paintings were stolen. The hallway door to the east has been left open to provide a clear view of the hallway, but the door in the north wall remains closed. The closed door is unlocked and leads into the **Servants Quarters (Area 3)**. A PC noticing the gouges in the wood-paneled inner walls might easily surmise that the looters were in a huge hurry to grab everything they could and leave before being discovered.

Ambush: Note that the three rascals in **Area 3** are most likely observing the PCs as they enter this room and may take action against them. See the **Combat Tactics** section of **Area 3**.

Treasure: Searching the area carefully (with a successful DC 20 Perception check) turns up a secret panel in the northern wall that slides down to reveal a compartment holding a light crossbow and several bolts. The light crossbow has ornate carvings on the stock along with delicate silver inlays, as well as 18 crossbow bolts.

Map 3: Hall of the Rainbow Mage

1 Square - 5 Feet

1st Level

2nd Level

3rd Level

4th Level

The Servant Quarters (CR 8)

Looters ransacked the small servants' quarters as effectively as the rest of the home. Several cots are turned on their sides, and the mattresses are slashed. Fragments of a broken wood chest cover the room along with small fragments of colored glass. Londar hired live-in servants and guards only when guests were staying with him. Londar placed great value on his privacy and generally had a coach drive the few cooks and food servers he did use back and forth to town.

Three adventurers hired by Baron Kurell hide in this room. Injured in a recent encounter with the wood golem in **Londar's Bedroom (Area 7)**, they finished resting and healing before hearing the PCs stepping on the broken glass on the floor of the **Entry Hall (Area 2)**. Already prepared to battle the wood golems in the office and bedroom, they instead prepare an ambush when they hear the PCs in the other room. If the PCs bypass this room, the looters wait until they are in the **Dining Room (Area 5)** and ambush them there.

Celadra   CR 4
XP 1,200
Human wizard 5
CN Medium humanoid (human)
Init +6; **Senses** Perception +1
AC 13, touch 13, flat-footed 11 (+1 deflection, +2 Dex)
hp 33 (5d6+15)
Fort +2, **Ref** +3, **Will** +5
Speed 30 ft.
Melee mwk dagger +3 (1d4/19-20)
Ranged mwk dagger +5 (1d4/19-20)
Special Attacks hand of the apprentice (7/day)
Wizard Spells Prepared (CL 5th; concentration +9)
  3rd—flame arrow, lightning bolt (DC 17)
  2nd—cat's grace, resist energy, web (DC 16)
  1st—burning hands (DC 15), burning hands (DC 15), mage armor, magic missile
  0 (at will)—dancing lights, daze (DC 14), detect magic, read magic
Str 10, **Dex** 14, **Con** 13, **Int** 18, **Wis** 12, **Cha** 8
Base Atk +2; **CMB** +2; **CMD** 14
Feats Brew Potion, Combat Casting, Craft Wondrous Item, Improved Initiative, Scribe Scroll, Toughness
Skills Appraise +10, Craft (alchemy) +12, Knowledge (arcana) +12, Knowledge (dungeoneering) +8, Knowledge (engineering) +8, Knowledge (geography) +8, Knowledge (history) +8, Knowledge (local) +8, Knowledge (nature) +8, Knowledge (nobility) +8, Knowledge (planes) +12, Knowledge (religion) +12, Spellcraft +12
Languages Abyssal, Celestial, Common, Draconic, Infernal
SQ arcane bond (wand of magic missile)
Combat Gear potion of cat's grace, potion of cat's grace, scroll of lightning bolt, summon monster ii (CL 5th), web (x2) (CL 5th), wand of magic missile; **Other Gear** mwk dagger, ring of protection +1, wizard spellbook, 43 gp, 97 sp, 32 cp
Special Abilities
Hand of the Apprentice (7/day) (Su) As a standard action, throw melee weapon (use Int instead of Dex) and instantly returns.

Krybern   CR 3
XP 800
Human unchained rogue 4
NE Medium humanoid (human)
Init +8; **Senses** Perception +7
AC 18, touch 14, flat-footed 14 (+3 armor, +4 Dex, +1 shield)
hp 26 (4d8+8)
Fort +2, **Ref** +8, **Will** +3
Defensive Abilities danger sense +1, evasion, uncanny dodge
Speed 30 ft.
Melee mwk dagger +8 (1d4+1/19-20) or
  mwk rapier +9 (1d6+4/18-20)
Ranged mwk composite shortbow +8 (1d6+1/×3) or
  mwk dagger +8 (1d4+1/19-20)
Special Attacks sneak attack (unchained) +2d6
Str 12, **Dex** 18, **Con** 13, **Int** 14, **Wis** 10, **Cha** 8
Base Atk +3; **CMB** +4; **CMD** 18
Feats Improved Initiative, Iron Will, Shield Proficiency, Weapon Finesse, Weapon Focus (rapier)
Skills Acrobatics +11, Appraise +9, Climb +8, Disable Device +13, Escape Artist +11, Knowledge (dungeoneering) +9, Knowledge (local) +9, Perception +7, Sleight of Hand +11, Stealth +11, Swim +8
Languages Common, Elven, Halfling
SQ debilitating injury: bewildered, debilitating injury: disoriented, debilitating injury: hampered, rogue talents (bleeding attack +2, weapon training), trapfinding +2
Combat Gear potion of cat's grace, potion of cure light wounds, potion of cure light wounds, potion of cure light wounds, potion of delay poison; **Other Gear** mwk studded leather, mwk buckler, arrows (20), mwk composite shortbow (+1 Str), mwk dagger, mwk dagger, mwk dagger, mwk rapier, 43 gp, 43 sp, 22 cp
Special Abilities
Bleeding Attack +2 (Ex) Sneak attacks also deal 2 bleed damage/round.
Debilitating Injury: Bewildered -2/-4 (Ex) Foe who takes sneak attack damage takes AC pen (more vs. striker) for 1 rd.
Debilitating Injury: Disoriented -2/-4 (Ex) Foe who takes sneak attack damage takes attack pen (more vs. striker) for 1 rd.
Debilitating Injury: Hampered (Ex) Foe who takes sneak attack damage has speed halved (and can't 5 ft step) for 1 rd.

Violet   CR 5
XP 1,600
Halfling fighter 2/unchained rogue 4
NE Small humanoid (halfling)
Init +8; **Senses** Perception +11
AC 18, touch 15, flat-footed 14 (+2 armor, +4 Dex, +1 shield, +1 size)
hp 37 (6 HD; 4d8+2d10+8)
Fort +7, **Ref** +10, **Will** +3 (+3 vs. fear)
Defensive Abilities danger sense +1, evasion, uncanny dodge
Speed 20 ft.
Melee +1 rapier +10 (1d4+5/18-20), mwk dagger +9 (1d3/19-20) or
  +1 rapier +12 (1d4+5/18-20) or
  mwk dagger +11 (1d3/19-20)
Ranged mwk shortbow +11 (1d4/×3) or
  mwk dagger +11 (1d3/19-20)
Special Attacks sneak attack (unchained) +2d6
Str 10, **Dex** 18, **Con** 14, **Int** 13, **Wis** 10, **Cha** 10
Base Atk +5; **CMB** +4; **CMD** 18
Feats Combat Reflexes, Improved Initiative, Two-weapon Defense, Two-weapon Fighting, Weapon Finesse, Weapon Focus (rapier)
Skills Acrobatics +15 (+11 to jump), Appraise +11, Climb +11, Disable Device +17, Escape Artist +13, Knowledge (dungeoneering) +6, Knowledge (engineering) +6, Knowledge (local) +6, Perception +11, Sleight of Hand +8, Stealth +17, Swim +4, Use Magic Device +9; **Racial Modifiers** +2 Acrobatics, +2 Climb, +2 Perception
Languages Common, Elven, Gnome, Halfling
SQ debilitating injury: bewildered, debilitating injury: disoriented, debilitating injury: hampered, rogue talents (hairpin trick, surprise attacks), trapfinding +2
Combat Gear potion of cat's grace, potion of cure moderate wounds; **Other Gear** +1 rapier, arrows (20), mwk dagger, mwk dagger, mwk dagger, mwk dagger, mwk shortbow, bracers of armor +2, cloak of resistance +1, ring of climbing
Special Abilities
Debilitating Injury: Bewildered -2/-4 (Ex) Foe who takes sneak attack damage takes AC pen (more vs. striker) for 1 rd.
Debilitating Injury: Disoriented -2/-4 (Ex) Foe who takes sneak attack damage takes attack pen (more vs. striker) for 1 rd.
Debilitating Injury: Hampered (Ex) Foe who takes sneak attack damage has speed halved (and can't 5 ft step) for 1 rd.
Surprise Attacks +2 (Ex) In surprise round, foes always flat-footed and add bonus sneak attack dam.

Tactics: Violet, Celadra, and Krybern have been a team for several years and work very well together. Celadra's spells are prepared with battling wood golems in mind so she has memorized more fire-based spells than she normally would. Upon hearing the PCs in the other room, Celadra casts *mage armor* on herself. The three move to the corners of the room farthest from the door and wait for the PCs to enter the room. Once the door opens, Celadra casts *web* into the entry hall to trap the PCs, while Violet and Krybern open fire with their bows. If the PCs are stuck in the web, the three soften them up with missile weapons and *magic missiles* from Celadra. If the PCs break or burn free, Violet and Krybern stand before the door to give Celadra protection and then the three looters flee through the broken windows.

If the PCs don't open the door within several minutes, Violet opens the door and stands aside to allow Celadra to cast *web*, and then the three use the tactics above. If the PCs have already moved on, they wait and ambush the PCs in the **Dining Room (Area 5)** using similar tactics.

Information: Capturing one of the three and coercing him or her to talk potentially provides useful information. Without magic or outright torture, a successful DC 18 Intimidate check is required to force one of them to talk. Baron Kurell hired the team to find an ancient text about a pyramid, a small silver and gold pyramid, and a large ruby. The baron paid 5000 gp in advance and agreed to pay another 10,000 gp upon completion of the mission with all other treasures kept by the trio. The information is useful but can't be used against the baron in a court of law because no written agreements or other witnesses exist.

4. The Kitchen

A massive iron stove stands in the center of the room with a large chimney leading up through the roof. Pots and pans are scattered across the floor, along with a variety of cooking utensils. Cabinet doors stand open, and the plates, bowls, and serving dishes that once occupied them have been thrown on the floor. Flour and sugar cover the floor of the small pantry in the west wall. Looters emptied every container and cabinet in search of hidden money. Doors into the hallway to the north and the large dining room to the east remain open, allowing a clear view into those rooms. A successful DC 13 Appraise check easily recognizes that some of the unbroken china left behind is quite valuable.

Treasure: Although somewhat difficult to transport, the unbroken china and glassware remaining behind are worth 350 gp.

5. The Dining Room (CR variable)

A stench of stale vomit fills the air of the dining room. That, along with the jumble of broken glass from the shattered windows, taints the view of this once-magnificent dining room. Pale wood paneling along the walls contrasts with the dark wood of the massive dining table and chairs in the center of the room. The table and chairs are in complete disarray, and whatever decorative vases or glassware once occupied the table has been stolen or broken. All but one of the small niches for statues and vases lining the walls are empty.

The single remaining statue is an ornate silver depiction of a dragon with its mouth open and ruby eyes flashing in anger as it prepares to breathe fire on its opponents. A master craftsman created the statue years ago for Londar before he worked his own spells on it. Before the other statues and vases were stolen, the silver dragon was the most valuable-looking piece in the dining room. It is really a complex magical trap.

Silver Dragon Trap CR 3
XP 800
Type magical; **Perception** DC 28; **Disable Device** special
EFFECTS
Trigger touch; **Reset** automatic
Effect If anyone other than Londar touches the statue, it "breathes" a *stinking cloud* (DC 14) that affects everyone in the room. The magic is permanent and can be triggered as often as once per round. The cloud dissipates through the broken windows 10 rounds after the trap is triggered. A *detect magic* reveals a complex magical aura surrounding the statue, but the trap cannot be identified by any other means. A successful *limited wish* or *wish* spell removes the enchantment, as does a successful *dispel magic* (DC 28). The magical effects must be removed before the statue can be transported and sold.
Treasure: The silver dragon statue is worth 1200 gp due to its exceptional craftsmanship and beauty.

6. The Guest Bedroom

Londar, an intensely private man, has only a single guest bedroom in his home. Designed for his niece Learah, it usually saw use only when she visited. Shattered glass from the single stained-glass window in the northern wall covers the room. All the drawers from the small dresser and desk in the room have been pulled out and overturned, and the blankets and sheets have been taken from the mattress. The mattress itself is slashed and torn apart, and several parts of the mattress are broken and dismantled. The only item of interest in the room is a small pool of blood along the windowsill. A successful DC 18 Survival or DC 10 Heal check determines the blood is less than a day old. A looter rested on the windowsill to dress her wounds after running from the golem's in **Londar's Bedroom (Area 7)**.

7. Londar's Bedroom (CR 6)

Double doors entering Londar's room were left closed by the last thief who entered and then fled the room. The doors are not locked. Londar created a **wood golem** to protect him while he was sleeping and to protect his room while he was away. The golem appears to be a simple wooden statue of a tall man holding a large mace in each hand. Londar created the construct with very specific orders: It utters a loud shriek similar to that of an *alarm* spell while it attacks anyone other than Londar who enters the room. Looters attempted to get past the golem but most met a bloody end. Broken glass is spread across the room along with the splintered furniture. Thieves broke the glass; their bodies broke the furniture as the golem tossed them about the room. Two ripe corpses remain in the room, both in an advanced state of decay.

Wood Golem CR 6
XP 2,400
hp 64 (Pathfinder Roleplaying Game Bestiary, "Golem, Wood")

Combat Tactics: The golem is keyed to Londar and attacks anyone else. It lets out a constant shriek as long as anyone is in the room and fights until destroyed. Fortunately, the golem is keyed to this particular room and does not chase fleeing victims. The golem has enough rudimentary programming to close the doors and stay away from the windows if the PCs attempt to use missile weapons against it from outside the room.

Examining the Room: If the golem is defeated or disabled, the PCs have an opportunity to search the room. Unfortunately, Londar had a passion for delicate porcelain and crystal, all of which was destroyed during the golem's battles with looters. One of the broken dressers has a drawer with a secret bottom (spotted with a DC 27 Perception check) holding several small, unmarked vials (*philter of love*, *potion of bull's strength*, *potion of enlarge person*, and a *potion of poison*). A search of the two corpses turns up a longsword, two daggers, and coins totaling 14 gp, 32 sp, and 55 cp.

8. The Living Room

Londar used his living room extensively, both for entertaining and for his own reading and relaxation. The curved end of the home marks the base of Londar's tower and has the only unbroken windows in the room. The rest of the room is now a complete wreck. Plush cushions that once lined the many chairs and sofas are slashed and shredded, and small tables throughout the room were broken in vain searches for secret compartments. A wide stairway climbs along the outer edge of the tower to its upper levels, while bloody handprints mark a door in the north wall. Bare spots on the walls indicate where tapestries or paintings once hung. Niches along the inner walls are all empty.

Blood left behind on the door to **Londar's Office (Area 9)** is old enough to be dried and flaking. Learah and the sheriff left the door unlocked after their search for Londar. They were unable to enter the office due to the golems guarding it but determined that he wasn't there.

9. Londar's Office (CR 8 or variable)

Londar never allowed his servants into his office nor did he ever do business here. His office is really a gateway down to the caverns beneath his home, a gateway he has kept well-guarded against invasion. The two stained-glass windows in this room are unbroken. Powerful magic rendered the stained-glass windows virtually unbreakable, and 2 **wood golems** guard the room against any unwanted intruders. The room was damaged during a battle with looters, but after they saw what the golem in the bedroom could do, looters left this room alone.

High niches along the walls hold a variety of delicate crystal vases and statues that are all lit from behind with magical lights. The crystal splits the light into a rainbow of colors that spills across the ceiling in a complex interweaving of color. The effect is a startling, hypnotic reminder of the reasons behind Londar being known as the Rainbow Mage and acts as a magical trap.

Wood Golem (2) CR 6
XP 2,400
hp 64 (Pathfinder Roleplaying Game Bestiary, "Golem, Wood")

Exterior Windows: 1/2 in. thick; Hardness 8, hp 30; Break DC 18. These stained-glass windows have been magically hardened, making them very difficult to break.

Tactics: The golems stand on each side of the doorway and turn to attack anyone entering through the door while emitting their piercing alarm wail. Neither golem leaves the office to chase intruders. They are programmed to close the door and stay out of sight to avoid missile fire and spells from outside the room.

Note: Damaging area effect spells stand a good chance of destroying items on the shelves and makes the secret door behind the bookcase more difficult to locate (requiring a successful DC 26 Perception check) but with the same possible modifiers described below).

Hypnotic Pattern Trap CR 2
XP 600
Type magical; **Perception** special; **Disable Device** special
EFFECTS
Trigger gaze; **Reset** automatic
Effect Staring at the pattern of colors on the ceiling for more than one round forces a DC 18 Will save to avoid gaining the dazed condition. Dazed characters are unable to act or think until the hypnosis is broken by somehow forcing the PC to stop looking at the pattern or by destroying the pattern itself. Breaking the hypnosis causes mental pain and anguish, forcing a second DC 15 Will save to taking 2 Int damage. A DC 20 Knowledge (Arcana) check allows someone to realize the colors could be dangerous and that breaking a single crystal vase or statue should disrupt the pattern and make it safe to look at the ceiling.

Examining the Room: A large ebonwood desk stands in the center of the office, and massive bookcases cover the inner walls. Various papers and books are scattered along the shelves. A successful DC 22 Perception check reveals a few arcane scrolls (CL 20; *darkvision, greater magic weapon, hold person, lightning bolt, improved invisibility, summon monster V*). The desk has several locked drawers that contain interesting items. A bookcase in the northeast corner of the office conceals a doorway (found with a successful DC 20 Perception check) that leads to a passage down to the caverns beneath the home. A dwarf or other character studying the construction of the home gains +2 on the Perception check to notice the secret door due to the missing space behind the wall in the living room and the wall in the corner of his office.

Londar's desk has a powerful trap yet contains only a few items of value. Attempting to open the drawers causes a crystal embedded in the top of the desk to emit a flash of brilliant red light that causes painful burns to anyone nearby. The red light is a powerful, concentrated form of heat that affects anyone within a 5-foot radius of the desk. The light passes above the desk, making it immune to the damage, but any items on top of it must succeed at a DC 10 Reflex saving throw or catch fire.

Crystal Light Trap CR 4
XP 1,200
Type magical; **Perception** DC 29; **Disable Device** DC 29
EFFECTS
Trigger touch; **Reset** automatic
Effect burning light (30 fire damage, DC 17 Reflex save for half damage); multiple targets (all creatures within 5 feet)

Londar kept his most valuable items hidden in his true library and vault within the caverns deep beneath his home. The trap on the desk was simply meant to further deter thieves to allow Londar time to prepare for battle. The desk drawers contain only divine scrolls *(death ward, restoration* x2*)* and a pouch containing 100 gp.

Londar's Tower (Areas 10–12)

Londar's Tower rises several floors above the main house. The living room of the home is the first level of the tower. Stairs circle the inner wall of the tower as they climb to the upper levels. A landing marks each level with a door blocking further progress up the stairs or into that particular floor. The three upper levels are devoted to storage or other special uses that Londar considered sage enough to house there. Doors in the tower generally have rather dangerous traps. Londar bypassed these traps — and all the traps in his caverns — using secret command words known only to him or by using *teleport* spells.

10. The Second Level of Londar's Tower (CR 6)

The stairs that lead up from **The Living Room (Area 8)** end before a solid stone door painted in fluorescent red. Soot marks along the walls surrounding the landing hint at a recent fire. The only features of the door are its bright red color and its strange lock. Anyone attempting to pick the lock or force open the door triggers the trap.

Red Stone Door: 9 in. thick; Hardness 8; HP 90; Disable Device 25; Break DC 30

Flame Strike Trap CR 6
XP 2,400
Type magic; **Perception** DC 30; **Disable Device** DC 30
EFFECTS
Trigger touch; **Reset** Automatic
Effect spell effect (flame strike, 8d6 fire damage, DC 17 Reflex save for half damage); multiple targets (all targets within 5 feet of the door)

Inside the Room: Once the door is opened, an apparently empty room and a stairway that continues upward along the outer edge of the tower is revealed. Londar used this room to store unused furniture and old items he didn't need anymore. The center of the room is enchanted so that any inanimate objects placed there become invisible within 2 rounds. A PC walking toward the center of the room bumps into the old furniture and can rapidly figure out what is there by feeling around. The items can be revealed with an *invisibilty purge* spell or by removing them from the middle of the room. None of the items is of any value to the party. Once reached, this room is relatively easy to guard and therefore a good place to rest.

11. The Third Level of Londar's Tower (CR 1)

Stairs from the second level rise to a small landing before a dull, featureless blue stone door. Anyone attempting to force the door or pick the lock triggers the release of oil from the holes along the floor. The oil pours across the landing and down the steps. The trap is difficult to locate but relatively easy to disable once discovered.

Blue Stone Door: 9 in. thick; Hardness 8; HP 90; Disable Device 25; Break DC 30

Oil Trap CR 1
XP 400
Type mechanical; **Perception** DC 28; **Disable Device** DC 18
EFFECTS
Trigger touch; **Reset** manual
Effect oil (1d6 damage from slipping and falling down the stairs, DC 18 Reflex avoids); multiple targets (all targets in front of door and on stairs)

Inside the Room: Opening the door reveals a well-appointed reading room decorated with beautiful crystal lamps, broad wool tapestries, and ornate wooden chairs with plush cushions. A beautiful full-sized mirror is molded to the stone of the floor in the center of the room, and the eastern portion of the circular room is decorated with colored stone inlays in the shape of strange runes along the walls and the floor. Stairs along the west wall continue their climb along the outside of the tower to its upper levels.

Londar generally avoided his traps and devices by simply *teleporting* from place to place or by using passwords known only to him. Rune-shaped decorations helped him key in on exact destinations and eliminated any chance of a failed *teleport*. *Detect magic* reveals nothing strange or magical about the symbols themselves but reveals extremely powerful magic surrounding the mirror. The mirror is a *mirror of random portals* (see sidebar) Londar created. When the mirror is activated, it generates a one-way portal to a random location throughout the world. Londar used the mirror to explore the world, always knowing he could *teleport* home when he needed to do so.

[BEGIN SIDEBAR]

Mirror of Random Teleportation

Aura moderate conjuration; **CL** 17th; **Slot** -; **Price** 73,500 gp; **Weight** 45 lbs.

DESCRIPTION

This odd mirror can be used to generate a one-way portal to random locations throughout the world. The location cannot be determined beforehand, and can be anyplace in the known world, including caverns, dungeons, forests, mountains, etc. The portal never opens up into rock or underwater, but can open to locations with no other exits.

Activating the mirror requires putting a gem worth at least 100gp to be put into the depression at the top of the frame. The mirror can only be activated once per day. Each mirror must be created in a particular location and does not function outside of that location.

CONSTRUCTION REQUIREMENTS

Craft Wondrous Item, *greater teleport*, *teleportation circle*; **Cost** 36,750 gp

12. The Fourth Level of Londar's Tower

Stairs from the third level of the tower end before a purple stone door that is marked with glowing runes. *Detect magic* reveals transmutation and evocation magic on the runes, but the door has no traps and is unlocked.

Purple Stone Door: 9 in. thick; Hardness 8; HP 90; Disable Device 25; Break DC 30

Inside the Room: A massive crystal ball occupies a circular table in the center of the room, and several strange silver bowls full of water rest on stands in different parts of the chamber. Runes and sigils decorate the north wall above a strange circle of inlayed stone. A small table against the west wall holds a number of carefully drawn maps.

Londar devoted the top of his tower to the creation of a scrying chamber that he used to spy on the important people and lands surrounding his home. He used this chamber to create intricate maps of the surrounding area and to record weaknesses of potential enemies. Carefully studying the map indicates that some of them were created as battle plans. PCs studying some of the notes and who succeed at a DC 18 Intelligence or Profession (soldier) check come to the conclusion that Londar was planning to take over the surrounding area by force, a rather shocking revelation considering his reputation as a well-liked, generous man.

Treasure #1: The crystal ball and scrying balls (non-magical) are of the highest quality and would fetch over 3000 gp on the open market. Unfortunately, everything bears Londar's symbol and can't be sold or openly transported locally. The maps and battle plans would be shocking to the local magistrate but are worth money only to Learah Relight who is willing to pay 1000 gp to prevent any public knowledge of Londar's "temporary madness."

Treasure #2: One of the drawers has a carefully hidden secret compartment that can be found with a DC 33 Perception check. It contains a *+1 ghost touch returning dagger* Londar forgot about.

Treasure #3: Beneath some of the maps is a letter written on thin parchment that reads, "L. It appears we are in agreement. The western mountains are yours, may your search of those ruins find success, and everything east and south of the Remick River shall be mine. As we discussed, the pyramid is necessary for success. I shall send a courier with funds sufficient to help acquire the final pieces of the device." While the letter is unsigned, a wax seal has been affixed to the bottom of the parchment. A successful DC 25 Knowledge (Nobility) check determines the seal is very similar to Baron Kurell's, but not similar enough to be certain of its source.

Treasure #4: Mixed in with some of the other maps and papers is a detailed map of the mountains west of the mansion and Hampton Hill. Known to most in the area simply as "the western mountains," Londar's map has an additional message that reads: "Batrie's Fall." A scrawled note near a mountain circled on the map reads: "Arn's? Hollow? Temple?" When combined with other information, the PCs can use this map to help locate Arn's Mountain where an ancient temple to Horgrim remains hidden.

Chapter 5: Beneath the Mansion

Additional Encounters in the Jungle Cavern

The GM may choose to include some of the following random events while in this cavern. Roll 1d20 for every 30 minutes in the cavern, an encounter already used counts as no encounter. The above should be used only once, if at all. GMs might decide to add more combat-oriented encounters to the jungle as it is a perfect place to add strange creatures *teleported* in from distant locations.

1d8	Encounter
1–2	A powerful roar reverberates through the trees and off the cavern walls followed by screeches and panicked birdcalls only to close with a distinctly uneasy silence.
3	A **tiger** bursts through the undergrowth and attacks the party.
4–5	A colorful bird charges from the treetops and attempts to chase the party away from its nest.
6	The party enters a small clearing only to notice 2 **chuul** at the same time they notice them.
7	Something screeches before running into the undergrowth, leaving behind only rustling leaves.
8–9	A pained wail echoes through the trees, followed by the call of a strange bird.
10–20	No encounter.

Chuul CR 7
XP 3,200
hp 85 (Pathfinder Roelplaying Game Bestiary, "Chuul")

Tiger CR 4
XP 1,200
hp 45 (Pathfinder Roleplaying Game Bestiary, "Tiger (Cat, Great)")

The Caverns (Areas 13□23)

Londar used the caverns below his home as a testing ground and as an extra layer of protection against invasion. Londar used magic and a charmed delver to create rooms hidden off the caverns as well as the tunnels connecting them. Londar installed permanent *teleportation circles* in several parts of the Under Realms and a distant jungle to keep his different caverns populated with creatures to study and experiment on. Some of Londar's research went into creating special forcefields he used to keep creatures in the various caverns apart. Once he finished the intricate network of caverns, he never had to travel through them. Each room he created has a special area with inlayed stone in the form of colored runes that gave Londar the exact coordinates for the use of *teleport* spells. All these areas are unique in design but none of the stonework is magical in nature.

Some of the creatures in the various caverns were deliberately summoned or *teleported* there by Londar; others simply wandered through *teleportation circles* and became trapped. The presence of the outside *teleportation circles* provides an opportunity for the GM to add new or different creatures the PCs have never before encountered. Several caverns include possible random encounter lists, but these lists should be considered optional and used only if the GM wants to create a more difficult adventure.

Forcefields: Forcefields dividing hallways and caverns are equivalent to *wall of force* spells that can be turned on and off with special dials. Londar created a system of dials that could be triggered only by a Small or Medium-size humanoid hand with a full complement of fingers. When turned, these dials open doors or turn off forcefields, and then slowly reset over a period of about 10 rounds (one minute). Once the dial resets, the door it opened closes or the forcefield it disabled goes back up. Forcefields follow all the rules of *wall of force* spells with respect to spells and attacks. The forcefields are difficult to notice without walking into them or hitting them with something, but PCs should soon recognize the dials to disable them and that the forcefields are always located at logical junctions.

13. Roughhewn Hallway (CR 4)

The stairs drop steadily into the ground in a steep spiral before finally ending at a wide, roughhewn hallway sloping downward to the south. The robed body of a wizard slumps on the floor near a pillar 30 feet down the hallway, which forks 30 feet past the pillar. The wizard used a *passwall* spell to get through the wall into the hidden passage he realized must be behind it. Unfortunately, he ran into a rather deadly trap. Cautious PCs recognize that the body and most of its clothing are horribly burned and that the stone wall near the body shows signs of great heat. A 5-foot strip of floor before the pillar is designed as a trigger for a **fire jet trap**. Anyone stepping on that area of the floor is engulfed in jets of fire from tiny nozzles in the walls.

Fire Jet Trap CR 4
XP 1,200
Type mechanical; **Perception** DC 26; **Disable Device** DC 28
EFFECTS
Trigger location; **Reset** Automatic
Effect fire jet (6d6 fire damage, DC 18 Reflex save for half damage)

Disabling the trap allows the PCs to examine the corpse. The powerful flames destroyed almost everything on the burned corpse, only a set of green robes survived (*robe of useful items* with 1 of each default patch and 2 random patches remaining) due to their magical nature.

Ten feet beyond the stone pillar is a forcefield (see above) that must be deactivated to travel any farther. PCs studying the pillar closely notice a dial with a depression the size and shape of a humanoid hand. Placing one's hand in the depression and turning the dial brings down the *wall of force*. Turning the dial begins a slow ticking sound as it begins to reset. Once it returns to its original position, the forcefield turns on again. Beyond the forcefield, a similar dial in the wall turns off the forcefield from the opposite side. Londar set up several such walls in different places throughout the cavern's halls to keep creatures safely confined.

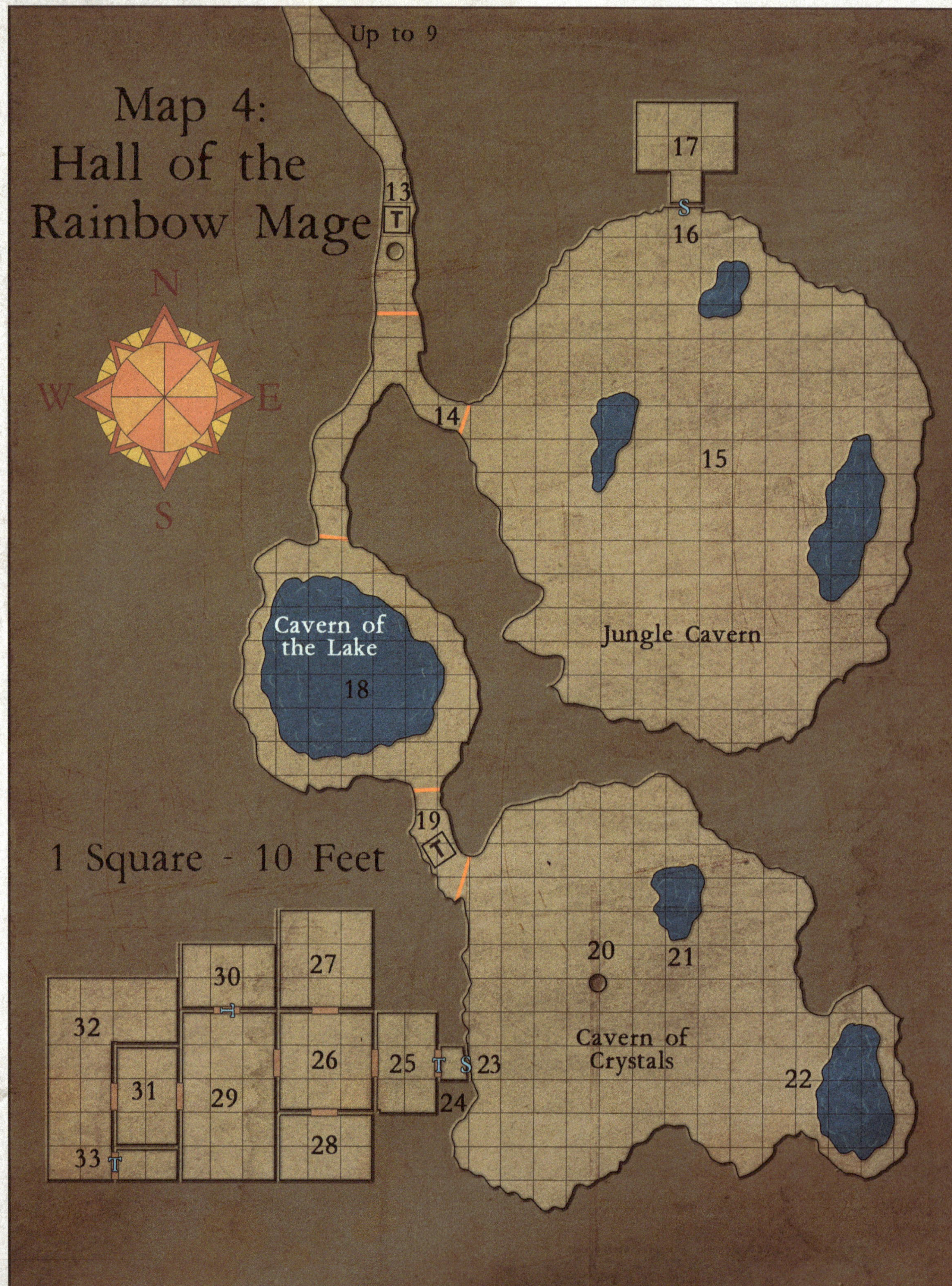

Up to 9
Map 4:
Hall of the
Rainbow Mage
N
W E
S
1 Square - 10 Feet
13 T
17
S
16
14
15
Jungle Cavern
Cavern of
the Lake
18
19 T
20
21
Cavern of
Crystals
22
30
27
32
26
25 T S 23
24
31
29
28
33 T

14. Before the Jungle Cavern

A shimmering forcefield blocks the entrance to a massive cavern lit with glowing stalactites and filled with jungle plants. Air on the opposite side of the *wall of force* is far hotter and more humid than the air in the hallway, causing the field to shimmer enough to be somewhat visible. A dial with a depression shaped like a human hand in the southern wall can be used to disable the field for 10 rounds. A second dial on the other side of the field can also be used to deactivate the field.

The Jungle Cavern

Londar loved the brightly colored creatures he saw while traveling in the jungle and endeavored to create his own jungle in this massive cavern. He used spells to permanently light the cavern from above and then teleported in large plants and a number of animals. While some of the plants don't grow very well, *teleportation circles* placed in several different jungles bring a constant influx of small jungle animals along with a few larger jungle creatures. *Teleportation circle* arrival locations identified on the map indicate regions where creatures might suddenly appear out of thin air. The cavern's ceiling rises approximately 80 feet above the floor with many of the jungle trees planted here reaching the top of the cavern and then bending along the ceiling. Birds, small monkeys, and other animals move through the twisted forest. Numbered locations indicate spots or encounters of particular interest.

15. Kunkthank's Ambush (CR 9)

Kunkthank (**tyrannosaurus rex**, but with Intelligence 4 due to a side effect of the *teleportation circle*) arrived here through one of the *teleportation circles* over a year ago. Although he stands slightly over 18 feet tall, he has found a particularly thick stand of jungle trees and undergrowth where he can hide and wait for food to wander by. While not overly intelligent, he knows exactly how close most prey needs to be before he charges forward and runs it to the ground. Few creatures ever get away from his brutal attacks.

Tyrannosaurus CR 9
XP 6,400
hp 153 (Pathfinder Roleplaying Game Bestiary, "Dinosaur, Tyrannosaurus")

Treasure: Kunkthank has a small cache of treasure hidden in a depression in the cavern floor near his ambush spot. Vines cover the hole, but a successful DC 18 Perception check allows a PC to notice green stains on the rocky ground where the vines are moved back and forth. His treasure includes some items acquired from two unlucky rogues that came through one of Londar's *teleportation circles*. In the depression is a *handy haversack* (empty), masterwork thieves' tools, 2 masterwork daggers, a rusted longsword, 18 pp, 87 gp, 93 sp, and 72 cp.

16. A Secret Door (CR 7)

The solid rock door sitting in the northern wall has carefully emulated the stone walls of the cavern, making it very difficult to spot (requires a successful DC 18 Perception check). PCs who spot the door also notice a dial with a human hand imprint in the rock several feet to the left of the door and automatically realize it must control a door or forcefield similar to those that the PCs have already bypassed. Placing a hand in the impression and turning the dial opens the door to reveal a small laboratory.

Heavy Stone Door: 3 ft. thick; Hardness 8; hp 280; Break DC 25

The door is a piece of the cavern wall carefully cut out to create a well-hidden door. It opens by a series of mechanical and magical mechanisms triggered by the dial in the stone wall beside it. A Small or Medium-sized humanoid hand with a full complement of fingers and a thumb is required to turn the dial; any other hand or appendage simply cannot bypass the magical protection placed upon it. Once turned, the dial slowly resets over a period of 10 rounds after which the door closes again.

A **chuul** set up an ambush (spotted with a DC 29 Perception check) by a small pond hidden by several thick trees and some heavy bushes. Intelligent enough to realize the dial in the wall controls a locking mechanism, it stands guard watching the dial and the adjoining doorway to learn who is responsible for its recent arrival here. The chuul presumes anyone opening or going through the door is the enemy that trapped it here and attacks. It would attempt to go through the door itself but is unable to turn the dial.

After falling through a *teleportation circle*, this chuul quickly assessed its situation and has made the best of a bad situation. It waits patiently, abandoning its vigil over the secret door only to hunt for a bit of food. Anyone attempting to open the door becomes a target for its anger.

Chuul CR 7
XP 3,200
hp 85 (Pathfinder Roelplaying Game Bestiary, "Chuul")

Tactics: The chuul hides in a small pool of water near the door. It bursts from cover and attacks anyone approaching the door or the lock, targeting the person closest to the door as its primary victim.

17. An Abandoned Alchemist's Laboratory (CR variable)

Glass objects, crystal flasks, and strange vases line shelves and benches throughout the room. Abandoned glassware here could fetch a total of 200 gp from an alchemist interested in purchasing it. Shelves along the back wall hold a variety of large bottles made of tinted glass, each with wax-sealed stoppers. A purple dial with a hand impression is beside a set of shelves in the north wall. If turned, this dial does not begin to reset like the dials that open doors or trigger the forcefields in the hallways. This dial needs to be turned for the west door in the **Large Laboratory (Area 29)** to be opened. A bench in the center of the room has been cleared of all glassware and holds only a single bottle with a cork stopper. Scrawled words on a piece of paper resting beside it read, "One wish left, don't push him."

Londar actually used this laboratory while experimenting on gorillas and other creatures. He abandoned it several years ago, but beforehand, Londar put a few items here to make life "entertaining" for anyone searching through the lab. Londar discovered a way to transform and imprison creatures in the large glass bottles along the shelves and on the bench. He used this method to store a few of his experiments and a few other creatures he intended to experiment on in the future. Breaking or opening a bottle releases the trapped creature. Creatures released in this manner suffer the stunned condition until the end of their turn following their release. Most of the creatures trapped in the bottles either attack anyone in the room or do their best to escape when finally released. While there is a **djinni** in a bottle on the bench, it was trapped in the bottle by Londar, can't cast any *wish* spells, and is VERY angry once it is finally released. PCs should be quite reasonably suspicious of both the bottle and the note. If they go ahead and open it, the djinni turns into a whirlwind as soon as it can act and travels through the room, shattering all the glassware and releasing the creatures trapped in the other bottles.

Djinni CR 5
XP 1,600
hp 52 (Pathfinder Roleplaying Game Bestiary, "Genie, Djinni")

Tactics: After recovering from its initial stunning, the djinni bellows with rage and uses its whirlwind ability to decimate the room. It sends shattered glassware throughout the room and breaks all the bottles on the shelves before using its *plane shift* ability to return to its home. If released in the laboratory, the djinni does not stay around to battle the PCs, though it would like to, because it is afraid of somehow being trapped again. Releasing the djinni outside the laboratory results in a full-scale battle from which the djinni flees only if mortally wounded.

The djinni breaks all the jars containing the bottled creatures (see sidebar) if he is released in the laboratory. Total chaos ensues: The pyrohydra basically attacks everything in sight; the troll attacks the PCs and tries to use them as a shield against the pyrohydra; and other creatures generally attack anyone next to them. Releasing all the creatures at once results in an encounter that should be considered CR 10 at a minimum. Wise PCs flee and let the released creatures destroy each other.

Creatures trapped in the bottles underwent a painful procedure against their will. Some failed enough saving throws that they did not survive, but most of the rest did. Creatures trapped in the bottles are not slaves of the person freeing them; in fact, they are more than likely going to attack as soon as they recover from their ordeal. There are 15 bottles total. If any are opened or destroyed, roll 2d8–1 and consult the following table.

Roll	Contents
1–2	**Kobold** (any kobolds released are frightened and attempt to run away or negotiate their freedom)
3	**Troll** (attacks the nearest creature)
4	**Ettercap** (if the door is opened, it attempts to flee; if the door is closed, it attacks the nearest creature)
5–7	Dead kobolds
8	**Griffon** (hungry and frightened, it attacks the nearest creature; attempts to calm or communicate with it suffer a –8 circumstance penalty)
9–10	**Bugbear** (attacks nearest creature)
11	**Pyrohydra** (attacks anyone and anything around it)
12	Dead griffon
13	**Shambling mound** (attempts to communicate unless attacked)
14	Dead bugbear
15	**Otyugh** (attacks nearest creature)

Bugbear CR 2
XP 600
hp 16 (Pathfinder Roleplaying Game Bestiary, "Bugbear")

Ettercap CR 3
XP 800
hp 30 (Pathfinder Roleplaying Game Bestiary, "Ettercap")

Griffon CR 4
XP 1,200
hp 42 (Pathfinder Roleplaying Game Bestiary, "Griffon")

Kobold CR 1/4
XP 100
hp 5 (Pathfinder Roleplaying Game Bestiary, "Kobold")

Otyugh CR 4
XP 1,200
hp 39 (Pathfinder Roleplaying Game Bestiary, "Otyugh")

5-headed Pyrohydra CR 6
XP 1,200
hp 47 (Pathfinder Roleplaying Game Bestiary, "Hydra, Pyrohydra (5-Headed)")

Shambling Mound CR 6
XP 2,400
hp 67 (Pathfinder Roleplaying Game Bestiary, "Shambling Mound")

Troll CR 5
XP 1,600
hp 63 (Pathfinder Roleplaying Game Bestiary, "Troll")

18. Cavern of the Lake (CR 7)

The hallway opens into a large cavern with a small lake in its center. A second hallway exits the cavern along the southern side with both exits from the cavern protected by forcefields operated by standard hand dials. Londar purchased an **aboleth** as an egg and let it grow up here specifically to provide a guardian for his deeper caverns. A narrow flagstone path closely follows the edge of the lake as it makes its way toward the southern exit, easily close enough to allow the aboleth the opportunity for surprise attacks. While it is a good guardian, this massive fish-like amphibian has no allegiance to anyone. It would happily destroy Londar but never got the chance. It knows about the forcefields that trap it here, but its lack of humanoid hands prevents it from inactivating them.

Aboleth CR 7
XP 3,200
hp 84 (Pathfinder Roleplaying Game Bestiary, "Aboleth")

Tactics: Keying the forcefield at either entrance to the cavern sets off an underwater alarm that only the aboleth can hear. This warning allows it to prepare for visitors. After determining which entrance the PCs are entering, the aboleth conceals itself in the lake and attempts to communicate with the party without revealing itself. During this conversation, it uses its probing telepathy to find out which party members are the most dangerous and then targets them with its enslave power. During battle, it attempts to use its tentacles to move creatures into the water so they suffer from the aboleth's mucous cloud.

Treasure: Several adventurers unfortunate enough to fall through the *teleportation circles* into Londar's caverns fell victim to the aboleth. It has collected their items into a small cache hidden at the bottom of the lake. Most of the items are decayed or rusted, but there is a *+1 spell storing dagger*, *+2 bracers of armor*, *clear spindle ioun stone*, *horn of fog*, 1000 gp ruby, an ivory tube containing 500 gp worth of diamond dust, and lost coins totaling 72 gp, 132 sp, and 259 cp.

19. A Short Hallway of Polished Stone (CR 4)

A different type of stone, greenish in hue and highly polished, lines the walls, floor, and ceiling of the short hallway connecting the lake cavern with another, larger cavern. The short, curving hallway is flanked by forcefields operated with standard dials. Characters entering the hallway notice that sound is somehow magnified and concentrated by the walls with a successful DC 20 Perform (any) check.

A 10-foot section taking up the center of the curving hallway is really a pressure plate triggering a powerful sonic trap that is concentrated and reinforced by the specially designed walls of the hallway.

Sonic Trap CR 4
XP 1,200
Type magical; **Perception** DC 31; **Disable Device** DC 33
EFFECTS
Trigger location; **Reset** Automatic
Effect Sonic Blast (4d6 sonic damage and deafness for 2d6 rounds; DC 19 Fort save for half damage and avoid deafness) Crystalline or glass creatures and objects take 15d6 sonic damage (DC 19 Fort for half), but objects stored in packs are buffered from the sound.

The Cavern of Crystals

The massive cavern is filled with strange crystals and bizarre stone structures. Patches of glowing moss cling to the floor and hanging stalactites shed an eerie light that is magnified by the many strange crystal growths throughout the cavern. Londar's latest attempt at creating an army resulted in strange humanoid creatures made of crystal and stone he named "chrystones." Londar used the natural crystal formations and stone of this cavern for his creations and imbued them with an ability to reproduce. Although chrystones have only rudimentary intelligence, they do have strange powers that make them extremely dangerous. While many still follow Londar's orders, others seek freedom. Some chrystones might attempt to communicate, while others simply attack the PCs as they have been trained to do. See **Appendix B: New Monsters** for statistics and description of these new creatures.

Sonic traps (see above) placed at the exits flanking this cavern are particularly deadly to the chrystone and were designed specifically to prevent their departure. The cavern itself is very rough, marked by small pools of water and a wide variety of stone stalagmites and stalactites, most of which have crystals of some sort imbedded in them. Creatures living in the cavern include the natural fungi and lizards present before Londar's modifications, the chrystones he created, and creatures arriving from *teleportation circles* placed in various caves and caverns throughout the world.

20. A Crystal Column (CR 9)

Londar's complicated spells gave the chrystones more intelligence and personality than he truly desired. Several of the chrystones used their *stone shape* abilities to create a massive column of various-colored crystals that shines with a soft light. The 5-foot-diameter column is perfectly smooth and made from a full spectrum of differently colored crystals. Soft light shining from within the column sheds multicolored light throughout the area. PCs with stonecunning or stone working abilities instantly recognize the superior craftsmanship that went into the creation of the single column.

The 5 **chrystones** that created this column are loyal to Londar; they made the rainbow-hued column as a tribute to their creator and master. When they hear the PCs approaching, they hide among the surrounding stalagmites and prepare an ambush. These particular chrystones are some of the first created by Londar and are the most loyal to him and his orders. While other chrystones might try to negotiate for their freedom, these attack anyone other than Londar.

Chrystone (5) CR 4
XP 1,200
hp 42 (Tome of Horrors Complete, "Chrystone")

Combat Tactics: The chrystones use their *color spray* breath weapon as they close in from all sides and join in melee combat. Creatures that are killed undergo death throes without giving any regard to their fellows. Their immunity to spells and lack of experience fighting tactically makes them fearless. Chrystones do not retreat when heavily injured and chase fleeing PCs no matter how badly they themselves are hurt.

Additional Encounters in the Cave

In addition to specific encounters at the marked locations, the GM has the option of using all or some of the following random encounters while the PCs explore the cavern. The GM might decide to use other exotic creatures that arrived via Londar's *teleportation circles* in place of these encounters. Roll 1d20 for every 30 minutes the PCs explore the cavern. Repeat encounters should be counted as no encounter.

1	A low hum moves through the cavern and causes the surrounding rock and crystal to vibrate.
2–3	The party is ambushed by a group of **3 chrystones**
4	The party hears the splashing of a **young black dragon** bathing in a nearby pool.
5	Shrill whistles pierce the air and echo off the cavern walls before fading to silence.
6	A **phase spider** attacks the party.
7	A small, harmless lizard leaps from a rock to a party member's pack, and then leaps off and flees into the cavern.
8	A **fungus gargoyle** attacks as the party walks by.
9–20	No encounter.

Chrystone CR 4
XP 1,200
hp 42 (Tome of Horrors Complete, "Chrystone")

Fungus Gargoyle CR 5
XP 1,600
hp 59 (Tome of Horrors Complete, "Gargoyle, Fungus")

Phase Spider CR 5
XP 1,600
hp 51 (Pathfinder Roleplaying Game Bestiary, "Phase Spider")

Young Black Dragon CR 7
XP 3,200
hp 76 (Pathfinder Roleplaying Game Bestiary, "Dragon, Black (Young)")

21. Slime Pool (CR 7)

A **black pudding** hides beneath the small pool of stagnant water, sliding out only when someone or something comes close enough for it to attack. Its location near a *teleportation circle* arrival spot provides it with a constant source of food. Chrystones living in the cavern are immune to its acid but have learned to stay away from it anyway.

Black Pudding CR 7
XP 3,200
hp 105 (Pathfinder Roleplaying Game Bestiary, "Pudding, Black")

Tactics: The ooze remains concealed in the pool of water and makes no effort to move or attack anything that doesn't approach the water. Enough creatures come to the water for a drink that it has a steady supply of food. Once a creature is within 5 feet, the ooze makes a swift attack and tries to grab and constrict the victim before sliding back into the pool.

22. A Shimmering Pool of Water (CR 8)

Water drips into the pool from the stalactites above, creating gentle ripples that shimmer due to the glowing crystals deep beneath the water. While the glowing crystals might appear attractive to adventurers, they are not very valuable and angering Yorliss is decidedly unhealthy. **Yorliss** is an elderly female water naga who made her home here after arriving through a *teleportation circle*. The pool itself is close to a *teleportation circle* arrival point that has provided Yorliss with plenty of food. She and the chrystones are content to leave each other alone because she has no desire for battle and the chrystones know her spells can cause them serious damage.

Yorliss' long, snake-like body is covered with emerald green scales. A series of orange and red spines run along her back and rise up when she is angered or frightened. Her face, though only vaguely human-like, is quite beautiful, and she has a charming personality. Her great age and constant food source have made her larger, stronger, and smarter than the average water naga. She has explored the cavern quite thoroughly and, if the PCs communicate with her, she can identify the location of *teleportation circle* arrival points, talk about where most of the chrystones can be found, and mention the location of a door she is unable to open (the door to Londar's laboratory). She knows nothing about Londar and has never communicated on any real level with any of the chrystones, so she doesn't know where they are from or how they came to be in the cavern.

Yorliss   CR 8
XP 4,800
Unique Giant water naga
N Huge aberration (aquatic)
Init +5; **Senses** darkvision 60 ft.; Perception +17
AC 21, touch 13, flat-footed 16 (+5 Dex, +8 natural, -2 size)
hp 92 (8d8+56)
Fort +9, **Ref** +9, **Will** +9
Speed 30 ft., **swim** 50 ft.
Melee bite +11 (3d6+7 plus poison), tail slap +6 (2d6+3)
Space 15 ft.; **Reach** 10 ft.
Sorcerer Spells Known (CL 7th; concentration +11)
  3rd (5/day)—hold person (DC 17), lightning bolt (DC 17)
  2nd (7/day)—fog cloud, invisibility, web
  1st (7/day)—charm person (DC 15), comprehend languages, grease, magic missile, true strike
  0 (at will)—detect magic, detect poison, disrupt undead, ghost sound (DC 14), ray of frost, read magic, resistance
Str 24, **Dex** 21, **Con** 24, **Int** 11, **Wis** 17, **Cha** 18
Base Atk +6; **CMB** +15; **CMD** 30 (can't be tripped)
Feats Combat Casting, Eschew Materials[B], Lightning Reflexes, Skill Focus (Perception), Skill Focus (Stealth)
Skills Bluff +8, Knowledge (local) +4, Perception +17, Spellcraft +11, Stealth +11, Swim +15
Languages Aquan, Common
SQ amphibious
Special Abilities
Poison (DC 21) (Ex) Bite—injury; save Fort DC 21; frequency 1/ round for 6 rounds; effect 1d2 Con; cure 2 consecutive saves. The save DC is Constitution-based.

Tactics: If the PCs approach the pool peacefully, she breaks the surface a safe distance away and greets the travelers. She hasn't had any intelligent company for a long time and is open to talking to the PCs and giving them any of the information mentioned above. If the PCs threaten or anger Yorliss, they soon discover she is a canny, dangerous foe. Yorliss remains in the water while casting spells at the PCs. She creates as much noise as possible to attract other creatures to the area (50% chance of 3 or more chrystones arriving in 5 rounds). If other creatures arrive, she casts a *web* around the PCs and any stalagmites and the stalactites surrounding them to make them sitting targets. Otherwise, she uses *charm person* on the most heavily armored PCs and *hold person* against any obvious spellcasters. If the battle begins to go poorly, she casts *fog cloud* to escape. She attempts melee combat only against single PCs and keeps to the water if the PCs stay in a group. If the PCs attempt to use missile weapons and spells against her, she swims beneath the water, casts *invisibility* and makes plans to ambush them later. She is very fast and sure in the water and attacks any PC foolish enough to try to enter melee combat with her there.

23. The Door to Londar's Laboratory (CR 9)

A well-concealed stone door similar to the one at **Area 16** is given away completely by a marble dial set into the wall beside it. Marked with the standard impression of a humanoid hand, it provides a clear indication that a door is nearby. Furthermore, the dial itself glows with a faint magical aura that makes it easy to see from 30 feet away. PCs within 30 feet of the dial notice it easily and those approaching the dial can make out the faint lines that indicate the presence of a door.

Heavy Stone Door: 3 ft. thick; 3 ft. thick; Hardness 8; hp 280; Break DC 25. This door is identical to the one found in **Area 16** and opens with the marble dial to its right.

While some of the original chrystones are blindly loyal, their offspring are more willful and intelligent. Several have made attempts to communicate to some drow that came through a *teleportation circle*. Although those attempts failed, they still have hopes of negotiating a way out of the cavern. They set up an ambush of sorts near the door to the laboratories. They use their stealth to look like surrounding stalagmites and come forward when the PCs approach the door. Although they retain the memories of their parental chrystones, they are more independent and have no loyalty to Londar. They simply want to escape the cavern and have lives of their own.

Tactics: These chrystones do not want to fight and attack only if forced. The leader, a chrystone with deep purple crystal along its arms and head, calls itself "Cliki" as it comes forward with its arms open in a gesture of peace. It attempts to communicate using some of the sounds it heard from the drow it met before, and then using some of the sounds that pass for the language created by its young race. Patient PCs may begin to understand that it is looking for a way to leave the cavern. Once communication is established, it offers several diamonds and emeralds — gems it knows other creatures find valuable — for help leaving the cavern.

It is quite possible the PCs misinterpret Cliki's overtures or refuse to deal with it. If the PCs attack, the chrystones make a fighting retreat using their *color spray* ability if needed. If Cliki is attacked or destroyed, the rest of the chrystones become enraged and attack the PCs to the best of their ability.

Chrystone (8) CR 4
XP 1,200
hp 42 (Tome of Horrors Complete, "Chrystone")

Londar's Laboratories (Areas 24–33)

All of these rooms were cut from the surrounding stone using magic and the assistance of a charmed delver. The ceilings are 20 feet high and lit with balls of glowing light unless otherwise stated. Any doors in this area not specifically listed as having traps or other locks have the following statistics:

Heavy Stone Door: 5 in. thick; Hardness 8; hp 90; Break DC 24. Turning the dial in the center of the door opens it. Only a Small or Medium-size humanoid hand with a full complement of fingers can turn the dial.

24. A Short Entry Hall

The door from the rough cavern (**Area 23**) opens to a short entry hall that ends before a **green stone door** (9 in. thick; Hardness 8; hp 90; Break DC 24). A stone dial similar to others throughout the caverns is placed in the exact center of the door. Stone used for the hallway and the door is the same material found in the hallway at **Area 19**, a hint to cautious PCs that another trap might be present. Turning the dial on the door opens it, but it also emits a high-pitched squeal that is specifically tuned to the structure of the chrystones and kills any chrystones who end their turn in the hall (Disable Device DC 29). PCs in the hallway find the high-pitched squeal painful, but any chrystones that might be with them must flee the area or shatter within one round.

25. A Quiet Sitting Room

Paintings depicting peaceful pastoral scenes line the walls, and small sofas and chairs are grouped around some low tables. The high-quality furniture has been kept clean and polished, almost as if someone has been here actively keeping it clean. Londar set up several different spells to help keep this room clean, for reasons he likely forgot long ago. Once the door in the east wall closes, the room can be considered a safe place to rest. It is devoid of traps and monsters, and there is little chance creatures enter the room through one of the doors.

Opening the door in the east wall triggers the sonic effect in **Area 24** unless it has been disabled (see description in **Area 24**). The door in the west wall is identical to the door in the east, with a hand-shaped depression marking the dial in the center of the door, but it is not trapped.

26. The Room of Symbols

Symbols, runes, and strange shapes created from colored stone have been inlaid into the stone walls and floor. Warm light flows down from the entire ceiling lighting the room as if it were in full daylight. Hand-shaped impressions mark stone dials in the center of the doors in each wall. A careful study of the runes and symbols with a successful DC 15 Knowledge (Arcana) check reveals that most are simply decoration, but some are protective runes and symbols meant to keep summoned creatures from traveling in or through the room. The light flowing down from the ceiling is, in fact, the equivalent of sunlight at high noon with the same effects on undead as normal sunlight. Any attempts to summon creatures into this room or have summoned creatures enter this room meet with complete failure due to the runes and symbols on the walls.

All the doors are identical and open easily with the hand dials in their centers. The doors remain open for 10 rounds before closing automatically.

27. The Coffin Room (CR 8)

Londar's decision to raise an army to take over the surrounding area first caused him to dabble in necromancy. His investigation into the necromantic arts was mostly disappointing, requiring more active control than he really wanted. When negotiations with a vampire went poorly, he simply sealed this room with the vampire in it and turned to other experiments. The vampire, though hungry, knows it can't exit without help. Daylight and magic runes in the room beyond effectively trap him here. Unlike other laboratory rooms, this room is cloaked in darkness that extends to the very doorway. PCs without darkvision require a light source to see.

The room is full of coffins, but most of them are open or broken. Three of the coffins are made of heavy stone while the rest are made of wood. The coffins once held minions of **Corl Krick**, the vampire Londar recruited to his cause. All the spawn and vampires in Corl's control were destroyed by the sunlight in the **Room of Symbols (Area 26)** in fruitless attempts to escape.

Corl Krick is an adventurer who deliberately chose to become a vampire when age began to slow him down. Londar recruited Corl, promising him great wealth and a lofty position when they finally conquered a kingdom of their own. Londar helped find victims for Corl to turn into spawn or additional vampires. Unfortunately, the army of undead that Londar envisioned required darkness to operate, and Corl desired more wealth and power than Londar was willing to surrender. A disagreement led Londar to trap Corl and his spawn in this room. Corl went mad. He sent his spawn through the door into the artificial sunlight to find an escape. All attempts failed, leaving him trapped here alone for years.

Corl Krick   CR 8
XP 4,800
Human vampire fighter 7
CE Medium undead (augmented humanoid, human)
Init +8; **Senses** darkvision 60 ft.; Perception +19
AC 28, touch 15, flat-footed 23 (+7 armor, +4 Dex, +1 dodge, +6 natural)
hp 59 (7d10+21); fast healing 5
Fort +6, **Ref** +8, **Will** +4 (+2 vs. fear)
Defensive Abilities channel resistance +4; DR 10/magic, 10/silver; **Immune** undead traits; **Resist** cold 10, electricity 10
Weaknesses vampire weaknesses
Speed 30 ft.
Melee +1 bastard sword +17/+12 (1d10+14/19-20) or
  slam +9 (1d4+3 plus energy drain)

Special Attacks blood drain, children of the night, create spawn, dominate (DC 14), energy drain (2 levels, DC 14), weapon training (heavy blades +1)
Str 24, **Dex** 18, **Con** —, **Int** 12, **Wis** 14, **Cha** 12
Base Atk +7; **CMB** +14; **CMD** 29
Feats Alertness, Blind-fight, Cleave, Cleaving Finish, Combat Reflexes, Dodge, Exotic Weapon Proficiency (bastard sword), Great Cleave, Improved Cleaving Finish, Improved Initiative, Lightning Reflexes, Power Attack, Toughness, Weapon Focus (bastard sword), Weapon Specialization (bastard sword)
Skills Acrobatics +9, Bluff +9, Climb +15, Perception +19, Ride +12, Sense Motive +12, Stealth +10; Racial Modifiers +8 Bluff, +8 Perception, +8 Sense Motive, +8 Stealth
Languages Common, Necronomus
SQ armor training 2, change shape (dire bat or wolf, beast shape II), gaseous form, shadowless, spider climb
Other Gear +1 chainmail, +1 bastard sword

Tactics: Corl's imprisonment has driven him insane, but it has done nothing to temper his combat ability. When he hears the door open, he assumes *gaseous form* and floats up near the ceiling. Keeping to the shadows, he slowly floats along the walls until he is near the doorway. He waits for all the PCs to enter the room before floating down behind them and returning to his standard form. Once in standard form, he greets the PCs. When the PCs turn to face him, he attempts to use his dominate ability on anyone wearing holy symbols or the most heavily armored party member. Afterward, he attacks using his bastard sword, reserving his slam attacks for a time when the party is reduced to a manageable size. Any charmed PCs are ordered to assist him in the battle. If things begin to go poorly, he uses his spider climb ability to retreat up the walls and to the ceiling where he again attempts to dominate additional PCs, focusing on PCs that clearly cast spells or wear holy symbols.

Treasure

Corl has hidden treasure in the three stone coffins, one of which is his. Holes along the lid and sides allow anyone in *gaseous form* to easily enter or leave the coffins.

Coffin #1: The first coffin contains a *potion of charm animal* and a *potion of clairvoyance*.

Coffin #2: The second coffin holds several tattered scrolls (you should choose five spells that the party lacks, plus *speak with dead*).

Coffin #3: Corl's coffin contains his equipment if he is killed here. In addition, it contains a small bag holding several pearls: 7 white pearls (100 gp each), 3 pink pearls (75 gp each), and 8 freshwater pearls (15 gp each) are mixed with a *Pearl of the Sirines* and a *pearl of the power (1st)*. Identifying and separating the magic pearl from the mundane ones requires *detect magic* or other means of magical identification. A bag containing 358 gp, 237 sp, and 82 cp rests in the bottom of the coffin along with a *+1 dagger*, masterwork bastard sword, a masterwork longsword, and a masterwork heavy crossbow.

28. A Huge Closet (CR 7)

At first glance, this room appears to be nothing more than a massive storage closet holding old broken glassware, furniture, rugs, and a few other items. Several of the items in the back of the room, including an old wooden chest, hint at potential hidden value. PCs exploring the room discover it is really where Londar trapped a **chaos beast**. The creature initially came through one of his *teleportation circles* and created havoc in one of his caverns, so Londar *teleported* it into this room and left it here as a deterrent to anyone lucky enough to get this far into his hidden domain. Designed as a lure to thieves, nothing of value is inside the room.

Chaos Beast CR 7
XP 3,200
hp 85 (Pathfinder Roleplaying Game Bestiary 2, "Chaos Beast")

Tactics: This horrid creature initially hides behind an old chair. It changes in appearance into a clawed monstrosity immediately before it attacks. It waits until a PC is within 5 feet before darting out to attack. Runes and symbols in **Area 26** prevent it from leaving the room, so PCs who flee are safe from its attacks. If PCs stay outside the room and attempt to attack with ranged weapons, the chaos beast reshapes itself to hide behind some solid objects and avoid their attacks.

29. A Large Laboratory (CR 7)

This massive 50-foot-by-30-foot room was Londar's main laboratory. Vials of foul-looking liquids and vases containing dried up herbs and unidentifiable items are stacked on the rows of shelves that cover all the walls. Altar-like tables and long, low benches line the center of the room. Some of the benches are covered with complex arrangements of delicate glassware while others are completely barren. The stone doors in the north and east walls are identical, but the stone door in the west wall is made of a strange purple stone covered with strange runes.

A successful DC 17 Knowledge (Arcana) check recognizes some of the tables as dissection tables and that much of the glassware is designed for specific alchemical purposes. A thorough search of the vials and bottles in the room reveals materials that would be valuable only to an alchemist, along with a few potions that are unidentified (antidotes for the following poisons: deathblade posion, black lotus extract (x2), and terinav root, a *potion of cure moderate*, 3 *potions of cat's grace*, and a *potion of lesser restoration*).

Trapped Drawer: A trapped laboratory bench drawer holds a spellbook containing a variety of different spells. Opening the drawer without uttering a password sets off a *fire trap* (CL 20; 1d4+20 fire damage; DC 20 Reflex save for half) that destroys the contents of the drawer and affects those nearby.

Spellbook: The laboratory drawer holds a spellbook marked "Utility" that contains the following spells: *enlarge person, reduce person, alter self, arcane lock, blur, darkvision, daylight, levitate, mirror image, shatter, dispel magic, gaseous form, summon monster III, tongues, globe of invulnerability, stoneskin, teleport, teleport, greater*.

Northern Door: The northern door (9 in. thick; Hardness 8; hp 90; Break DC 24) opens with a standard dial like other doors throughout the caverns but is trapped. The dial on this door is keyed precisely to Londar's handprint. While any humanoid hand can open it, anyone other than Londar triggers a blast of liquid air that freezes everything within a 10-ft. radius of the door.

Ice Blast Trap CR 7
XP 3,200
Type magical; **Perception** DC 29; **Disable Device** DC 28
EFFECTS
Trigger touch; **Reset** Automatic
Effect Ice Blast (8d6 cold damage; DC 21 Reflex save for half); multiple targets: everything within a 10 ft. radius of the door
Stone Door in the West Wall: The door in the west wall (5 in. thick; Hardness 15; hp 90; Break DC 30) is not trapped, but cannot be opened unless the purple dial in the **Abandoned Alchemist's Laboratory (Area 17)** has also been turned. Londar enchanted the stone of the door and created two locks as a failsafe in the event one of his laboratory creations somehow attempted to open the door. The PCs must break down the door if they did not locate that dial.

30. Teleport Chamber

A decaying corpse rests in the center of an intricate pattern of multicolored tiles set into the floor. These tiles provided Londar with exact *teleport* coordinates. Londar used this as his main teleport chamber for coming to his laboratory and separated it from the rest of his laboratory only for safety reasons. The room wasn't used for anything else and has no other decorations or items. The rotting corpse is, in fact, Londar. He *teleported* here as part of a *contingency* spell and was attempting to make it to his stock of antidotes and potions in the laboratory when the poison finally killed him. His rotting hand is wrapped around an empty, unmarked potion vial. While the secluded nature of the chamber prevented any scavengers or maggots from getting at the body, bacteria have already begun their slow decay of the corpse. PCs might wish to somehow *speak with dead* or use other spells to communicate with Londar. For the purpose of spells, Londar has been dead for 4 weeks plus the number of days it has taken PCs to get this far. Londar generally answers poorly worded questions with riddles or questions, but carefully worded questions provide useful information (see Londar's Information sidebox). Londar felt safe and really wasn't carrying much with him when he left for his niece's wedding, so his corpse carries less treasure than the PCs would normally hope.

Treasure: Londar's corpse wears a signet ring (20 gp) that should make it clear that this is his corpse. They can also find the following items: a brightly colored *cloak of resistance +2*, a *ring of protection +2*, a *wand of fireball* (CL 10, 27 charges), a *wand of stoneskin* (CL 10, 12 charges), a money bag holding 58 gp, 73 sp, and 2 cp, and a *blessed book* containing the following spells: 1st—*alarm, charm person, color spray, mage armor, shield*; 2nd—*arcane lock, invisibility, see invisibility, web*; 3rd—*dispel magic, fireball, haste, major image*; 4th—*dimension door, rainbow spear*, wall of fire*; 5th—*contact other plane, geas, rainbow staff*, teleportation circle*; 6th—*contingency, programmed illusion, sunbeam*; 7th—*magnificent mansion, prismatic spray, teleport, greater*; 8th—*control weather, dominate monster, mind blank*; 9th—*gate, teleport other*, prismatic wall, time stop*.

* Spell created by Londar that appears in **Appendix E: New Spells**.

Londar's Information

If the PCs use a *speak with dead* spell (a scroll with this spell is found in **Area 27**) to question Londar, they can learn some useful facts. A few sample questions and answers are listed below. The GM needs to adjudicate other questions as Londar's corpse avoids giving information about what *Horgrim's Pyramid* does, specifically naming Baron Kurell, or telling the PCs how to open his vault.

Question	Response
Who killed you?	Thieves, who else? Lucky bastards, too. Poisoned me.
Why were you killed?	I suppose the baron didn't pay my bills as he promised. Probably wants the pyramid for himself.
What bills?	The bills the baron was supposed to pay.
Which baron?	The one that was supposed to pay the thieves' guild.
What pyramid?	*Horgrim's Pyramid.*
What does the pyramid do?	Enough to kill for.
Why do you owe the thieves' guild money?	We hired Alfguir to steal a few things for us.
How do you open the vault?	I generally just turn the dial with my hand.
Is the vault trapped?	Certainly.

---

31. The Summoning Chamber (CR 7)

This summoning chamber is heavily warded and protected. Summoned creatures cannot even touch the doors, let alone escape. Powerful runes and symbols adorn the walls and ceiling and prevent summoning anywhere other than the center of the circle of runes in the middle of the room. These same runes prevent any form of ethereal travel or *gate* or *teleport* spells. Londar used this chamber to summon and talk to demons and other powerful creatures and depended on his protective spells to keep the summoned creatures trapped here until he released them.

Londar's most recent discussion was with a demon named **Iriala** who remains trapped in the room since the mage's death. Iriala desperately wants to escape the room but knows the only way out is to be invited by someone unaffected by the imprisoning spells. Londar normally entered through the western door from the library, and his long absence bothers Iriala, who fears being forgotten by the mage or of something happening to Londar. Upon hearing the click of the door mechanism, Iriala prepares to meet anyone coming through as described below.

Iriala CR 7
XP 3,200
hp 84 (Pathfinder Roleplaying Game Bestiary, "Demon, Succubus")

Tactics: Iriala has been trapped for more than a month. The magic of the room prevents them using their etherealness. They must be invited out of the room by another free-willed being (charmed characters or NPCs do not count). Once free of this room, they can use all their abilities.

Iriala's primary goal is to obtain their freedom. When the door from the laboratory, a door Londar never used, opens, they use their change shape ability to take the shape of a handsome male human wearing expensive clothing. Using that form, Iriala greets the PCs joyfully and thanks them for rescuing him. Claiming to be a kidnapped victim, Iriala begs the PCs to escort him out of "Londar's horrible dungeon." Iriala uses different tactics against the PCs depending upon whether or not they invite them to travel with them, thereby releasing them, or see through their ruse and refuse to help them.

If the PCs invite them along, they continue in their male human form, with the goal of letting the PCs obtain treasure for them before they flee. They surreptitiously attempt to *charm* any character that shows interest, but take advantage of their energy drain only in privacy. Otherwise, they wait for a good moment to loot the characters before fleeing through the Ethereal Plane. They use any charmed PCs to foster confusion and use their energy drain ability on any PC they attack. If the battle goes against them, Iriala flees to the Ethereal Plane, stealing as many items as possible.

The PCs are likely to find Iriala's male form and story of kidnapping different enough to be believable, but they might also notice that the doors out of the room open easily and might wonder why he didn't try to leave on his own. If the PCs see through their ruse and refuse to release them, Iriala flees.

32. Londar's Library (CR 9)

Londar's library is, in a word, magnificent. Londar *teleported* highly paid craftsmen into the room along with the wood and materials they needed to do their work. Dark brown leather chairs surround mahogany tables in the center of the room, and mahogany bookcases with intricate carvings line the walls all the way up to the high ceiling. Rolling ladders attached to the bookshelves allow access to books on the highest shelves. A diffuse light comes down from the ceiling, lighting the room evenly for reading and studying. Beautiful wool rugs cover the stone floors in all but the northeast corner, which is coated with colored tiles in the shape of intricate runes. The only doors in the room include the stone door leading back into the **Summoning Chamber (Area 31)** and the heavy steel door into **Londar's Vault (Area 33)** located at the southernmost end of the east wall.

Books lining the shelves cover a wide variety of subjects and include works of poetry and fiction along with texts on warfare, military organization, construction, and other rather dry subjects. Londar knew where he put different books and never took the time to organize his library beyond keeping books he used most often on the lower shelves. Books containing magic spells are mixed together with the other texts and take some searching to identify.

The library is protected by 3 **wood golems** keyed specifically to Londar. These golems are similar to those in **Area 7** but are made from the same mahogany as the rest of the furniture in the library and are carved in the form of robed humans with clenched fists.

Wood Golem (3) CR 6
XP 2,400
hp 64 (Pathfinder Roleplaying Game Bestiary, "Golem, Wood")

Tactics: The golems rush forward, screeching their alarm, and attack anyone other than Londar. They close for melee combat with their chosen target(s) and fight until destroyed. These golems follow fleeing characters as far as the **Laboratory (Area 29)** but go no farther. Doors that close automatically and prevent their return to the library might effectively trap them in a different room.

Battle with the wood golems stands a chance of damaging books and other items in the library. The GM should carefully monitor the use of any area spells or fire-based spells and inflict damage on items within the library as needed.

Treasure: Finding the various spellbooks requires some time searching, so each spellbook is given a different DC. PCs searching with the assistance of a *detect magic* spell receive a +2 circumstance bonus on their search for spellbooks.

Spellbook #1: DC 13 Perception check; contains the following spells: 0—all; 1st—all. This book is trapped with the *explosive runes* spell (CL 20) triggered by anyone reading the first page. It is a DC 18 to save against the spell.

Spellbook #2: DC 15 Perception check; contains the following spells: 7th—*banishment, force cage, phase door, prismatic spray*; 8th—*greater planar binding, prismatic wall*; 9th—*prismatic sphere*. This book is trapped with the *sepia snake sigil* spell triggered by anyone reading the 50th page. It is a DC 18 to save against the spell.

Spellbook #3: DC 22 Perception check; contains the following spells: 7th—*prismatic spray, sequester, teleport, greater*; 8th—*charm monster, mass, iron body*; 9th—*teleport other**.

Spellbook #4: DC 25 Perception check; contains the following spells: 2nd—*blur, continual flame, detect thoughts, flaming sphere, mirror image, rope trick*; 3rd—*fireball, fly, glyph of warding, hold person, tiny hut, lightning bolt*; 4th—*dimensional door, fire shield, rainbow spear**. This book is trapped with *explosive runes* exactly the same way as spellbook #1.

Spellbook #5: DC 30 Perception check; 4th—*arcane eye, charm monster, greater invisibility, fabricate, ice storm, locate creature, rainbow spear**; 5th—*contact other plane, dominate person, dismissal, rainbow staff**.

* Spell created by Londar that appears in **Appendix E: New Spells**.

Treasure: In addition to the spellbooks, several other interesting texts are stored in the library. Each requires a DC 20 Perception check to find:

- Two matched books known as the *Arcanari**
- *Jaerel's Jungle Guide**
- Several ancient texts describing the process to magically harden and reinforce stone (worth 2000 gp)
- Book describing how to create wood golems found throughout Londar's home (worth 1000 gp)
- Book describing several foul uses for dragon blood (worth 300 gp)

* See **Appendix D: New Magic Items**

The ornate wool rugs are heavy and difficult to move but have a total value of 2700 gp.

33. Londar's Vault (CR 15)

The massive steel vault is covered with strange, glowing runes and sigils that surround yet another handprint lock. While any small or medium-size hand can unlock the vault, only Londar's hand can open the vault without setting off a very deadly *chain lightning trap*.

Steel Vault Door: 15 in. thick; Hardness 15; hp 180; Break DC 35. The enchanted steel door is counterweighted to open and close easily once unlocked.

Chain Lightning Trap CR 15
XP 51,200
Type magical; **Perception** DC 31; **Disable Device** DC 31
EFFECTS
Trigger touch; **Reset** none
Effect spell effect (empowered chain lightning, 13d6 electricity damage plus 50%, DC 24 Reflex save for half); multiple targets (up to 13 secondary targets within 30 ft. of primary target, DC 22 Reflex save for half)

Note: If the PCs haven't learned caution after the door to the **Teleport Chamber (Area 30)**, this trap has the potential to kill many in the party.

In addition to spellbooks containing all or some of the spells found in **Areas 29, 30, and 32** (GM's choice), the PCs find a book describing a process to colorize spells and a variety of papers and documents describing Londar's experiments. When combined with the maps and battle plans found in the **Fourth Level of Londar's Tower (Area 12)**, the papers and documents the PCs find here provide undeniable proof that Londar was planning to brutally conquer the surrounding area with the help of an unidentified baron.

Treasure: *Rainbow bracers*, rainbow ring*, rainbow crossbow*, Horgrim's Pyramid*, Korik's Ruby*, the Decaying Book**, and gold and gems with a total value of 45,000 gp.

* See **Appendix D: New Magic Items**

After learning what happened to Londar, the party is almost certain to return to Hampton Hill with their newfound knowledge, treasure, and possibly Londar's corpse.

Ambush! CR 8

Unfortunately, **Ander Fierk** has been scrying on the party to determine whether or not they have been successful. Once he learns they have some of Londar's spellbooks and papers, he decides to ambush the party along the road back to Hampton Hill.

Tactics: Ander, in his quest for power and knowledge, has joined forces with Baron Kurell. His mission is to obtain Londar's spellbooks, notes, and any evidence mentioning the baron. He casts *alter self* to alter his appearance to avoid being identified in the event he fails or someone gets away. He then casts *fly*. Once prepared, he flies above the path or road the PCs are using and waits for them to approach his position. He attempts to capture the PCs with a *black tentacles* spell. If the battle goes against him, Ander is a coward; he uses his *fly* spell to remain high above the PCs and rains fireballs down on them. He retreats if he takes more than 20 points of damage and leaves the area to meet with Baron Kurell (see below).

Ander Fierk CR 8
XP 4,800
Male human wizard 9
CE Medium humanoid (human)
Init +1; **Senses** Perception -1
AC 14, touch 12, flat-footed 13 (+2 armor, +1 deflection, +1 Dex)
hp 41 (9d6+9)
Fort +4, **Ref** +5, **Will** +6
Speed 30 ft.
Melee +2 dagger +8 (1d4+4/19-20)
Ranged mwk light crossbow +6 (1d8/19-20)
Special Attacks hand of the apprentice (7/day)

Wizard Spells Prepared (CL 9th; concentration +13)
5th—dominate person (DC 19)
4th—black tentacles, summon monster IV, summon monster IV
3rd—fireball (DC 17), fireball (DC 17), fly, summon monster III
2nd—fog cloud, invisibility, resist energy, shatter (DC 16), web (DC 16)
1st—burning hands (DC 15), burning hands (DC 15), disguise self, mage armor, shield
0 (at will)—daze (DC 14), detect magic, ghost sound (DC 14), read magic

Str 14, **Dex** 13, **Con** 10, **Int** 19, **Wis** 8, **Cha** 12
Base Atk +4; **CMB** +6; **CMD** 18
Feats Brew Potion, Combat Casting, Craft Wand, Craft Wondrous Item, Empower Spell, Maximize Spell, Quicken Spell, Scribe Scroll
Skills Appraise +16, Craft (alchemy) +16, Fly +13, Knowledge (arcana) +16, Knowledge (dungeoneering) +8, Knowledge (engineering) +8, Knowledge (geography) +8, Knowledge (history) +16, Knowledge (local) +8, Knowledge (nature) +8, Knowledge (nobility) +8, Knowledge (planes) +8, Knowledge (religion) +8, Linguistics +8, Spellcraft +16
Languages Abyssal, Celestial, Common, Draconic, Infernal, Sylvan
SQ arcane bond (masterwork light crossbow), metamagic mastery (1/day)
Combat Gear *potion of cat's grace, potion of cure light wounds, potion of invisibility, potion of invisibility, scroll of alter self (CL 9th), greater invisibility (CL 9th), summon monster iv (CL 9th), wand of fireball (CL 9th, 36 charges), wand of maximized magic missile (CL 9th, 18 charges),* tanglefoot bag (2); **Other Gear** *+2 dagger,* crossbow bolts (20), mwk light crossbow, *bracers of armor +2, cloak of resistance +1, ring of protection +1,* ander fierk's spellbook, 121 gp, 97 sp, 78 cp

Special Abilities
Hand of the Apprentice (7/day) (Su) As a standard action, throw melee weapon (use Int instead of Dex) and instantly returns.
Metamagic Mastery (1/day) (Su) Spend 1 use per spell level increase to apply a known metamagic feat for free.

Arriving in Hampton Hill

After the ambush, the PCs are likely injured, tired, angry, and somewhat suspicious. Finally reaching Hampton Hill doesn't turn out to be very relaxing.

Their return is met with joy and sorrow as other things have happened in their absence. After their return, Sheriff Hamra Ranthas summons the PCs. Hamra and the mayor inform the PCs that Baron Kurell and his men tortured and left for dead Xanthaque, an elderly elven witch living in town. Xanthaque did not reveal what they were searching for but did tell the sheriff that she gave them wrong directions. The sheriff tells the PCs that pigeons have gone out with information about the baron's destination and that the king has sent guards to arrest him. Based on comments Xanthaque made, Hamra is concerned about potential threats to the town. She asks the PCs to speak to Xanthaque and ensure there are no other threats to Hampton Hill.

Returning Londar's corpse and the incriminating papers to Learah Relight should garner a reasonable monetary reward and a small experience point reward. Upon the return of her uncle's corpse, Learah makes immediate plans to have him *resurrected*. Learah also most likely claims her father's spellbooks as her property by right, though she allows PC spellcasters to copy spells from them. She also may (at your discretion) claim any of the magic items recovered from the mansion as hers by inheritance.

Attempts to contact Ander Fierk (presuming he escaped the ambush without being identified) end in failure. Questions regarding Ander's whereabouts cause several people to say that he left with Baron Kurell, a rumor Learah and Xanthaque can confirm (see below).

Xanthaque's Tale

If the PCs follow up on the sheriff's request and visit Xanthaque (female elf wizard 7 / loremaster 5), she weaves a tale that sends them off on another, possibly more dangerous, journey.

Despite the healing and ministering she has received, Xanthaque's age makes recovery from her ordeal rather lengthy. Xanthaque informs the PCs that Baron Kurell is really a cleric worshipping Orcus and that he somehow found out about an artifact known as *The White Eye*. While she doesn't know the exact details about the eye, she knows it is an extremely powerful, evil relic. Xanthaque provides the PCs with sketchy information about a forgotten evil god known as "Horgrim" and the great battles between his forces and forces worshipping Arn (see the information previously provided regarding Arn's Mountain).

If the PCs provide her with the *Decaying Book* (**Area 33** of the **Mansion**), maps, and other documents found in **Areas 12** and **33**, she interprets the book and tell the PCs the properties of the activated pyramid. If the PCs let her, she dispels some of the spells on the pyramid and asks them to melt it down. Although she is unable to identify the exact powers the eye is supposed to possess, she is certain that it is extremely powerful and should never find its way into the wrong hands. She tells the PCs that she sent Baron Kurell in the wrong direction but believes he will escape capture and eventually discover the eye's location.

The maps and notes discovered in Londar's mansion and library allow her to provide the PCs with a location for "Arn's Mountain," a hollow mountain reported to hold an ancient temple to Horgrim, the last known refuge for Horgrim's followers and *The White Eye*. If the PCs seem hesitant, Xanthaque describes the vast wealth Horgrim's followers reportedly hid deep inside their temples and even goes as far as to offer a few magic items. After her torture, she is desperate to foil any plans the baron might have and is honestly afraid of the powers the eye might possess.

Continuing the Adventure

Learah recovers her beloved uncle's corpse and travels to a major city to have him *resurrected*. Londar's paranoia leads him to *teleport* to a distant jungle hideaway and begin making new plans. While he might eventually plot against the PCs, he has more pressing plans to make regarding Alfguir and the baron and is desperately short of funds. If the PCs introduce some of the items they found as evidence against Baron Kurell and Londar, they find that their information simply isn't important when compared to Xanthaque's testimony about the baron's torture.

The PCs might decide to act on information suggesting Alfguir is somehow responsible for Londar's death or that he is a member of the thieves' guild. If they question Alfguir, they find themselves up against an intelligent, wily thief who has learned many tricks for fooling spells aimed at determining truth (see below).

Questioning Alfguir

Alfguir is a successful merchant and a successful thief due to his intelligence. He does an excellent job of avoiding accusations and redirecting accusations made against him. If the PCs do question Alfguir, he avoids telling direct lies, but also avoids revealing much of the truth. One point that should be remembered is that Alfguir suspects his people killed Londar but doesn't know for certain, and he did not order them to do so. Londar's death disappoints him because all he really wanted was payment. This means that he can honestly say he did not know about or order Londar's death. If asked if he is a thief, Alfguir replies, "Well, someone always claims a merchant has robbed them, so I suppose you can find someone that will say I am." If asked if he is a member of the thieves' guild, Alfguir replies, "I am a member of many guilds, some admittedly with bad reputations, but all traveling merchants must make these sacrifices."

In general, the PCs do not have enough information to accuse Alfguir of breaking any laws, and he avoids giving them any. Alfguir makes certain to depart for distant cities if he discovers the PCs have any inkling of his true business. If the PCs are clever enough about their questioning and avoid making any accusations, Alfguir might reveal he was hired to "acquire" a few rather strange items pictured in a book and used his contacts to eventually purchase them for Londar (Diplomacy check DC 20).

Chapter 7: Arn's Mountain

Background

Horgrim's followers once captured vast territories, but their success also led to their downfall. Using the many relics and artifacts they possessed depended upon cooperation, teamwork, and a strict adherence to hierarchy. Political ambitions and infighting broke down the hierarchy, leading many different factions to break apart, with each taking different relics and pieces of relics with them. Forces worshipping the good gods were quick to take advantage of their lack of order. Successive battles broke down and destroyed many of the different factions until one main faction remained. A last effort was made to create a hidden temple within the recesses of a hollow mountain. Designed as a place to gather Horgrim's remaining forces and artifacts and eventually rebuild the great armies they once possessed, it became a focal point not just for Horgrim's followers, but also for followers of the good gods, particularly Arn, one of Horgrim's main opponents.

Several rangers dedicated to Arn discovered the hollow mountain and instigated an all-out attack against the temple hidden within it. After terrible losses, Arn's forces took the cavern and trapped all of Horgrim's followers inside their temple. All efforts to invade the temple itself were repelled, sometimes by traps, other times by soldiers or magic. Arn's forces had few remaining leaders after these battles, but all of them reached the same conclusion: The cost of taking the temple was too high. It would be easier to keep the denizens of the temple trapped inside until they died of starvation, thirst, or old age.

The rock of the high ceiling was imbued with magical sunlight using complex rituals, and magical creatures were asked to guard the temple and prevent Horgrim's trapped followers from ever departing. With the outside of the temple securely guarded, the priests and faithful servants to Horgrim inside used their time to create numerous deadly traps to help protect their relics from Arn's forces. Some of the followers chose death, while others willing turned to a life of undead servitude in Horgrim's name. A few chosen followers were frozen in time, awaiting a day when they could again form armies in Horgrim's name and march forth on the world.

Over the centuries, some guardians left for other duties or died without passing the duty to another. A few magical creatures remain, guarding the temple as a duty handed down through generations with no real knowledge of why. Years of constant sunlight and moisture, along with seeds brought in by passing birds and animals, helped the cavern develop lush, rich vegetation that supports a variety of wildlife.

Arn's Mountain

Bright, magical sunlight constantly flows from the high ceiling of the hollowed-out mountain to feed the many plants and mosses that grow in the moist, warm air. A number of animals make their winter, or even permanent, homes here, with some of them growing far larger than normal. The high ceiling varies from 600 to 800 feet above the rolling floor and the hollowed-out mountain itself has a radius of roughly 2000 feet. A strange, tiered temple stands in the southwest corner, oddly free of the many vines and mosses that cover almost every other surface. While there are numerous exits and entrances to the hollow chamber, most are quite small, and all are at least 100 feet above the ground, forcing creatures entering or leaving to either climb the walls or fly. Numerous pools of water dot the cavern, along with clusters of large trees grown from seeds carried by birds or other animals.

The most dangerous creatures in the cavern are undoubtedly the **couatl** that stand watch over the temple. Other creatures in the cavern are generally frightened enough of armed humanoids to stay far away. The only creature that might cause trouble is the tiger lord that doesn't like anyone interfering with its territory (see **Area A**).

Horgrim, God of War and Magic

Alignment: Lawful Evil
Domains: Evil, Law, Magic, War
Symbol: A black spearhead covering a gold disc that represents an eclipse.
Worshippers: Evil monks, warriors, wizards, and nobles.
Favored Weapons: Shortspear, staff

Horgrim is commonly depicted as a handsome male figure in black robes wielding a shortspear. Almost forgotten now, Horgrim was a popular god several millennia ago but political fighting among his priests led to a rapid decline. Horgrim's theology is straightforward: Magic is a tool used to enforce the law of might upon all. Some scholars use ancient references to Horgrim as a god of magic and darkness to support the claim that Horgrim's role as a war-god is a secondary result of this theology. Any modern priests or worshippers of Horgrim must practice their faith in secrecy because there are no known active temples. According to ancient texts, worship services included a gathering at dusk and a simple, unified chant of, "Power shall bring the darkness that makes all equal before Horgrim." At the height of their power, Horgrim's worshippers counted many wizards, warriors, and nobles among their number. Many of Horgrim's priests studied wizardry and warfare to better serve their god. Priests and wizards led the many wars Horgrim's followers fought to expand his domain and were usually seen at the front of the battle line. Sketchy records indicate the priests and followers of Horgrim created a number of powerful relics that are lost or forgotten. The few existing relics that can be traced back to Horgrim's worshippers are powerful enough to lend credence to these rumors.

The Guardians

Any creature entering the mountain is watched carefully by the few guardians that remain. After a few minutes, one of the **couatl** guarding the temple approaches the PCs to determine their purpose. The main remaining guardian for the cavern is **Souref**, an ancient couatl, who is supported by two younger **couatl** named Shiviec and Rivarn. Any of these creatures is a formidable opponent; all three together are particularly deadly. All of them possess gold tattoos embedded into the scales of their chest that they can activate at will with a number of special effects as described below. Shiviec and Rivarn are a mated pair and are always found together. If only one is seen, the other is usually hiding nearby. Souref is often encountered alone, but the other two are always close enough to rapidly come to his aid.

Souref   CR 16
XP 76,800
Advanced couatl cleric of Arn 10
LG Large outsider (native)
Init +8; **Senses** darkvision 60 ft., detect chaos, detect evil, detect good, detect law; Perception +38
AC 25, touch 14, flat-footed 20 (+4 Dex, +1 dodge, +11 natural, -1 size)
hp 297 (22 HD; 10d8+12d10+186)
Fort +19, **Ref** +17, **Will** +26
Speed 20 ft., fly 60 ft. (good)
Melee bite +26 (1d8+12 plus grab and poison)
Space 10 ft.; **Reach** 5 ft.
Special Attacks channel positive energy 11/day (DC 23, 5d6), constrict (1d8+12), holy lance (5 rounds, 1/day), poison
Spell-Like Abilities (CL 9th; concentration +17)
Constant—detect chaos, detect evil, detect good, detect law
At will—detect thoughts (DC 20), ethereal jaunt (CL 16th), invisibility, plane shift (DC 25)
Domain Spell-Like Abilities (CL 10th; concentration +19)
12/day—rebuke death (1d4+5), touch of good (+5)
Sorcerer Spells Known (CL 9th; concentration +17)
4th (6/day)—holy smite (DC 22), ice storm
3rd (8/day)—dispel magic, flame arrow, lightning bolt (DC 21)
2nd (8/day)—acid arrow, blur, calm emotions (DC 20), web (DC 20)
1st (8/day)—alarm, detect undead, magic missile, shield, shocking grasp
0 (at will)—dancing lights, daze (DC 18), detect magic, detect poison, ghost sound (DC 18), mending, open/close (DC 18), read magic
Cleric Spells Prepared (CL 10th; concentration +19)

5th—dispel evil[D], flame strike (DC 24), flame strike (DC 24), raise dead, summon monster V
4th—divine power, holy smite[D] (DC 23), neutralize poison, restoration, spiritual ally, summon monster IV
3rd—create food and water, glyph of warding, magic circle against evil[D], searing light, summon monster III, trial of fire and acid (DC 22)
2nd—align weapon (good only)[D], augury, bull's strength, consecrate, silence (DC 21), summon monster II, suppress charms and compulsions
1st—bless, command (DC 20), comprehend languages, divine favor, entropic shield, protection from evil[D], sanctuary (DC 20), summon monster I
0 (at will)—create water, light, purify food and drink (DC 19), stabilize
D Domain spell; Domains Good, Healing
Str 26, **Dex** 18, **Con** 26, **Int** 21, **Wis** 28, **Cha** 26
Base Atk +19; **CMB** +28 (+32 grapple); **CMD** 43 (can't be tripped)
Feats Alertness, Combat Casting, Dodge, Empower Spell, Eschew Materials[B], Improved Initiative, Inscribe Magical Tattoo, Iron Will, Lightning Reflexes, Quicken Spell, Still Spell, Turn Undead
Skills Acrobatics +19 (+15 to jump), Bluff +14, Craft (tattoo) +30, Diplomacy +33, Fly +21, Heal +13, Knowledge (arcana) +20, Knowledge (history) +9, Knowledge (nature) +8, Knowledge (nobility) +9, Knowledge (planes) +9, Knowledge (religion) +20, Perception +38, Sense Motive +38, Spellcraft +30, Survival +21, Use Magic Device +33
Languages Celestial, Common, Draconic, Elven, Sylvan; telepathy 100 ft.
SQ healer's blessing
Special Abilities
Cleric Channel Positive Energy 5d6 (11/day, DC 23) (Su) Positive energy heals the living and harms the undead; negative has the reverse effect.
Combat Casting +4 to Concentration checks to cast while on the defensive.
Empower Spell Numeric effects of a spell are increased 50%. +2 Levels.
Healer's Blessing (Su) Your cure spells are empowered for free.
Holy Lance (5 rounds, 1/day) (Su) Touched weapon temporarily becomes holy.
Poison - STR Damage (DC 24) (Ex) Bite—injury; save Fort DC 24; frequency 1/minute for 10 minutes; effect 1d4 Str; cure 2 consecutive saves. The save DC is Constitution-based.
Quicken Spell Cast a spell as a swift action. +4 Levels.
Rebuke Death (12/day) (Sp) As a standard action, touch heals 1d4+5 dam to negative HP target.
Still Spell You can cast a spell with no somatic components. +1 Level.
Touch of Good +5 (12/day) (Sp) Grant +5 to skill checks, ability checks and saving throws for 1 rd.
Turn Undead (DC 23) Your Channel Energy can make undead in 30 ft flee for 1 min.
Description and Personality: Souref is a large serpent with feathered wings. Age has deepened the bright colors of his wings rather than fading them, making him even more colorful than the young couatl that assist him. Souref is vain, confident in his strength, beauty, and faith to Arn. Souref provides healing to those in need, but only if asked properly. Souref is resolute in his duty to prevent evil creatures from leaving the temple, and to keep evil magical items from being taken from it. In all the years here, he has only had two major battles. One with a creature that tried to flee the temple, and another with adventurers who entered the cavern with "evil hearts." Nothing would please him more than destroying some of the evil artifacts hidden in the temple, though he isn't even certain what those items might be. In the past 1000 years, he has witnessed three groups enter the temple. Two groups never emerged; the third fled the temple, bloody and terrified. Even after being healed, those adventurers decided against trying to enter the temple again. Souref would love to destroy any evil items the PCs find during their exploration. PCs who willingly surrender powerful evil items for destruction might receive an item from Souref's treasure chest (See **Area D**) as a reward.

Shiviec and Rivarn (2) CR 10
XP 9,600
hp 126 (Pathfinder Roleplaying Game Bestiary, "Couatl")
Description and Personality: Shiviec and Rivarn are a mated pair, though it appears that only couatl can tell them apart. The beautiful creatures joined Souref in guardianship of the temple approximately 50 years ago. They are far more playful, friendly, and outgoing than their elder counterpart, but possess less knowledge about the temple. Compliments on their beauty appeals to their vanity and makes them far more receptive to requests for aid.

Map 5:
Arn's Moutain
1 Square - 100 Feet
A
E
B
D
Temple
C
Major Cave Entrances
100 Feet above Cavern Floor
N
W
E
S

General Tactics: As guardians, the couatl must prevent evil creatures from leaving the temple and prevent the removal of powerful, evil items. They have nothing against adventurers entering the temple or taking the treasures hidden within, but their oaths force them to attack any creatures identified as evil. All of them *detect evil* before greeting any new creatures in the cavern. They ask the PCs why they have come to the cavern and how they knew about it. If asked, the couatl provide most of the background information on the temple, but this knowledge is told from the perspective of Arn's followers and is heavily biased. If the couatl trust the PCs' intention, they welcome them to the cavern and tell them they can do whatever they want in the temple so long as they do not remove any evil relics or artifacts from the mountain; such items must be destroyed. Each time the PCs prepare to leave the cavern after exploring the temple, one of the couatl activates its *detect thoughts* tattoo and questions them again. This time they just want to ensure that the PCs are not leaving with any evil-aligned, powerful magic items. If the PCs say they do not know, or are uncertain, the couatl ask them to show all the items they recovered, promising they can keep any non-evil items. A lie results in a request to empty their backpacks; if the PCs do not comply, all three couatl attack.

Tactics: The magic tattoos (see sidebox) prevent *banishment* or similar attacks from working on the couatl. The couatl generally consider physical combat beneath them and depend heavily on their spells to soften up their opponents before risking their beautiful bodies and plumage in physical combat. The first action any couatl takes when going into battle is to activate its *haste* tattoo. With all of his age and wisdom, Souref is far less forgiving than the younger couatl. Souref believes his actions are necessary for protecting the world outside the mountain and, after using the *haste* and *protection from energy* tattoos, wades into combat. In the unlikely event that one of the other two couatl is in trouble, Souref casts *sanctuary* on himself while he makes new plans.

GM Note: A fight with the couatl at the PCs' present level is almost certain suicide. If the PCs end up in a fight and realize this, they should be given one opportunity to drop their weapons and surrender.

Keyed Locations

Several locations inside the hollow mountain are potentially dangerous. The couatl warn the PCs of the more dangerous locations if they are treated politely. If the PCs are rude, or if the couatl don't trust them, the couatl don't give the PCs any warnings. They fly high into the air and watch how the PCs work their way through any problems.

A. Dire Tiger's Lair (CR 8)

A stand of large trees surrounds an obvious home for an extremely large animal. A dire tiger made its way inside the mountain while traveling as a druid's companion. The druid visited Souref, and the dire tiger decided it wanted to stay and play so the druid left it here. A collar around the massive beast's neck allows it to shrink itself enough to climb up one of the exits when food inside the mountain becomes scarce. The creature is intelligent enough to avoid armored characters, but defends the small, tree-shaded area that it considers home. The tiger is a source of potential problems toward the end of the adventure. If the PCs staked horses or pack animals outside the mountain someplace, it is very likely the tiger kills and eats them if they aren't protected somehow.

Tactics: Generally, the diretiger doesn't attack anyone unless its home is invaded. If the tiger lord does feel a need to fight, it pounces on the most lightly armored character (it learned once before that metal doesn't taste good) and tears at them until dead. It is intelligent enough to flee if badly injured. It is also intelligent enough to guess that adventurers might leave something tasty to eat outside the mountain. If it notices adventurers inside the mountain, it climbs out to scout for an easy meal. The dire tiger eats one unattended horse or pack animal per week (chosen randomly), leading to potential problems when the PCs want to leave. If Uvear (**Area G**, Wilderness) is guarding the pack animals, the dire tiger leaves them alone. The PCs can communicate with it if they choose, but it is very wary of them and unwilling to be anyone's companion.

Tiger, Dire CR 8
XP 4,800
hp 105 (Pathfinder Roleplaying Game Bestiary, "Tiger, Dire")

B. Assassin Vine (CR 3)

Numerous vines crawling across the rocks and bushes surround a small pool of water. One of these vines is an **assassin vine** that waits for thirsty victims.

Assassin Vine CR 3
XP 800
hp 30 (Pathfinder Roleplaying Game Bestiary, "Assassin Vine")

Tactics: The vine waits patiently for prey to approach the water before attempting to grab it. A few small animal corpses hidden beneath the leaves and vines in the area mark the roots of the plant (can be spotted with a DC 22 Perception check).

C. Peaceful Pool

A slow trickle of water flows from the ceiling high above to splash into a peaceful pool of water. Vines cover several stone benches looking over the pool as well as several small statues. Clearing the vines away from the statues reveals stone figures of men and women with robes and staves facing toward the water. The entire area is considered *hallowed* ground due to the many rituals and spells performed upon it by the clerics and paladins of Arn. This area is an excellent place to rest, heal, and plan.

D. Souref's Cave

Souref lives in this small cave near the top of the hollow mountain. The cave is difficult to detect (can be spotted with a DC 27 Perception check) due to the magical sunlight pouring down from the ceiling and can be reached only with a *fly* or *levitate* spell, or some other means of flight. Souref is profoundly insulted if anyone enters the cave without an invitation and resorts to violence to expel them (see statistics above). Even Shiviec and Rivarn call to him from outside the cave and wait for an invitation before entering.

Permanent *daylight* spells along the ceiling of the small cave provide steady light. A small altar dedicated to Arn faces east, but no other furniture is in the room. Beneath the altar is a heavy wooden chest (unlocked, no traps) that contains a vast array of items collected over the years by Souref and his predecessors.

Treasure: The chest contains more than 100,000 gp worth of various gems and coins, and a number of magical weapons, armor, and other items: *+3 longsword, +3 bastard sword, +3 great sword, +3 short spear, +3 dagger, +2 staff, +2 dagger of returning, +2 scimitar, +2 adaptive composite longbow, +2 dwarven plate, +3 mithral chainmail, plate armor of the deep, +3 studded leather, darkwood shield, +3 bracers of armor, +2 amulet of natural armor, boots of speed, boots of levitation, boots of elvenkind, cloak of the bat, cloak of elvenkind, +2 headband of alluring charisma, +2 belt of incredible dexterity, harp of charming, lens of detection, pearl of power (3rd), efficient quiver, rope of climbing,* and a *robe of useful items.*

If the PCs voluntarily turn over evil-aligned items such as *The White Eye* and *amulets of the dark sun*, Souref rewards them with a few items from his treasure chest. The GM should choose items that fit the classes and levels of the PCs and the power level of the campaign.

E. Shiviec and Rivarn's Lair

The mated couatl have a small home here that is usually used only for short rests and private time. The smooth-walled cave is 600 feet above the floor of the hollow mountain and requires some means of flight to reach. Nothing of value is stored here because the pair gives any items they discover to Souref to store in his cave. Couatl are intensely private with regard to their homes; any invasion of this home results in attack.

F. The Temple

The temple to Horgrim is detailed in the next chapter.

Chapter 8: Horgrim's Temple Level 1

The massive temple stands in the southwest portion of the vast, hollow mountain. Each of its four sides is exactly 300 feet or was when it was first constructed. Three tiers rise above the temple, each much smaller than the last, before finally reaching a pyramid-shaped top. Each tier is approximately 30 feet tall, with the final pyramid at the top measuring 60 feet in every direction. While the stone building is ancient, the engineering and construction were extremely skilled. Horgrim's faithful hollowed out the mountain to create a nice, dark place to build a grand temple dedicated to the god of war and darkness. Although Horgrim's faithful lost the hollow mountain to forces of the good gods long ago, the sturdy temple remains unconquered. Outer walls of the lower portions of the temple are 20 feet thick, only thinning to 10 feet or less toward the top of the temple. Various minerals contained in the stone prevent scrying in or out of the temple, interfere with all divination spells, and make *passwall* spells half as effective as normal. In addition, the minerals in the stone make it resistant to *stone shape* and similar spells that shape or change the nature of stone. These spells are only half as effective in terms of volume and duration. The thickness of the walls combined with the strange nature of the stone makes using spells to create an entrance to the temple extremely difficult but not impossible.

Keyed Locations

The Doors to the Temple

Three doors are evenly spaced along the base of each face of the temple, with the central door always being a set of double doors. Only one of the 12 doors leads deeper into the temple and allows access to other levels; some of the other doors lead to other regions of the first level and contain various treasures and keys that make entering the higher levels of the temple somewhat easier. Several doors are simply traps, while others lead to rooms that are cleverly designed traps, or both. Numbering of the doors and rooms starts in the northwest corner on the western side of the temple and continues around the temple in a clockwise direction. All upper tiers are completely devoid of any type of windows or doors, leaving these 12 doors as the only visible entrances.

1. Iron Door

The humid air has added a patina of rust to the solid door. It is unlocked and opens easily.

2. Room of Broken Stone

Broken rocks cover the floor, all of them clearly from the ceiling above. This room was designed as a trap, with the ceiling designed to collapse on anyone attempting to pass through the room. Many years ago, several unfortunate adventurers fell victim to the trap, leaving only their broken bones behind as a testament to their failure. A thorough search of the room finds remains from at least 5 individuals, but no treasure. Narise (see **Area 3**) looted these corpses years ago and then moved the rubble back over the bodies. Dust covers a small open area before the door in the west wall. Someone took the time to move the rubble away from the door to open it, but dust coating the floor shows nobody has been here for a very long time.

A careful search through the rubble (and a successful DC 30 Perception check) locates the trigger mechanism used to collapse the ceiling. While the trap has already been triggered, identifying this mechanism gives a character +2 to spot similar traps on this level.

3. Narise's Greeting Chamber (CR 13)

Flickering lamps shed a shadowy, uneven light throughout the beautifully decorated room. Velvet-covered sofas and chairs surround mahogany tables. Delicate tapestries depicting bloody battles decorate the walls, and a soft rug covers the floor. All of the items in the room have an air of great age yet are clearly cared for. One of the tapestries on the southern wall conceals a series of evenly spaced holes that **Narise** (female **vampire**) travels through in gaseous form to reach her special burial chamber (**Area 4**). The wall is 3 feet thick (Hardness 8; hp 180, Break DC 24) and must be broken down or passed through using *gaseous form* or *passwall* spells. Narise uses this room as her "greeting chamber" when she is fortunate enough to have victims to toy with. There haven't been any visitors in centuries, so Narise generally keeps up this room and patrols the halls (**Areas 41–47**). If the PCs haven't met Narise in **Areas 41–47**, they definitely meet her here.

Narise   CR 10
XP 9,600
Human vampire sorcerer 9
CE Medium undead (augmented humanoid, human)
Init +8; **Senses** darkvision 60 ft.; Perception +21
AC 25, touch 16, flat-footed 20 (+2 armor, +1 deflection, +4 Dex, +1 dodge, +7 natural)
hp 104 (9d6+72); fast healing 5
Fort +12, **Ref** +10, **Will** +11
Defensive Abilities channel resistance +4; DR 10/magic, 10/silver; Immune undead traits; Resist cold 10, electricity 10
Weaknesses vampire weaknesses
Speed 30 ft.
Melee slam +7 (1d4+4 plus energy drain)
Special Attacks blood drain, children of the night, create spawn, dominate (DC 20), energy drain (2 levels, DC 20)
Sorcerer Spells Known (CL 9th; concentration +15)
  4th (5/day)—bestow curse (DC 20), dimension door, lesser globe of invulnerability, shout (DC 20)
  3rd (7/day)—dispel magic, haste, hold person (DC 19), lightning bolt (DC 19)
  2nd (8/day)—alter self, darkness, invisibility, invisibility, see invisibility
  1st (8/day)—comprehend languages, disguise self, identify, mage armor, magic missile, obscuring mist
  0 (at will)—dancing lights, daze (DC 16), detect magic, ghost sound (DC 16), mage hand, mending, open/close (DC 16), read magic
  Bloodline Arcane
Str 16, **Dex** 19, **Con** —, **Int** 15, **Wis** 14, **Cha** 22
Base Atk +4; **CMB** +7; **CMD** 23
Feats Alertness, Bestow Luck, Combat Casting, Combat Reflexes, Defiant Luck, Dodge, Eschew Materials, Great Fortitude, Improved Initiative, Inexplicable Luck, Iron Will, Lightning Reflexes, Skill Focus (Spellcraft), Toughness
Skills Bluff +18, Diplomacy +15, Intimidate +10, Knowledge (arcana) +14, Knowledge (religion) +6, Perception +21, Sense Motive +12, Spellcraft +17, Stealth +17, Use Magic Device +10; Racial Modifiers +8 Bluff, +8 Perception, +8 Sense Motive, +8 Stealth
Languages Common, Draconic, Necronomus
SQ arcane bond (amulet of natural armor +1), bloodline arcana (+1 DC for metamagic spells that increase spell level), change shape (dire bat or wolf, beast shape II), gaseous form, metamagic adept (2/day), new arcana, shadowless, spider climb
Other Gear amulet of natural armor +1, bracers of armor +2, cloak of resistance +1, ring of protection +1
Special Abilities
Defiant Luck (2/day) Reroll a natural 1 on a save, or force a reroll of a critical hit confirmation roll.
Inexplicable Luck (1/day) Gain +8 bonus to a single roll, or +4 after the roll is made.

Personality: Narise was a vain sorceress who accepted vampirism as a way to preserve her beauty and serve Horgrim as a guardian for the temple and the treasures hidden within it. She did not know she would be given what she feels is a relatively minor and immensely boring job. She knows a bit about the design of the temple, but next to nothing about the treasures it was built to guard. She enjoys using her powers to confuse and trick people, and relishes destroying good clerics and paladins. The first few decades brought occasional explorers and adventurers, but since that time, Narise has had few visitors and is bored and restless. She desires companions to spend her time with and gets very excited at the prospect of finding, or creating, some.

Tactics: Noise in either **Area 2** or **Area 5** alerts Narise to possible visitors. Narise is vain and overconfident, but not foolish. She greets the party in a friendly manner, joking with them by saying such things as "I keep telling you people I don't want to be rescued." Then she plays along with whatever presumptions the PCs make. While she talks to the party, she looks for characters bearing holy symbols that might indicate clerics or paladins. Her first aggressive action is to attempt to use her charm ability on the most heavily-armed fighter in the party. She continues attempting to charm other characters until she is noticed, at which point she promptly moves away from the party and prepares for battle. The following round, she uses children of the night to summon allies. She uses any charmed characters to defend her by having them attack their friends. She does her best to stand back and enjoy the battle, casting periodic spells to increase the chaos of the area. If the PCs overcome her charm ability, she enters melee combat with the character she considers most dangerous, usually a cleric, paladin, or elven character. Narise is bold, but not foolish; if she is brought to fewer than 20 hp, she assumes mist form and flees through cracks in the wall to her special burial chamber.

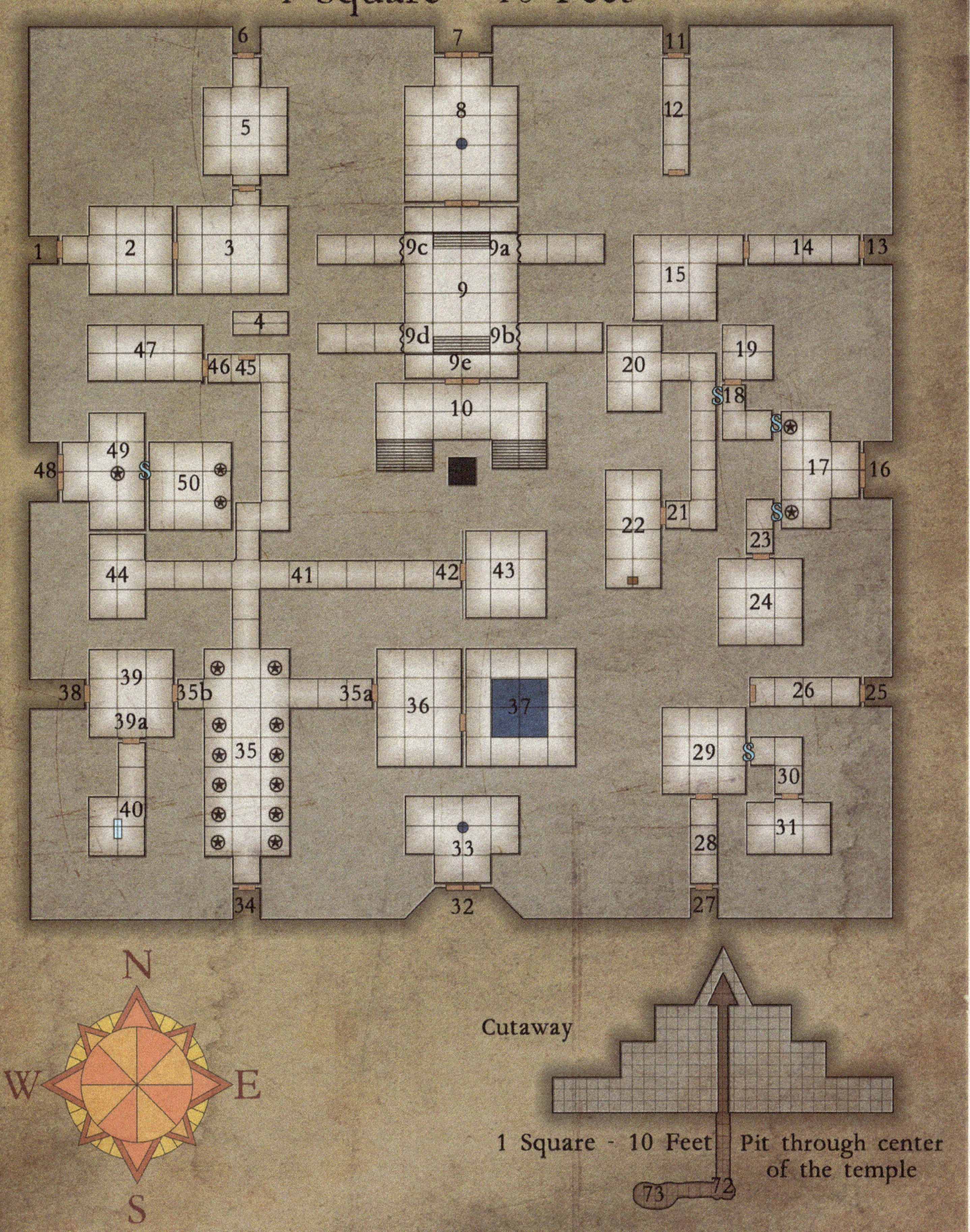

Map 6: Horgrim's Temple
1 Square - 10 Feet
N
W
E
S
Cutaway
1 Square - 10 Feet
Pit through center of the temple

4. Sealed Chamber

Narise has her coffin here as well as all her special treasures. Her special burial chamber was constructed with narrow gaps and cracks in the 3-foot-thick stone walls (Hardness 8; hp 180, Break DC 24) between **Areas 3** and **45**, allowing her to act as a guardian for those portions of the temple. The walls in those locations must be broken down or breached with *passwall* or *gaseous form* spells to reach the chamber. If the PCs somehow enter this room without already meeting Narise, she is drawn back to her chamber within 1d4 rounds by the noise they make. Narise attacks anyone in her private chamber, using all her spells and abilities as described in the tactics section of **Area 3**.

Narise rests in a stone coffin (18 in. thick; Hardness 8; hp 90; Break DC 24; DC 22 Strength check required to move the lid). While she does store some of her treasure in the massive chest at the foot of the coffin, the main items are in a hollow chamber beneath the coffin. A careful search (DC 27 Perception check) of the coffin reveals holes along the bottom. Narise passes through the holes in gaseous form to obtain or store items.

Treasure #1: The chest contains a black velvet cloak decorated with small diamonds (800 gp), 3 hats of various styles (45 gp each), and a collection of silk scarves (30 gp each) that cover small bags with the following treasure: a gold bracelet studded with six diamonds (2000 gp), an emerald pendant on a gold chain (600 gp), an ornate silver bracelet (400 gp), and three ivory tubes filled with 250 gp of diamond dust each.

Treasure #2: A DC 28 Strength check is required to move the coffin aside and get to the primary stash of treasure containing a *+2 heavy mace, +1 dwarven waraxe, +1 adaptive composite longbow, +1 chain shirt, scrolls of acid arrow (CL 3rd), darkvision (CL 3rd) x2, speak with dead (CL 7th), and spell immunity (CL 7th)* and *potions of intelligence, heroism, swimming, and vision.*

5. The Red Path (CR 4)

Red stepping-stones create a winding path leading through the room from the northern door (**Area 6**) to the southern door with a large, flat red stone before each door. Faded tile mosaics decorate the walls with pictures of rocky hills and strange, twisted forests. Approximately 20 holes line the walls of the room at a height of 3 feet. Almost anyone glancing into the room (DC 5 Perception check) easily determines the holes are part of some sort of dart or arrow **trap**. A desiccated corpse in the center of the room provides another hint of danger. But what actually triggers the trap? A character examining the stepping-stones easily ascertains the red stepping-stones are linked to some sort of mechanical mechanism. What is not obvious is the fact that the red stepping-stones prevent the firing of darts while people are in this room. The entire floor, including the stepping-stones, is a weight-sensing mechanism that controls the firing of darts through holes in the wall. As long as one person stands on a red stepping-stone, the darts do not fire. If anyone is in the room without someone standing on a red stepping-stone, the darts fire at a rate of 20 per round. While the trap is difficult to disable, it is easy to avoid once the triggering mechanism is understood.

Hail of Darts Trap CR 6
XP 2,400
Type mechanical; **Perception** DC 25; **Disable Device** DC 30
EFFECTS
Trigger location; **Reset** manual
Effect Atk 20x +8 ranged (1d4+1); multiple targets (all targets in room)

Note: An unsuccessful Perception check leads the character to believe that the stepping-stones are a trigger for the trap rather than a mechanism to keep the darts from firing. The trap is extremely clever, but purely mechanical. After 100 darts (5 rounds), the dart-firing mechanisms are empty and emit only hollow clicks.

Treasure: A rogue began a solo exploration of this area several centuries ago, and now only her desiccated corpse remains. It is so dry that it turns to dust at the merest touch. The only items that survive are a *+1 dagger* with an ivory hilt, a *+1 ring of protection*, a gold amulet (350 gp) and loose coins totaling 32 gp, 45 sp, and 72 cp. The coins are very ancient; a successful DC 23 Knowledge (History) check determines the coins are approximately 750 years old.

6. Iron Door

Iron Door: 2 in. thick; Hardness 10; hp 90; Break DC 28; Disable Device DC 20

The plain iron door shows no signs of rust but is clearly quite ancient. When viewed from the outside, scratches around the ancient lock suggest other people have done some "work" on the lock without the proper key. PCs who approach the door from the inside (**Area 5**) find the door easy to open. The locking mechanism is connected to the inner doorknob.

7. Lead Double Doors

Lead Double Doors: 10 in. thick; Hardness 15; hp 300; Break DC 28; Disable Device DC 40; SR 22; DR 5/-; Resist fire 25

Enchanted to harden the lead and make the doors impervious to heat and magical attacks, the doors are resistant to magic as well as physical blows. This, combined with the complex lock, makes the room virtually impossible to open without the **twisted lead key** (Key T1) found in **Area 22**. When they are finally opened, the doors emit an ear-piercing squeal.

8. Darkened Room

The lead double doors open to reveal a room full of dark, roiling mist. While the mist glows magically and seems horribly ominous, it is designed only to cloak light sources and make them ineffective. All light sources attract the strange, magical mist, with normal lanterns and torches so effectively cloaked that they shed no light whatsoever. Magical light sources and spells produce a shadowy, uneven light to a maximum 5-foot radius. The only features of the room include a stone fountain in the center of the room and a set of rune-covered copper double doors set in the southern wall.

The stone fountain (Hardness 8; hp 90; Break DC 24; SR 16) in the center of the room exudes the strange black mist. Mist pours from the extended arms of a tall, thin wizard to flow down his body into a basin surrounded by serpent-like figures before swirling out of the basin and spreading throughout the room. The fountain shows a variety of different magic when studied with the use of *detect magic*. Destroying the fountain stops production of the mist and the remaining mist fades within 8 hours, enabling the use of normal lights.

Copper Double Doors: 5 in. thick; Hardness 15; hp 150; Break DC 28; Disable Device DC 40; SR 24

These rune-covered doors are enchanted to harden the copper and make the doors impervious to magical attacks. This makes the door very difficult to open without the **copper lion key** (Key T2) found in **Area 43**.

9. Large Tiled Room

Large globes of glowing light hover inches below the high ceiling and illuminate a large room coated floor to ceiling with colored porcelain tiles. The colored tiles form a mosaic depicting furious black dragons battling groups of poorly equipped elves. The central section of the room is approximately 4 feet lower than the 10-foot landings in front of the north and south doors. Small, low steps lead down from the north and south landings to the central room where four hallways appear to extend to rooms filled with weapons, armor, or treasure. PCs who enter the lower portion of the room to look down the hallways might notice the floor is covered with traces of white, powdery dust (DC 20 Perception check). Only a very knowledgeable alchemist (with a successful DC 34 Craft [Alchemy] check) recognizes the powder as Zhilac powder, a compound that can be mixed with acid to produce a deadly gas.

The entire room is actually a very deadly trap designed to prevent invaders from reaching the silver doors at the south end of the room. Illusions cloak the hallways (**9a–9d**) and conceal a large volume of acid behind a magic barrier. The porcelain tiles are immune to the acid, so the walls and floor effectively contain the horribly caustic substance.

9a.–9d. Illusion-Cloaked Chambers

Illusions cloaking these chambers make them appear to be hallways extending to large rooms filled with weapons (**9a**), armor (**9c**), or chests of treasure (**9b** and **9d**). In reality, they are 10-feet-wide, 10-feet-tall, 30-feet-deep chambers coated with porcelain tiles holding a potent acid. PCs attempting to enter these hallways encounter a strange, flexible barrier that appears to be some version of a *wall of force* spell. Attempting a *dispel magic* on a barrier, or any physical attack with a weapon, automatically dispels the illusions and barriers on all four hallways and releases a sudden flow of acid into the entire central section of the room. *Detect magic* reveals a variety of different types of magic at the junction of each hallway. Spells such as *true seeing* reveal the true nature of the hallways, but any attempt to disbelieve the complex illusions requires a successful DC 32 Will save.

Acid Trap CR 6
XP 2,400
Type magical; **Perception** see above; **Disable Device** N/A
EFFECTS
Trigger *dispel magic*, physical attack on one of the hallway barriers, opening door 9e; **Reset** none
Effect see below

Acid Trap

Only glass, porcelain, or pure gold items resist the acid. Water, wine, or ale is useful for rinsing or diluting the acid. Medium-sized or larger characters standing near the north or south ends of the room can attempt to leap onto the higher landings and avoid acid damage with a successful DC 18 Reflex save; all others must swim or wade out of the acid. Those caught in the acid suffer 2d4 acid damage at the start of their turn.

Poison Gas Trap

The acid mixes with the Zhilac powder coating the floor to release a cloud of poisonous gas that fills the entire room within one round (no attack roll necessary). Anyone still in the room one round after the acid is released must either attempt to hold their breath or breathe the gas. All breathing the deadly fumes must succeed at a DC 16 Fortitude save each round to avoid suffering 1d4 temporary Intelligence and 1d4 temporary Wisdom damage. Victims recover 1d4 Intelligence and Wisdom damage every 20 minutes when removed to fresh air.

Once the trap is triggered, the southern door is very difficult to reach. The poison gas fades and loses effectiveness after 24 hours, but the acid remains a potent barrier that must be overcome. The silver double doors at the southern end of the room are covered with a variety of runes that pulse with a faint purple light.

9E. SILVER DOORS

Silver Double Doors: 3 in. thick; Hardness 15; hp 100; Break DC 28; Disable Device DC 40; SR 28

The silver doors are designed to be opened with an **ornate silver key (Key T3)** found in **Area 50**. Enchantments on this door are similar to those on the lead and copper doors above. Attempts to damage the door with spells or to unlock the door with a *knock* spell must overcome it's spell resistance. The acid and gas traps described above are immediately triggered when the door is opened, if they have not been triggered already. Magical protections designed to prevent the triggering of the trap when the key was used faded several centuries ago. Any means used to open the doors triggers the trap and creates a barrier the PCs have to overcome when leaving the temple.

10. WIDE LANDING

Twin stone stairways to the east and west lead upward to the next level of the temple (**Area 51**). The silver doors in the south wall can be closed to prevent any poison gas from coming into this room. There are no markings on the walls or stairways to hint at what might lie in either direction.

11. SIMPLE STONE DOOR

Simple Stone Door: 4 in. thick; Hardness 8; hp 60; Break DC 28; Disable Device DC 15

The lock on this ancient door is so easy to pick that it almost seems broken.

12. HALL FULL OF RUBBLE

Rubble from the collapsed ceiling lines the floor, making it quite difficult to pass through the oak door at the very end of the hall. Despite its careful framing and solid appearance, the oak door leads nowhere. The entire room was designed as a trap triggered by a pressure plate in the center of the hall. A careful character searching through the rubble with a successful DC 30 Perception check locates the trigger mechanism used to collapse the ceiling. Although already triggered, identifying the mechanism gives the character +2 on checks to identify similar traps on this level. The rubble also contains the remains of the unwary adventurer killed by the trap.

Treasure: A careful search (DC 25 Perception check) turns up skeletal remains wearing *+1 full plate*, a *+2 bastard sword*, a *+1 ring of protection*, a *ring of minor acid resistance*, an ancient gold amulet shaped like a spider, and a decaying leather pouch containing 5 pp, 39 gp, and 20 sp.

13. ORNATE STONE DOOR

Ornate Stone Door: 10 in. thick; Hardness 8; hp 120; Break DC 28; Disable Device DC 27

Ornate engravings of hawks and eagles adorn the heavy stone door. The delicate artwork conceals the complexity of the lock used to seal it as well as the deadly poison needle trap the lock once contained.

14. HALL FULL OF RUBBLE

On the surface, this room appears to be exactly the same as **Area 12**. The trap, its trigger, and the collapsed ceiling are indeed the same, but the decaying oak door at the back of this room leads into another chamber. If the PCs search this room, they find that the unfortunates that triggered this trap escaped, with rogues being as likely to locate the trigger mechanism as above.

The door is old, but still very sturdy. It is unlocked but opens out into the room. Several bits of rubble must be removed before the door can be opened.

Heavy Oak Door: 3 in. thick; Hardness 8; hp 30; Break DC 22

15. HALL OF BROKEN STATUES

At first glance, the room appears to be full of rubble. Broken granite and marble statues — items where craftsmen failed to make their mark or cracked the stone with their chisels — line the room in uneven rows. Most of the statues are of wizards or witches, while others depict monsters or strange, warped creatures. Although the broken statues are of no value, a beautiful flute made of a strange black metal lies forgotten beneath some broken rock and can be found with a DC 22 Perception check.

FLUTE OF THE BLACK SUN

Price 16,000 gp; **Slot** none; **CL** 5th; **Weight** 3 lbs.; **Aura** moderate abjuration and transmutation

Ancient elven runes adorn the black metal flute along with an elven symbol representing the sun. The alloy of silver, steel, and several rare minerals that create its black coloration helps prolong notes played on the flute and give it a beautiful tone. Anyone playing the flute gains a +4 circumstance bonus on Perform (wind instruments) checks due to its exceptional craftsmanship. In addition, the flute can be used to cast *darkvision* once per day, and, if held or played, grants cold resistance 15.

Cost 8,000 gp; **Feats** Craft Wondrous Item; **Spells** *darkvision, protection from energy*

---

16. STEEL DOUBLE DOORS

Steel Double Doors: 2 in. thick; Hardness 12; hp 80; Break DC 30; Disable Device DC 22

The enchanted doors are sturdy, solid, and so well constructed that it is easy to believe they were recently made and installed. Opening the doors releases a cloud of dried pollen from a pink lotus flower.

Pink Lotus Flower Pollen Trap CR 2
XP 600
Type mechanical; **Perception** DC 17; **Disable Device** DC 21
EFFECTS
Trigger touch; **Reset** none
Effect poison (pink lotus extract)
Pink Lotus Extract
DETAILS
Type poison (inhaled); **Save** Fortitude DC 13; **Onset** 1 minute; **Frequency** once for 1d4+1 hours
EFFECT
2 STR damage, 2 DEX damage, and -4 to disbelieve illusions of all types.

17. GAS-FILLED ROOM (CR 7)

A thick, swirling gray mist fills the room. Strange static barriers in the doorway to the east and the secret doors in the northwest and southwest corners contain the mist. While these barriers contain the gas in the room effectively, they can be touched or walked through without any harm, giving only the vague feeling of static electricity. The wet, poisonous mist hides 4 **mummies** and two statues of wizards in the west corners of the room. Secret doors hidden behind each statue lead deeper into the temple.

Poison Gas
DETAILS
Type poison (inhaled); **Save** Fortitude DC 16; **Onset** immediately;
   Frequency 1/round with in room
EFFECT
-4 to attack rolls, saving throws, and AC for 2d4+6 rounds. The
poisonous gas protects the mummies with its moistness while it
weakens characters entering the room. Fire-based attacks and spells
used in the room do only half damage. The gray mist also makes the
use of ranged weapons and spells difficult as it prevents any form of
vision beyond 10 feet.

Mummy (4) CR 5
XP 1,600
hp 60 (Pathfinder Roleplaying Game Bestiary, "Mummy")

Gear *Amulet of the Dark Sun* (See Appendix)

Tactics: The mummies use the swirling mist to help cloak their movements as
they move up to attack. They attack any living creature in the room mercilessly
until destroyed. Their job is to guard this room against intruders coming from any
direction. They do not leave the room to chase fleeing characters.

Note: Although the mummies do not chase fleeing PCs, the poisonous gas makes
them much more dangerous and difficult to defeat. PCs defeating the mummies
receive an additional 1,600 experience bonus due to their added turn resistance and
difficulties caused by the poison gas.

Secret Doors: 2 in. thick; Hardness 8; hp 20; Perception DC 20. Once the panel
of stone is easily recognized as a hidden door, it is easy to open.

18. Before a Stone Door

The featureless hallway ends before a plain stone door to the north and a secret
door in the west wall.

18a. Plain Stone Door

Although the door is unlocked, it has no handles or clear sign of which direction
it opens. A short investigation quickly determines the door slides to the right.

18b. Secret Door

Due to a gap in the wall, this door can be found with a successful DC 16
Perception check.

19. Shield Room (CR 9)

A silver shield rests on a pedestal in the center of the room and sheds a faint blue
magical light. Large metal shields coated with red enamel decorated with the faces
of snarling hell hounds line the walls. A *detect magic* spell reveals an aura on all
the shields in the room. Touching or moving shields on the wall has no effect, but
touching the shield on the pedestal or attempting to remove one of the red enamel
shields from the room releases the 7 **hell hounds** magically trapped in the red
shields. The hell hounds leap out of the red enamel shields and attack anyone in
the room.

Hell Hound (7) CR 3
XP 800
hp 30 (Pathfinder Roleplaying Game Bestiary, "Hell Hound")

Combat Tactics: The hell hounds begin with a breath weapon attack and fight
characters in the room first, then track down any fleeing characters using scent once
everyone in the room has been killed or forced to flee. They fight to the death and
track fleeing PCs anyplace they decide to run. If the PCs hide behind a closed door,
the hell hounds repeatedly ram the door to knock it down.

Treasure: The silver shield is a *+1 light mithral shield* decorated with delicate
engravings. The seven remaining shields are masterwork light steel shields coated
with red enamel.

20. Abandoned Storeroom

The large room has wide shelves and racks along the wall but nothing of value is
in the room. This room provides a relatively safe place to rest if a recent opponent
is not tracking the PCs.

21. Heavy Lead Door (CR 7)

The hallway turns slightly before ending in front of a sturdy lead door. Glowing
runes run all along the outer edge of the door and circle the strange doorknob in its
center. Opening the unlocked door summons a **naunet protean** into the hallway.

Naunet Protean CR 7
XP 3,200
hp 94 (Pathfinder Roleplaying Game Bestiary 2, "Protean, Naunet")

Tactics: The protean is almost as surprised at being suddenly summoned amid
the PCs as they are. It tears into the most lightly armored foe near it with frightening
ferocity. The creature doesn't know why it was summoned and believes the PCs are
attempting to enslave it. It fights to the death, pursuing any fleeing PCs to the limit
of its ability.

22. Lead Room (CR 8)

The walls, ceiling, and floor of this large room are coated with enchanted lead
that nullifies any attempt to use magic to see into the room from outside. The only
item in the room is a simple wood chest (Hardness 4; hp 10; Break DC 10; DC 25
Disable Device check) resting against the south wall. A **darkling sentinel** stands
in front of the chest, remaining motionless until someone enters the room. PCs
remaining outside the room can study it and the chest from a distance, but anyone
entering the room is immediately attacked.

Darkling Sentinel   CR 8
XP 4,800
LE Medium outsider (evil, lawful)
Init +0; **Senses** blindsight 60 ft., darkvision 60 ft.; Perception +14
AC 23, touch 10, flat-footed 23 (+13 natural)
hp 58 (9d10+9)
Fort +4, **Ref** +6, **Will** +8
Defensive Abilities shatter; **Immune** acid, blindness, deafness,
   disease, hunger/thirst, poison; SR 19
Speed 30 ft.
Str 20, **Dex** 10, **Con** 13, **Int** 10, **Wis** 14, **Cha** 12
Base Atk +9; **CMB** +14; **CMD** 24
Feats Cleave, Cleaving Finish, Great Cleave, Improved Cleaving
   Finish, Power Attack
Skills Appraise +12, Knowledge (arcana) +12, Knowledge (planes) +12,
   Perception +14, Sense Motive +14, Spellcraft +12
Languages telepathy 40 ft.
SQ crystalline armory
Special Abilities
Cleave If you hit a foe, attack an adjacent target at the same attack
   bonus but take -2 AC.
Cleaving Finish Make additional attack if opponent is knocked out
Crystalline Armory (At will) (Su) Darkling Sentinels can form weapons
   from their crystalline bodies as a free action. They may form any
   simple or martial melee or thrown weapon. They commonly form
   greatswords for melee and throwing axes for thrown combat.
Improved Cleaving Finish May use Cleaving Finish any number of
   times/round
Power Attack -3/+6 You can subtract from your attack roll to add to
   your damage.
Shatter (At will) (Su) When a Darkling Sentinel is struck by a melee or
   sonic attack it may voluntarily shatter under the force of the blow as
   a free action. The sentinel's body fragments into a shower of shards
   and reforms immediately afterwards. The sentinel takes no dam
Spell Resistance (19) You have Spell Resistance.
Telepathy (40 feet) (Su) Communicate telepathically if the target has a
   language.

Tactics: The sentinel was summoned from a distant world and placed here to guard the key hidden in the chest. It attacks any creature that doesn't utter the worlds "Darkness is truth" before entering the room. It initially stands in front of the chest but immediately charges the doorway as soon as anyone enters without saying the proper phrase. It is bound to servitude within this room until it is destroyed and, hating the servitude, refuses to communicate even with characters who somehow learn its command phrase.

Treasure: The chest contains an ornate **lead key shaped like an eagle with a forked tail (Key T1)** that fits the door in **Area 7**, a *+2 dagger* bearing serpentine symbols engraved on the blade, an ivory tube holding 500 gp of diamond dust, and a pouch containing an adamantine ring shaped like a hell hound biting its tail (*minor ring of cold resistance*), 4 rubies (600 gp each), 6 agates (200 gp each), and 7 small bloodstones (50 gp each).

23. Ornate Gold Door

The short hallway bends to the south to end at an ornate gold door. Glowing with a strange magical light and decorated with ornate filigrees and beautiful designs, the door appears far more imposing than it really is. The only magic on the gold door is the magic shedding the pale green light, and there are no traps. While the door appears to be made of solid gold, the interior core is made of lead and only the outer coating is gold. Separating the gold from the lead is costly, but the effort still garners a profit of 800 gp to anyone willing to remove the door.

24. Dourala's Room (CR 0 or 9)

Dust-covered velvet cushions line several long sofas and small chairs surrounding a single stone statue in the center of the room. The statue depicts a female human in ornate plate armor swinging a large sword with both hands. Her expression is an odd mixture of pain and rage and bewilderment that is so deeply detailed that the statue seems alive. A successful DC 13 Knowledge (Arcana) check quickly determines that the statue is a victim of a *flesh to stone* spell. Dourala, a faithful servant to Horgrim, was unknowingly turned into a statue in the middle of a battle. Certain that the forces of good would return her to flesh and provide them with a powerful spy, Horgrim's minions left the statue here.

If the PCs return Dourala to flesh, use the statistics and tactics described below. She carries an *amulet of the dark sun*.

Dourala   CR 8
XP 4,800
Human fighter 9
LE Medium humanoid (human)
Init +4; **Senses** darkvision 60 ft.; Perception +1
AC 21, touch 10, flat-footed 21 (+11 armor)
hp 76 (9d10+27)
Fort +9, **Ref** +4, **Will** +5 (+2 vs. fear)
Speed 30 ft.
Melee +1 greatsword +17/+12 (2d6+11/19-20)
Special Attacks weapon trainings (heavy blades +2, spears +1)
Str 19, **Dex** 10, **Con** 14, **Int** 8, **Wis** 12, **Cha** 13
Base Atk +9; **CMB** +13; **CMD** 23
Feats Improved Initiative, Leadership, Mounted Archery, Mounted Combat, Point-Blank Shot, Power Attack, Precise Shot, Ride-by Attack, Weapon Focus (greatsword), Weapon Focus (lance), Weapon Specialization (greatsword)
Skills Handle Animal +13, Ride +9
Languages Common
SQ armor training 2
Combat Gear ring of animal friendship; **Other Gear** +2 full plate, +1 greatsword, amulet of the dark sun, cloak of resistance +1

Tactics: Dourala is not particularly bright, but she instantly recognizes that drastic changes have occurred since the middle of her last battle. She returns her sword to the sheath on her back if returned to flesh and calmly asks how the battle is going, waiting to see what the answer is before she mentions which side she is actually on. When informed of the time that has gone by, she gets extremely upset, and becomes even more upset when she is unable to locate her lance or bow. Dourala offers to travel with the party a bit before going her own way. If the party accepts, she does her best to quietly sabotage them, attacking openly if she is discovered. Her skills are aimed at battle, mostly leading mounted knights on horseback, not delicate subterfuge. If the PCs are suspicious or disrespectful, Dourala draws her sword and attacks. She does her best to damage the party and then makes a fighting retreat out of the temple to escape and find reinforcements.

25. Plain Stone Door

The featureless door has no visible knob but slides to either side when pushed carefully.

26. Short Hallway (CR 8)

The simple hallway appears to end at a warped oak door but is really a trap. Anyone stepping into the center of the room triggers a pressure plate that causes the ceiling to collapse.

Collapsed Ceiling Trap CR 8
XP 4,800
Type mechanical; **Perception** DC 28; **Disable Device** DC 18
Trigger location; **Reset** repair
  Effect falling ceiling (8d6 bludgeoning and piercing, DC 25 Reflex for half); multiple targets (all targets in hallway)

27. Ornate Stone Door (CR 8)

Ornate Stone Door: 10 in. thick; Hardness 8; hp 120; Break DC 28; Disable Device DC 27.

Carvings of lions and strange, twisted animals cover the entire surface of the door. Opening the door sprays everyone within 10 feet of the entrance with insanity mist.

Insanity Mist Trap CR 8
XP 4,800
Type mechanical; Perception DC 25; Disable Device DC 20
EFFECTS
Trigger location; **Reset** repair
Effect poison gas (Insanity mist); never miss; onset delay (1 round); multiple targets (all targets in a 10-ft.-by-10-ft. area)

28. Short Hallway (CR 8)

This hallway is identical to the one in **Area 26**. The hallway possesses the exact same trap as the area described above but the brittle oak door at the end of the hall is real. The door is unlocked and opens easily.

Collapsed Ceiling Trap CR 8
XP 4,800
Type mechanical; **Perception** DC 28; **Disable Device** DC 18
Trigger location; **Reset** repair
  Effect falling ceiling (8d6 bludgeoning and piercing, DC 25 Reflex for half); multiple targets (all targets in hallway)

29. The White Room

Hexagonal white porcelain tiles cover the walls, floor, and ceiling of the entire room. All the tiles are highly polished and free of dust, but the east wall is marred by streaks of dried blood. A *detect magic* spell reveals a faint abjuration aura on the entire room, but the magic of the room is designed only to keep it dust-free. A secret door (can be found with a DC 17 Perception check) is in the center of the east wall. Dried blood has caked along a few cracks in the wall, making the door easier to locate. Once opened, it reveals a short hallway with dried spots of blood along the floor and walls.

30. Dragon Scale Door (CR 8)

A strange door made from the scales of a blue dragon stands at the end of the hallway. Streaks of dried blood decorate the walls as well as the scales making up the door. A *detect magic* spell easily discerns a powerful magic aura on all the individual scales making up the door. A complex magical trap breaks the door into its individual scales and sends them flying through the hallway if the door is touched. Dried blood in the hallway comes from some adventurers who fled the temple several hundred years ago.

Dragon Scale Door Trap CR 8
XP 4,800
Type magical; **Perception** DC 29; **Disable Device** DC 29
Trigger touch; **Reset** automatic after 5 rounds
Effect dragon scale blast (12d4 slashing damage; DC 18 Reflex for half); multiple targets (all targets within 20 ft. of the door in the hallway)

Clever PCs might hurl an item down the hall, let the trap fire, and run down the hall to enter the room (**Area 31**). The trap is also triggered when touched on the opposite side, but the scales only blast into the hallway and not back into the room.

31. THE DRAGON ROOM (CR 10)

Dust covers the varied decorations and furniture in what is apparently a living room. The furniture and decorations have a dragon theme and are also made from dragon bone, scales, claws, or horns. Most of the items, while valuable, are heavy and difficult to transport. Included among the items is a small life-like statue of a red dragon. The statue is a magic construct made from bone and scale fragments from an ancient red dragon that imbue it with supernatural strength. It is a potent guardian against anyone daring to enter the room.

Red Dragon Statue   CR 9
XP 6,400
N Small construct
Init +4; **Senses** blindsight 60 ft., darkvision 60 ft., low-light vision; Perception +0
AC 25, touch 15, flat-footed 21 (+4 Dex, +10 natural, +1 size)
hp 85 (14d10+10)
Fort +4, **Ref** +8, **Will** +4
DR 10/magic; **Immune** construct traits, acid, cold, fire; **Resist** electricity 30, sonic 30; **SR** 20
Speed 10 ft., fly 90 ft. (good)
Melee bite +27 (1d2+12), 2 claws +27 (1d3+12)
Special Attacks breath weapon 30 ft. cone; 2d6 sonic damage (DC 17 Fortitude negates deafness)
Str 34, **Dex** 18, **Con** —, **Int** —, **Wis** 10, **Cha** 10
Base Atk +14; **CMB** +25; **CMD** 39
Skills Acrobatics +4 (-4 to jump), Fly +10
Special Abilities
Breath Weapon (DC 17) (Su) 30 ft. cone; 2d6 sonic damage (DC 17 Fortitude negates deafness)

Note: Dragon statue can be found in **Appendix B: New Monsters.**

Tactics: While the magic and items used in its creation were potent, the dragon statue does not have a complex program. It attacks anyone who isn't wearing an *amulet of the dark sun* by breathing on them and swooping down on them to make bite and claw attacks. It is programmed only to guard this room and won't leave under any circumstances.

Treasure: The furniture is worth more than 5000 gp in a major city but would require a large wagon to transport. A detailed search (DC 30 Perception check) of the room reveals a *wand of magic missile* (CL 9th) with 30 charges made from dragon bone and *+2 bracers of armor* made from the scales of a gold dragon.

32. OBSIDIAN DOUBLE DOORS

Obsidian Double Doors: 4 in. thick; Hardness 8; hp 60; Break DC 28; Disable Device DC 25.

The highly polished stone doors show no sign of age, yet the stone around them is clearly ancient. Though they do not glow with any obvious magic, any damage done to the doors "heals" magically within 24 hours.

33. SKELETON WARRIORS (CR SPECIAL)

The room is a strange and frightening sight to anyone opening the door. A collection of armored **skeletons** stand at attention in neat, tight rows broken only by a small fountain in the center of the room. The mindless creatures were part of the army defeated when the cavern outside the temple was lost to the forces of Arn. Unlike most such creatures, these stand motionless, waiting for orders. The clerics and wizards that once controlled them are long dead. The creatures act only if attacked.

The foul green liquid in the basin of the fountain looks and smells dangerous but is harmless unless consumed (characters must succeed at a DC 12 Fortitude save or suffer 1d4 Con damage). A *purify food and drink* spell cleanses the fountain of the poison but doesn't change its murky nature.

Treasure: Hidden in the fountain (DC 30 Perception check) is a *pearl of power (2nd)*, a *ring of swimming*, and a *strand of prayer beads*.

Skeleton (30) CR 1/3
XP 135
hp 4 (Pathfinder Roleplaying Game Bestiary, "Skeleton")

Tactics: Designed as low-level troops, they respond only to orders or to being attacked. Skeletons surviving an attack of any type charge forward to engage their aggressors and fight with single-minded ferocity. Only their previous orders keep them in the room; they follow fleeing characters out of the temple despite the dangers they face outside the room.

34. THE LION DOOR

The massive bas-relief of a roaring lion thrusting its head out of the door conceals the doorknob used to open it. One must reach their hand inside the lion's mouth to find and turn the doorknob. *Detect magic* reveals a powerful aura around the lion's head, but no traps are on the door.

35. HALL OF HEROES

Six statues of armed warriors are spaced 10 feet apart along both the east and west walls with gaps left where hallways extend to the east and west. The 12 statues are carved from the same stone used for the temple walls. Craftsmanship and detailing on each of the statues is superb, with each figure standing in a heroic pose, haughty and confident in their skill. Statues on both sides of the room are identical and depict the following (moving north to south): a tall male human in full plate wielding a greatsword; a thin male elf in leather armor holding a bow; a female human in chainmail wielding a longsword; a female human in spiked full plate wielding a longsword; a male elf wearing leather armor wielding a mace; and a male human in scale mail wielding a pike. It is impossible to determine who the statues represent as there are no signs or messages describing them anywhere in the room.

A *detect magic* spell reveals a faint aura around each statue, but none of the statues is magical or animated in any way. When the PCs look down the hallways running to the north, east, and west, they notice the east and west hallways end at stone doors (**35a** and **35b**), and the north hallway continues through an intersection and bends in the distance.

36. BARRACKS (CR 10)

Back in a time when the temple had living servants, this stale-smelling room housed many of them. Long rows of beds line the east wall, separated only enough for a person to climb between them — with the exception of a larger gap in front of a stone door. Chests at the foot of each bed are thrown open and ancient clothing and bedding is thrown about as if a tornado or whirlwind burst through the room recently. Although the room doesn't appear guarded, two of the temple's servants was changed into **fallen** as punishment when the battle outside the temple went poorly.

Fallen (2) CR 8
XP 4,800
hp 93 (Pathfinder Roleplaying Game Bestiary 6, "Fallen")

Treasure: When the room was abandoned, almost everything of value was taken, but a thorough search of the entire room (DC 24 Perception check) turns up a *+2 staff, cloak of arachnida, +1 cloak of resistance, stone of alarm, stone salve, 2 amulets of the dark sun*, a platinum ring studded with moonstones (500 gp) and an ornate silver bracelet (250 gp).

37. THE BATH HOUSE (CR 8)

Humid air scented with perfume fills the air as tendrils of steam rise from the large pool of water in the center of the room. Created as a bath house for some of the faithful servants serving the temple, the magic spells purifying the water and keeping it warm and clean still function. Sweet, warm air makes the room especially relaxing and pleasant. Steps lead down into the warm pool of water, welcoming anyone interested in taking a bath, and soft sofas and chairs surround the quiet, bubbling pool. Soft towels and robes hang from pegs on the south wall. Disturbing portrayals of murder adorn tapestries along the remaining walls, jarring the otherwise peaceful feel of the room. Horgrim confined an ancient **erinyes devil** known as Lourecious to this room for being overly ambitious and acting against some of his interests. Her confinement ends when she converts one good creature to the worship of Horgrim, a task made virtually impossible by the fact that not a single living creature has entered the room since she was placed here.

Lourecious CR 8
XP 4,800
hp 94 (Pathfinder Roleplaying Game Bestiary, "Devil, Erinyes")

Tactics: Although the room is beautiful and comfortable, Lourecious has been waiting for someone to enter it for years and is surprised when someone does. Startled enough that there is no time to cloak her real form, she decides against the attempt. Making no effort to cloak what she is, she greets the PCs in a friendly, charming manner. Her goal is not to slaughter the PCs but rather their conversion to evil, particularly to worshipping Horgrim so she can be freed. If she convinces a good-aligned PC to swear an oath of allegiance to Horgrim, she is free to leave. At first, she simply makes conversation, asking the PCs how they arrived here and informing them she is "trapped by ancient promises" and would like to escape. She offers to assist the PCs but claims she can't leave unless someone utters an oath "to return to Horgrim what he desires when Lourecious is done helping me." The oath can vary; she is trying to make the PCs promise to worship Horgrim (what he desires) while making them think they simply need to return her to this room. Most PCs are suspicious of any agreements with devils and are unlikely to make such a promise.

If the PCs attack or refuse to swear any sort of oath, she gets frustrated. She flies to the farthest side of the bathing pool from the PCs and pulls out her weapons.

Treasure: Lourecious hid a bag of gems at the bottom of the pool (can be found with a successful DC 25 Perception check). The gems are a black pearl (500 gp), a silver pearl (100 gp), 5 moonstones (50 gp), 12 moss agates (10 gp each), 5 freshwater pearls (10 gp each), and a blue quartz gem (10 gp).

38. Cracked Stone Door

Ancient attacks on the door left cracks and gaps that are now filled with dust and dirt.

39. The Mirror Room (CR 8)

Mirrors line all the walls and a glass column stands in the center of the room. The column glows with a faint, almost indiscernible light that causes reflections in the mirrors to act like swift-moving shadows that dart across the walls. The faint lighting is insufficient to create reflections the crystalline horrors can use to manifest themselves. Brighter lighting brought into the room creates such a disturbing series of reflections that many people become dizzy (characters must succeed at a DC 13 Fortitude save or suffer -2 on all rolls and checks while in the room). While the PCs adjust to the many confusing images, the first PCs to enter the room are attacked by their own reflections as 3 **crystalline horrors** manifest out of the mirrors and attack.

Crystalline Horror (3) CR 5
XP 1,600
hp 59 (Tome of Horrors Complete, "Crystalline Horror")

Tactics: Once they manifest, the crystalline horrors attack any living creatures in the room without mercy.

Most PCs quickly realize the attacks have something to do with the mirrors. While some might stay and fight the creatures, wise PCs leave the room and cast spells into the room to break the mirrors or cloak them in darkness and thus eliminate the threat.

Mirrors (36): Hardness 4; hp 15; Break DC 18

The magically hardened mirrors are immune to acid, lightning, fire, and poison damage. Extreme cold makes them brittle (Hardness 2; Break DC 10) but does only half damage, sonic damage ignores hardness. The large mirrors are arranged in panels all along the walls. If the PCs decide to use spells to shatter the mirrors from outside the room, use the statistics presented here as an average and make the three mirrors used to manifest the crystalline horrors the last to break. PCs attacking mirrors physically may use a successful DC 15 Intelligence check to determine which of the mirrors might be the culprit. On a failed check, or random attack, use random dice (1 on 1d12) to determine whether a horror's mirror is struck.

While all doors leading out of the room are unlocked, they are covered with mirrored glass on this side, making them difficult to locate (can be spotted with a successful DC 20 Perception check). Shattering all the mirrors makes the doors visible, but also covers the floor with enough sharp, broken glass shards to make the floor difficult terrain.

40. The Glass Sarcophagus (CR 0 or CR 10)

A crystal chandelier sheds a soft magical light on an ornate glass sarcophagus that fills the small room at the end of the short hallway. Red velvet carpeting covers the floor and the raised stone platform that the transparent coffin rests on. Violet curtains on the stone walls highlight the transparent coffins and its skeletal inhabitant. The creature within appears to have once been an extremely tall elf with folded wings. Glowing purple letters along the one side of the transparent coffin read, "Huvarial, Arn's failed champion." While letters on the opposite side proclaim, "Even the brightest lights learn the power of the night."

Huvarial, was a great hero in her day, but her exploits are entirely forgotten now (a successful DC 35 Knowledge [History] check reveals her name and story). Huvarial was brought down in the battle for the outer cavern and dragged into the temple, causing despair among her supporters. Loss of her leadership was a major factor in the decision to leave the temple trapped in a cavern of sunlight. Unfortunately for Huvarial, she was not dead, only disabled. Horgrim's faithful brought her into the temple and changed her into a vampire before trapping her in the glass coffin.

Transparent Stasis Coffin: Hardness 8; hp 30; Break DC 28

The "glass" is actually stone magically treated to make it transparent. Huvarial was subdued and placed in the magic sarcophagus, and then frozen in time with powerful spells. Opening the coffin by any means ends the magic keeping her in stasis. Counterweights make the lid easy to open.

Huvarial   CR 10
XP 9,600
Half-celestial half-elf vampire fighter 3/sorcerer 4
CE Medium outsider (augmented humanoid, elf, human, native)
Init +9; **Senses** darkvision 60 ft., low-light vision; Perception +16
AC 23, touch 16, flat-footed 17 (+5 Dex, +1 dodge, +7 natural)
hp 86 (7 HD; 4d6+3d10+56); fast healing 5
Fort +10, **Ref** +9, **Will** +9 (+1 vs. fear); +2 vs. enchantments
Defensive Abilities channel resistance +4; **DR** 10/magic, 10/silver; **Immune** sleep, undead traits; **Resist** acid 10, cold 10, electricity 10; **SR** 21
Weaknesses vampire weaknesses
Speed 30 ft., fly 60 ft. (good)
Melee slam +12 (1d4+10 plus energy drain)
Special Attacks blood drain, children of the night, create spawn, dominate (DC 19), energy drain (2 levels, DC 19), smite evil 1/day (+6 attack and AC, +7 damage)
Spell-Like Abilities (CL 7th; concentration +13)
  3/day—protection from evil
  1/day—aid, bless, cure serious wounds, detect evil, holy smite (DC 20), neutralize poison, remove disease
Bloodline Spell-Like Abilities (CL 4th; concentration +10)
  9/day—heavenly fire (1d4+2 divine energy)
Sorcerer Spells Known (CL 4th; concentration +10)
  2nd (5/day)—acid arrow
  1st (8/day)—bless, magic missile, ray of enfeeblement (DC 17), true strike
  0 (at will)—dancing lights, detect magic, ghost sound (DC 16), mending, open/close (DC 16), read magic
  Bloodline Celestial
Str 25, **Dex** 20, **Con** —, **Int** 14, **Wis** 18, **Cha** 22
Base Atk +5; **CMB** +12; **CMD** 28
Feats Alertness, Arcane Armor Training, Arcane Strike, Combat Casting, Combat Reflexes, Dodge, Eschew Materials, Exotic Weapon Proficiency (bastard sword), Improved Initiative, Lightning Reflexes, Power Attack, Skill Focus (Sense Motive), Toughness, Weapon Focus (bastard sword)
Skills Acrobatics +12, Bluff +14, Fly +9, Knowledge (arcana) +12, Perception +16, Sense Motive +24, Spellcraft +12, Stealth +13; Racial Modifiers +8 Bluff, +10 Perception, +8 Sense Motive, +8 Stealth

Languages Celestial, Common, Elven
SQ armor training 1, bloodline arcana (summoned creatures gain DR 2/evil), change shape (dire bat or wolf, beast shape II), elf blood, gaseous form, shadowless, spider climb

Special Abilities
Heavenly Fire (1d4+2 divine energy, 9/day) (Sp) Ranged touch attack harms evil and heals good. Neutral unaffected.

Tactics: Her transformation into a vampire is already complete, with darkness and hatred completely consuming her nature. This hatred is aimed at anything to do with Horgrim's minions and the temple as it is at any living creature. With more time to assess her situation, she would certainly use more devious tactics, possibly even allying herself with the PCs to destroy the temple. Unfortunately, she wakes up naked, and her armor and weapons are nowhere to be found. She has no idea that she was frozen in time and acts on her previous plans to exact vengeance on the next person she sees. Although she is alert and awake immediately, she blinks and acts disoriented as she looks around the room while attempting to use her dominate ability on the nearest PCs. Unless attacked, she climbs slowly out of the coffin without speaking or responding to questions. She then stretches her wings and leaps up to the ceiling where she hangs with her spider climb ability and orders any dominated PCs to attack remaining party members. She exclusively uses her bite attacks and stays in physical combat unless severely injured. Severe injuries lead her to fly up to the ceiling, where she hangs face down casting *magic missile* and *acid arrow* while attempting to dominate heavily armored PCs. Huvarial's resting place is in this room; she fights until destroyed because she has nowhere else to flee. If the PCs flee, Huvarial makes plans to hunt them down. Huvarial is not familiar with the layout of the area, having only been imprisoned here; she uses great caution when searching the halls and rooms nearby.

Treasure: Unknown to Huvarial, her armor and weapons are hidden (can be found with a successful DC 25 Perception check) in a hollow chamber inside the stone pedestal that the coffin rests on. The hidden chamber contains the following items: a *+2 mithral shirt*, *+2 bastard sword* ("Light's Cleaver") with symbols representing the sun engraved on the blade, *+1 keen long sword*, *+1 amulet of natural armor* and a *+1 ring of protection*.

41. DEAD END

The hallway ends at a wall bearing a lengthy message written in dark green letters, "Put faith in Horgrim's darkest night and pass through solid rock." The message refers to the fact that the wall is a *permanent image* (a successful DC 20 Will save disbelieves). Characters without sight due to blindness or complete darkness do not see the illusion and boldly step through it to continue down the hallway. Although it has other sensory elements, the illusion is triggered by sight. Someone feeling the wall while looking at it believes they are feeling solid stone, but if they close their eyes and continue feeling the wall, those senses soon fade, and the wall no longer seems to exist. Anyone looking down the hall with a *true seeing* spell sees only a long hallway ending before a copper door.

42. ENGRAVED DOOR

Engravings on the copper door include a variety of complex runes and strange symbols along with the words, "In the end, only the darkness is real." A detailed representation of Horgrim as a tall human in robes holding a shortspear is engraved immediately beneath the strange statement. None of the engravings gives any hint how to open the door, which has no visible door knob or locking mechanism.

Engraved Copper Door: 2 in. thick; Hardness 15; hp 80; Break DC 28; Disable Device DC 20; SR 24

Powerful magic spells cast on the door give it some magic resistance, making it very difficult to open by magical means. Various runes on the door must be touched in a particular order. A clever rogue can eventually determine the proper sequence through trial and error.

43. COPPER ROOM (CR 9)

Beaten copper, complete with odd lumps and strange depressions, cover the walls, floors, and ceiling of the room. An insect-like **copper golem** with a circular head and eight legs ending in razor-sharp blades stands over a copper chest in the center of the room. The statue is a magical construct programmed to attack anyone not wearing an *amulet of the dark sun* and keep them away from the chest.

Copper Golem CR 9
XP 6,400
N Large construct
Init -1; **Senses** darkvision 60 ft., low-light vision; Perception +0
AC 22, touch 8, flat-footed 22 (-1 Dex, +14 natural, -1 size)
hp 96 (12d10+30)
Fort +3 **Ref** +2 **Will** +3
Defensive Abilities DR 10/adamantine; **Immune** construct traits, magic
Speed 20 ft.
Melee 4 slams +17 (2d10+6+1d6 electricity)
Special Attacks Electrical conduction, electrical shock (3d6 electricity, DC16 Reflex for half)
Str 23, **Dex** 8, **Con** -, **Int** -, **Wis** 11, **Cha** 1
Base Atk +12; **CMB** +19; **CMD** 28
Languages none
Special Abilities
Electrical conduction (Su) A copper golem deals 1d6 points of electrical damage with a touch. Creatures attacking a copper golem with unarmed strikes, natural attacks or metal weapons take this same electrical damage each time one of their attacks hits.
Electrical shock (Su) A copper golem can release a bolt of electricity every 4 rounds for 3d6 damage, DC 16 Reflex save for half.
Immunity to magic (Ex) A copper golem is immune to spells or spell-like abilities that allow spell resistance. Certain spells & effects function differently against it as noted below:
A magical attack that deals fire or cold damage slows a copper golem (as the slow spell) for 2d6 rounds, with no saving throw.
A magical attack that deals electrical damage breaks any slow effect on the golem and heals 1 points of damage for each 3 points of damage the attack would otherwise deal. If the amount of dealing would cause the golem to exceed its full normal hit points, it gains any excess as temporary hit points. A copper golem gets no saving throw against attacks that deal electrical damage.

Note: Copper golem can be found in **Appendix B: New Monsters**.

Copper Room: Copper on every surface of the room helps retain and magnify electric charges. All attacks inflicting lightning damage do double damage in this room.

Tactics: The statue has razor-sharp tips at each end of its powerful legs and uses them very effectively. It releases its electric charge at the first person to enter and charges the doorway to defend the room. A massive reach and the ability to use multiple attacks make it an effective guardian. It focuses all its attacks on the first person to enter the room, only spreading its attacks if someone attempts to sneak past it. The construct is programmed to fight until destroyed.

Copper Chest: 1 in. thick; Hardness 15; hp 80; Break DC 28; Disable Device DC 35

The lid of the small chest has an engraved description that is a mirror image of the symbols on an *amulet of the dark sun* that is part of the locking mechanism. Any *amulet of the dark sun* can be used to unlock the chest.

Treasure: The main item of importance in the chest is a **delicate copper key shaped like a lion (Key T2)** that opens the copper doors in **Area 8**. The key rests on top of a collection of 1500 copper coins, copper bracers with black enamel trim, a copper *ring of protection +1*, a thin copper wand (*lightning bolt*, 18 charges), a copper-tipped darkwood wand (*restoration*, 9 charges), 5 golden yellow topaz germs (500 gp each), and 4 amber gems (100 gp each).

44. THRONE OF NIGHT (CR 7 OR 0)

The hallway opens into a large room with strange, twisted engravings of skeletons and strange bone figures decorating every wall. A massive throne of pure black stone rests against the south wall, beckoning someone to sit in it. Polished and smooth, the stone is still somehow non-reflective and seems to soak up any light that hits it. Any PC able to *detect magic* or *evil* instantly discovers a vast, evil power emanating from the throne, a throne once used to help create undead to support Horgrim's armies. Anyone sitting on the throne risks a terrible fate.

The Throne of Night: This powerful item is imbued with terrible magic through numerous dark, necromantic rituals. Made of simple black stone, it soaks up light as easily as it does a creature's lifeforce. Dead humanoid creatures seated on the throne are engulfed in swirling shadows only to emerge a minute later with the flesh burned from their bodies as animated skeletons. Living creatures that sit on the throne must succeed at a DC 15 Reflex save to leap off the throne quickly enough to avoid the swirling shadows. Those who fail are engulfed in the swirling shadows and forced to make a DC 15 Fortitude save or die as the flesh and lifeforce are stripped from the character's body as they are turned into an animated skeleton. Success indicates characters escape the burning shadows, suffering only 5d6 negative energy damage.

Destroying the Throne CR 7: Characters recognizing the immense evil of the throne might decide to destroy it. Although not a true living beast, the throne does have its own defenses. Attacks against the throne release waves of electrical energy once every round (2d8+4 electricity damage to everyone within 10 ft., DC 18 Reflex save for half). The throne has 300 hp, fast healing 5, DR 10/magic, and SR 28. When destroyed, the throne explodes in a blast of raw energy with a 20-foot radius blast; characters must succeed at a DC 20 Reflex save or suffer 10d6 fire damage (half damage on a successful save).

Treasure: Once destroyed, the throne leaves behind broken gems that were used during its initial creation. A patient wizard can collect 2000 gp worth of diamond dust, 1500 gp worth of ruby dust, and 1500 gp worth of emerald dust for use as spell components.

45. WORN TAPESTRY

A worn tapestry with a portrayal of a human riding the back of a black dragon hangs on the wall in the center of the hallway. The odd placement of the tapestry suggests something may be hidden behind it. Anyone searching the wall behind the tapestry (DC 15 Perception check) finds long grooves or slots in the stone that appear to lead to an open or hollow area behind the wall. These grooves provide Narise (see **Areas 3–4** above) with access to these hallways using her gaseous form. She doesn't usually come through this hallway unless she hears a great deal of noise, or if she has recently encountered the PCs. If Narise has already encountered the PCs, or if the PCs make a great deal of noise, there is a 40% chance that Narise ambushes the PCs somewhere in **Areas 41–47**. In that instance, she forgoes any play and simply uses the battle tactics mentioned in **Area 3**. The wall between this section of hallway and her **Sealed Chamber (Area 4)** is 3 feet thick (Hardness 8; hp 180; Break DC 24) and must be broken down or bypassed with *passwall* or *gaseous form* spells.

46. BRITTLE OAK DOOR

Although once a sturdy, solid door, this portal has become brittle through the passing of time. The unlocked oak door opens easily but has a rather interesting **trap**.

Alarm Trap CR 1
Type magical; **Perception** DC 25; **Disable Device** DC 25
  Trigger touch; **Duration** 1 round; **Reset** automatic; **Bypass** arcane switch (Knowledge (arcana) DC 15 to determine)
Effect Opening the door triggers an *alarm* spell that lasts for 1 round unless the words "Love Horgrim" are spoken. While the alarm spell does no damage, it alerts Narise (**Areas 3–4**) that someone is in the hall.

47. ANCIENT ARMORY (CR 8)

Racks of greatswords, pikes, shortspears, and longspears are evenly spaced throughout the room. Although extremely old, the weapons are still in excellent shape, possibly because a **fallen** watching over the room polishes and oils them continuously.

Fallen CR 8
XP 4,800
hp 93 (Pathfinder Roleplaying Game Bestiary 6, "Fallen")

Treasure #1: Of the more than 100 weapons lined up in the racks, a number are masterwork quality weapons: 10 greatswords, 8 pikes, 6 shortspears, and 6 longspears.

Treasure #2: One cleric took the time to create a secret hiding place beneath one of the weapon racks (DC 30 Perception check) where he hid several "personal" items in a small leather bag. The decaying leather bag contains a *pale blue rhomboid ioun stone* (+2 Str), a mithral *+1 ring of protection*, a *necklace of fireballs (Type III)*, a *+2 headband of inspired wisdom*, a flawless emerald (5000 gp), 4 fire opals (1200 gp each), a black pearl (500 gp), 3 violet garnets (400 gp each), and 9 bloodstones (50 gp each).

48. BLACK METAL DOORS

Black Metal Doors: 1 in. thick; Hardness 15; hp 120; Break DC 30; Disable Device DC 27

These plain black doors are made of a mysterious alloy that is so heavily enchanted that it defies identification. While the lock can be picked, the **lead key (Key T1)** found in **Area 22** opens this door as well as the double lead doors (**Area 7**).

49. SMOKE-FILLED ROOM (CR 15)

Thick gray smoke pours out of the room when the doors are opened. The smoke dissipates quickly when it leaves the room, but the amount of smoke within the room doesn't change. Bitter and dry, the harmless smoke causes a bit of coughing and concern. A large marble statue of a serpent-like creature with three heads stands in the center of the room surrounded by four brass barriers. Smoke flows from the braziers in a steady stream, filling the room with bitter fumes. Although the smoke is not poisonous, it reduces all forms of vision to a maximum of 10 feet no matter what form of lighting is used. In addition, it conceals a **mummy lord** that guards the room against anyone not wearing an *amulet of the dark sun*.

Mummy Lord CR 10
XP 9,600
hp 103 (Pathfinder Roleplaying Game Bestiary 5, "Mummy Lord")

Brass Braziers: These items glow with several types of magic when studied with the aid of a *detect magic* spell. Covering the braziers with a blanket or some other item stops the flow of smoke. A *dispel magic* cast directly on one of the braziers (DC 23) eliminates the magic on that brazier and stops the smoke. Once the flow of smoke from all four barriers is stopped, the room can be cleared of smoke in 1d4 hours if the doors are left open.

Tactics: Once a faithful cleric of Horgrim, the mummy lord retains much of its prior knowledge and experience, making it a very deadly foe. It senses the PCs enter the room and moves out of its strange coffin quietly. The smoke gives it extra time to prepare, so it takes the opportunity to cast *protection from good* and *bull's strength* on itself and then casts *desecrate* before finally moving into battle. It does its best to attack and destroy anyone attempting to use fire-based spells or weapons on it, usually attempting a *hold person* spell first.

Examining the Room: Other than the statue and braziers, the only other item in the room is a sarcophagus that stands upright against the wall directly behind the statue. The sarcophagus is the mummy's resting place, and a cleverly designed secret door leading into another room. Smoke in this room makes it extremely difficult to recognize this, but if the braziers are covered and the smoke dissipates, locating the secret door gets much easier (the door can be found with a successful DC 36 Perception check, DC 18 Perception check without smoke). The door is counterweighted to allow the entire sarcophagus and door to slide to one side without much effort.

50. SILVER ROOM (CR 8)

Flaking silver paint covers the walls, floor, and ceiling. Peeling paint and silver fragments on the floor suggest the silver was a late addition to the room. Standing on silver pedestals are 2 **magnesium golems**. Each golem attacks as soon as someone enters the room. Only a cleric devoted to Horgrim wearing an *amulet of the dark sun* can command the golems to stop and freely surrender the fragment of the **ornate silver key (Key T3)** each carries.

Magnesium Golem (2) CR 6
XP 2,400
hp 64 (Tome of Horrors Complete, "Golem, Magnesium")

Tactics: The golems approach anyone entering the room. If a cleric of Horgrim does not show a holy symbol and utter the proper words within 2 rounds, they attack, focusing on lightly armored characters first.

Treasure: The body of each golem is worth 3000 sp and the ruby in each golem's head can be broken into 500 gp worth of ruby dust. A single piece of an ornate silver key is embedded in the chest of each golem next to a reversed engraving of an *amulet of the dark sun*. Placing an amulet into the engraving releases the piece of key. The two fragments fit together to form an **ornate silver key (Key T3)** that fits the silver double doors in **Area 9 (Door 9e)**.

Chapter 9: Horgrim's Temple Level 2

The second level of the temple is quite like the first. The outer walls are 20 feet thick and both inner and outer walls are made of the same material. Rooms and hallways have no lighting unless otherwise stated.

51. Chamber of Faces (CR 10)

Twin stairways climb up to a large room. Bas-relief carvings along the walls depict elegant humans and elves standing at attention. Some of the figures wear armor, while others have on robes, but all the carvings are detailed to the point that each figure seems life-like. Strange symbols are painted on the floor using dark reddish-black paint. Any magic the symbols once possessed has faded. Each figure is a follower of Horgrim who volunteered to meld with the stone wall and await a priest to reverse the spells that placed them there. Unfortunately, the magic that kept their souls from departing failed long ago. A *dispel magic* (DC 30) cast directly on a bas-relief carving has a small chance of expelling the body of the victim, but none of the carvings gives rise to a living being.

A set of ornate double doors is at the southern end of the room. The doors are unlocked, though one of the **fallen** described below does have a key that can be used to lock them.

The room is heavily guarded. Anyone climbing one of the sets of stairs is attacked by 2 **fallen** as soon as they reach the top.

Fallen (2) CR 8
XP 4,800
hp 93 (Pathfinder Roleplaying Game Bestiary 6, "Fallen")

Note: One of the fallen has a key to the double doors described above.

52. Hall of Honor

Small statues and plaques fill niches along the long, wide hallway stretching to the east and west. The hallway bends north at its eastern- and westernmost limits before ending in front of double doors.

53. Frost-Covered Doors

The hallway ends before a set of steel doors covered with frost. The rune-coated doors are cold enough that they are painful to touch, dealing 1d6 cold damage whenever touched.

54. Room of Ice (CR 7)

Icicles hang from the ceiling, which glows with an odd blue light, and strange ice sculptures dot the room. The room is so extremely frigid that everyone inside suffers 1d4 points of cold damage for every round they remain in the room. The extreme, magical cold of the room makes fire-based spells half as effective in terms of size, duration, and damage. Thick coats of ice cover a set of steel double doors in the north wall, as well as all the walls. A huge **ice elemental** guards the room; it creates strange, twisted sculptures and odd ice carvings during its long, boring tenure.

Huge Ice Elemental CR 7
XP 3,200
hp 95 (Pathfinder Roleplaying Game Bestiary 2, "Elemental, Ice (Huge)")

Tactics: Before attacking, this creature attempts to communicate in its guttural language. It was summoned here and bound to the room as a guardian. All it knows is that it is supposed to guard the doors against anyone who doesn't have an *amulet of the dark sun*. The ice elemental is willing to trade the key to the north door in exchange for an amulet, which it uses to exit the room and return to its own plane of existence. The creature communicates very slowly and isn't very intelligent. By now, the PCs are probably used to attacking rather than negotiating. It focuses melee attacks on one target at a time, doing its best to kill one creature before moving on to the next.

Steel Double Doors: 5 in. thick; Hardness 15; hp 150; Break DC 30; Disable Device DC 40; SR 24

Approximately 1-foot-thick ice (Hardness 2; hp 30; Break DC 12) covers the doors and must be broken away to reveal them. Faint runes near the lock suggest that it has been magically hardened and enhanced. The extremely complex lock requires a **special key (Key T4)**.

Map 7: Horgrim's Temple - Level 2

1 Square - 10 Feet

Map 7: Horgrim's Temple
Level 3

1 Square - 10 Feet

Map 7: Horgrim's Temple
Level 4

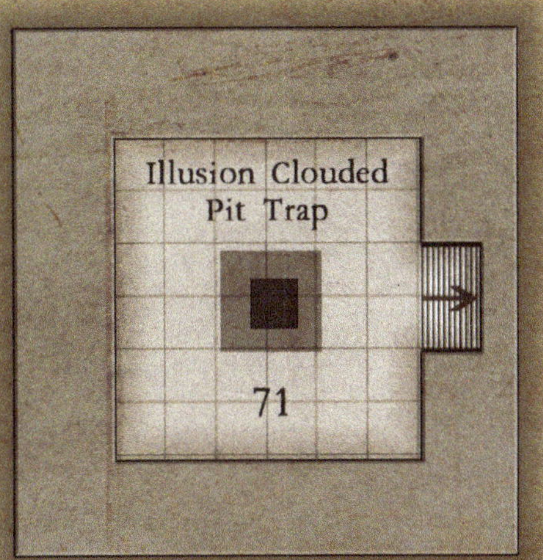

1 Square - 5 Feet

55. Shattered Room

Ages ago, this large room contained a variety of furniture, sofas, chairs, tables, but now only broken fragments remain along the outer walls of the room. The devastation appears to be focused in the center of the room where an explosion threw everything into the walls with such force that virtually everything is shattered and broken. A lich left to guard this room eventually went insane. Without spellbooks to study or a particular task to fulfill, he decided that his continued existence was no longer fulfilling. Using *passwall* spells, he was able to obtain his phylactery from its hiding place in the walls of the temple. He brought it into the center of the room and attempted to destroy it. This act instantly brought down Horgrim's wrath and set off a detonation of such force that the ceiling and floor show signs of melting and cracking. Even the walls show cracks where furniture was crushed against it.

Dwarves or other characters with stonecunning instantly recognize hints that stonework was done to close off a wide doorway in the northern wall. The stone that was used matches the other stone used to make the temple, but its placement, and the cracks that run through it, suggest there was once a wide doorway here. Followers of Horgrim sealed this doorway, once the main passage to upper levels of the temple, after losing the battles outside the temple.

Bone fragments from the several skeletons left behind to serve the lich are strewn about the debris, along with a few treasures. One important item is a **twisted metal key** (Key T5, DC 28 Perception check). Once an ornate silver key with delicate filigree around the outer edges, it is now bent beyond usefulness. It was designed to open the door in **Area 59**. A character making a careful study of the item can use information from the key to gain a +15 circumstance bonus on checks to open the lock on the door in **Area 59**.

Treasure: A thorough search (DC 28 Perception check) of the entire room takes several hours but turns up a few worthwhile items: a *+2 rapier, wand of restoration (8 charges), a ring of jumping,* a number of small gems, including a star-cut ruby (2500 gp), a tiny emerald (1500 gp), 12 black pearls (apparently from a necklace, 350 gp each), 15 pieces of polished jade (150 gp each), and 8 moonstones (50 gp each).

56. Red-Hot Doors

Glowing double doors at the end of the hallway shed enough heat to warm the hallway significantly. The doors are searing hot — so hot that they appear close to melting yet are somehow resisting for the moment.

Searing Hot Double Doors: 10 in. thick; Hardness 15; hp 300; Break DC 30

The doors inflict 1d8+4 fire damage on anyone touching them and 3 fire damage per round on anyone starting their turn within 5 feet.

The doors are made of a mysterious alloy enchanted to resist very high temperatures. Although the doors are unlocked, they open outward and must be pulled firmly (a successful DC 15 Strength check opens the doors).

57. Room of Fire (CR 9)

The doors open to reveal a room filled with darting flames and molten rock. The walls and floor are magically enchanted to resist the heat and the presence of a 1-foot-deep pool of molten rock that fills the room. The fantastic heat inflicts 5 fire damage per round on anyone starting their turn in the room, and anyone stepping into the molten rock is subject to additional 2d4 fire damage per round at the start of their turn. Overwhelming magical heat in this room makes cold-based spells half as effective in terms of size, duration, and damage. The large black doors at the north end of the room appear remarkably cool when compared to the boiling rock and flames that surround them. Unfortunately, a greater **fire elemental** is looking for someone to wreak vengeance on after being trapped here for thousands of years. The elemental does everything it can to slaughter anyone entering the room.

Greater Fire Elemental CR 9
XP 6,400
hp 123 (Pathfinder Roleplaying Game Bestiary, "Elemental, Fire (Greater)")

Tactics: The elemental has been trapped here for so long that it is mindless in its rage. All it knows is that it has been abandoned by the mages that initially summoned it here. Enough time has gone by that it has forgotten what its duties are, or how it might be able to leave the room. It can leave the room only if it is "released" by a priest of Horgrim or freely given a holy symbol of Horgrim. Even if the PCs manage to do this, it is upset enough that it is unlikely to care. It attacks one character at a time, trying to burn them to a crisp before moving on to others.

58. Sitting Room

Elegant sofas and chairs are organized into several sitting areas. Despite its great age, the furniture is in excellent condition. Everything in the room is clean, dust-free, and in some cases highly polished. Niches along the outer walls hold small statues and figurines made of porcelain. **Skeletons** stand in each of the corners of the room. The four skeletons are not outfitted for battle; they hold serving trays and cleaning cloths, making them appear to be servants of some type. Depending on the actions of the PCs, this room should be a safe place to rest and recuperate.

A small fountain is in the northeast corner of the room, but no water is in the basin. Cabinets along the west wall hold a variety of liquors and wines, and jars contain the desiccated remains of what might once have been food. Sealed bottles of liquor and wine are still consumable, but the rest is beyond rescue.

A set of ancient oak double doors in the north wall leads into another room.

Tactics: These skeletons are servants that haven't had anyone to serve for many centuries. They do not initiate combat but fight back if attacked. They silently serve the PCs any liquor or wine that is specifically requested and simply ignore requests they cannot fulfill. If the PCs make no aggressive actions against the skeletons, they simply stand in their corners, moving only to polish furniture or to clean the room.

59. Priests' Quarters (CR 11)

The opulent decorations and furniture of the room indicate it was once home to only the highest ranking and most loyal followers of Horgrim. Gold, silver, and a strange, dark metal were used to create a figure of Horgrim as a tall human holding a spear standing before a circle of complete darkness adorning the west wall. A total of eight beds occupy the room, each spaced close together along the outer walls, and each having a large wooden chest at its foot. Several chairs surround low tables in the center of the room, along with a single wooden bench facing the west wall. Rods along the ceiling allow the various beds in the rooms to be cloaked by curtains, giving the occupants some privacy. In general, the room has an air of a military barracks, albeit a barracks decorated with wealth and style. Four serving **skeletons** similar to those in **Area 58** stand in each corner of the room.

A slow, rasping noise — like the heavy breathing of a sick patient — comes from the ornate double doors in the north wall. The noise is particularly disconcerting because it appears to be coming from the doors themselves.

None of the chests in the room is locked but they give up few treasures.

Treasure #1: The unlocked chests contain a *+2 dagger,* 3 *+1 maces,* 4 *+1 cloaks of resistance* decorated with holy symbols to Horgrim, various masterwork daggers, maces, morningstars, and various pieces of decaying clothing.

Treasure #2: One of the chests has a false bottom (DC 28 Perception check) that conceals *+1 bracers of armor,* arcane scrolls (*blink, fly, lightning bolt,* and *fireball*) (CL 5th), and a *wand of fireball (20 charges).*

Ornate Double Doors: 10 in. thick; Hardness 15; hp 300; Break DC 28; Disable Device DC 40; SR 30

The beautiful doors are made of an alloy of several different metals that gives it a rainbow-like sheen on a background of black. Enchantments add to the strength of the door and make it very resistant to magic spells. As the ornate engravings and decorations would suggest, the lock for the door is extraordinarily complex. The ornate keys fitting the door have all been lost or destroyed, except for the key found in **Area 55** (Key T5). While this key is also bent and broken, a careful study gives a careful character a +15 circumstance bonus on checks to open the lock. Oddly enough, the breathing the PCs hear comes from the doors. Several priests and wizards used a series of spells to trap a **horned devil** within the door.

Release Devil Trap: A *magic mouth* appears on the door and asks for the "password." If the proper reply is not uttered within 2 rounds, a **hamatula devil** is released from the door to attack anyone in the area. The password is "wiyeth," an ancient term for darkness (can be recalled with a DC 35 Knowledge [History] check). *Detect magic* reveals a powerful magic aura around the door, and *detect evil* exposes a powerful evil aura, but there is no physical sign of a trap. The spell can be dispelled (DC 25) but doing so releases the devil and inflicts 24 points of damage on it.

Barbed Devil (Hamatula) CR 11
XP 12,800
hp 138 (Pathfinder Roleplaying Game Bestiary, "Devil, Hamatula (Barbed Devil)")

60. Narrow Hallway

The double doors open into a narrow hallway that extends past a wider hallway only to reach a dead-end. A massive black circle made of metal is bonded to the stone floor in the center of the wide hallway immediately before a set of stone steps heading up to the next level of the temple (**Level 3, Area 61**).

Chapter 10: Horgrim's Temple Level 3

The outer walls of the third level of the temple are only 10 feet thick but both inner and outer walls are made of the same stone as the rest of the temple. Rooms and hallways on this level have a strange type of lighting that enables anyone with low-light vision or darkvision to see perfectly. Characters unable to see under these conditions need additional light sources. Unless otherwise noted, all the doors on this level are identical oak doors (unlocked) decorated with a carving of Horgrim depicted as a tall human male in robes holding a shortspear in his left hand.

61. Small Landing

Wide stairs climb up from the second level of the temple to reach a small landing with wooden doors to the east and west. The south wall is decorated with a brightly colored painting portraying a tall human male in black robes standing atop a mountain with his hands outstretched as if giving a blessing.

62. Preparation Room (CR 8)

Various chalices, scepters, vases, and braziers rest on a long table in the center of the room, and a variety of jars line the shelves along the east wall. Open cabinets in the southeast corner hold a variety of black-and-red colored linen cloths. Even the uninitiated instantly recognize this area as a room for clerics to prepare for holy ceremonies. An open doorway in the north wall leads to another storage room, and a closed oak door is to the south. Anyone entering the room without wearing an *amulet of the dark sun* is immediately attacked by a **fallen**.

Fallen CR 8
XP 4,800
hp 93 (Pathfinder Roleplaying Game Bestiary 6, "Fallen")

63. Storage Chamber

The door to this chamber was left open so long that it sagged away from the frame and can no longer be closed. Casks of scented oil, unholy water, and other liquids line the room, all obviously meant to be used in religious ceremonies and rituals.

64. Adoration Chamber (CR 10)

This massive chamber is organized like a large church, only there are no benches, just faint dark lines along the stone floor where worshippers are expected to stand. A large mirror framed with black metal stands behind a plain altar resting on a raised platform on the west side of the room. Several oak doors dot the north and east walls. Horgrim requires only simple services from his followers, expecting them to show their faith by their everyday actions rather than in ceremonies. These "adorations" usually took place at sunset and included simple statements of faith in Horgrim followed by a pledge to spread this faith in Horgrim followed by a pledge to spread this faith to all lands. The black-framed mirror was once used as a portal between this temple and another a great distance away. Several clerics and warriors faithful to Horgrim fled through the portal when their efforts here failed. Unfortunately, they fled to a temple that had already been discovered and defeated by Arn's forces and were instantly captured. Other clerics forcefully moved and deactivated the portal to prevent any further desertions.

A **fallen** stands behind the altar flanked by 2 **lead skeletons**. They attack anyone who dares enter the room without displaying an *amulet of the dark sun*.

Fallen CR 8
XP 4,800
hp 93 (Pathfinder Roleplaying Game Bestiary 6, "Fallen")

Lead Skeleton (2) CR 7
XP 3,200
hp 75 (Tome of Horrors Complete, "Skeleton, Lead")

Treasure: The lead skeletons have been studded with a variety of valuable gems along their ribs, teeth, and eye sockets. These gems include 4 large rubies (2000 gp each), 18 small diamonds (700 gp each), and 12 small emeralds (500 gp each).

65. Room of Coffins

Simple stone coffins are lined up against the east wall. The unadorned stone coffins are the final resting places for the clerics and wizards that lived out their final days in the temple creating the traps designed to prevent the forces of Arn or any other good god from violating it. A thorough investigation of all the coffins turns up only bones; all those interred here were placed into their coffins completely naked.

66. Burial Chamber

While high-raking priests and warriors merited burial in their own coffins lined up in the **Room of Coffins** (**Area 65**), lower-ranking personnel merited simple burial in a stack of small stone cubicles along the east wall. Small stones cover each square hole, with only the empty spots left uncapped. Based on the number of stone caps, more than 50 people were laid to rest here. Additional openings reach the ceiling, adding another 20–30 places for further burials. As in **Area 65**, everyone buried here was buried free of clothing or belongings.

67. Small Library (CR 7)

Heavy stone shelves reach from the floor to ceiling all along the outer edges of the room, and several solid stone tables stand in the center of the room. A strange metal ladder with wheels at the feet and a guide along the ceiling allows access to books on the highest shelves. The dry room has preserved the ancient texts but left almost all of the parchment pages extremely brittle. Any fire in the room creates a horrible inferno as flames leap from book to book all along the shelves. Many of the texts describe tactics for warfare, weaknesses of certain ancient armies, as well as weather patterns and trade routes. Although the information in those texts is hopelessly outdated, their great age makes some of them valuable to some collectors.

A **lead skeleton** stands watch here. The high priest that stationed it here ordered it to attack anyone other than him, presuming he would be back later to change those orders.

Lead Skeleton CR 7
XP 3,200
hp 75 (Tome of Horrors Complete, "Skeleton, Lead")

Tactics: The jewel-studded skeleton ferociously attacks the first PC to enter the room. Although not really programmed to do so, it makes its attacks immediately inside the doorway, thus restricting who might be able to enter melee combat with it. Once it tastes battle, it chases any fleeing PCs until it is completely destroyed.

Note: Any fire-based spells used in this room destroy all the non-magical books.

Treasure: Prying the gems off the skeleton turns up two large rubies (1500 gp each) and 12 small emeralds (500 gp each). While only a few of the ancient texts could be considered collector's items, those 20 books fetch a total of 8000 gp in a major city. A very careful study (DC 32 Perception check) reveals a book titled *Iliachoam's Beasts and Saddles* (detailed in **Appendix D: New Magic Items**).

68. Small Library (CR 10)

On its surface, this room appears identical to the **Small Library** (**Area 67**). The shelves, ladder, and tables are the same. The books are quite different, however. All the books, whether mundane or magical, have bindings and covers made from scales of various types of dragons. All the mundane texts in the room are as dry and subject to burning as those in **Area 67**, but many of the texts here are enchanted against fire and other damage. These books include tomes of spells, texts designed to make shadow and illusion magic more powerful, and detailed discussions of Horgrim and the various spells and powers he offers his faithful followers. Perusing the texts is difficult, however, as the room is guarded by a small **blue dragon statue**.

Blue Dragon Statue　　CR 9

XP 6,400

N Small construct

Init +4; **Senses** blindsight 60 ft., darkvision 60 ft., low-light vision;
　Perception +0

AC 25, touch 15, flat-footed 21 (+4 Dex, +10 natural, +1 size)

hp 85 (14d10+10)

Fort +4, **Ref** +8, **Will** +4

DR 10/magic; **Immune** construct traits, acid, cold, electricity; **Resist**
　fire 30, sonic 30; **SR** 20

Speed 10 ft., fly 90 ft. (good)

Melee bite +27 (1d2+12), 2 claws +27 (1d3+12)

Special Attacks breath weapon 30 ft. cone; 2d6 sonic damage (DC 17
　Fortitude negates deafness)

Str 34, **Dex** 18, **Con** —, **Int** —, **Wis** 10, **Cha** 10

Base Atk +14; **CMB** +25; **CMD** 39

Skills Acrobatics +4 (-4 to jump), Fly +10

Special Abilities

Breath Weapon (DC 17) (Su) 30 ft. cone; 2d6 sonic damage (DC 17
　Fortitude negates deafness)

Note: Dragon statues can be found in **Appendix B: New Monsters**.

Combat Tactics: The statue has a simple directive: Attack anyone not wearing
an *amulet of the dark sun*. When the door is opened, the statue takes flight and
circles the perimeter of the room. It attacks anyone entering without the required
amulet first with its breath weapon and then with its bite and claw attacks. Once the
door is opened, the statue chases fleeing opponents. It is unable to open the door
itself. If the door is closed, it simply returns to its resting position.

Note: Use of fire-based spells destroys any non-magical texts and stands a good
chance of damaging or destroying spellbooks and other magical texts.

Treasure: The shelves are lined with a wide variety of books including non-
magical texts worth a total of 2000 gp to an avid collector. Among the enchanted
books are *Iliachoam's Trainer's Guide*, *Instruments of the Vearlik*, and a variety of
spellbooks that include the following spells: 0—all; 1st—*alarm*, *burning hands*,
color spray, *comprehend languages*, *etch stone**, *feather fall*, *mage armor*, *magic
missile*, *shield*, *floating disc*; 2nd—*alter self*, *arcane lock*, *blur*, *darkness*, *detect
thoughts*, *invisibility*, *knock*, *levitate*, *mirror image*; 3rd—*dispel magic*, *explosive
runes*, *fireball*, *gaseous form*, *haste*, *hold person*, *lightning bolt*, *protection from
energy*, *stinking cloud*, *suggestion*; 4th—*arcane eye*, *confusion*, *contagion*,
dimension door, *ice storm*, *wall of fire*, *wall of ice*; 5th—*animate dead*, *passwall*,
stone shape, *telekinesis*, *teleport*, *wall of force*; 6th—*contingency*, *programmed
image*.

* The spell *etch stone* is detailed in **Appendix E: New Spells**.

69. Rune-Coated Steel Door

The steel door is covered with glowing pink runes surrounding a cloaked figure.
Words engraved beneath the cloaked figure read, "Death is the entrance to new
life."

Steel Door: 2 in. thick; Hardness 15; hp 90; Break DC 28; Disable Device DC
40; SR 22

The door is difficult to open without the proper key (**Key T6** found in **Area 64**).
Once opened, the door reveals a short hallway.

70. Short Hallway (CR 9)

Glowing runes decorate the walls of the short hallway as it approaches a small
wooden door near its very end. Two **lead skeletons** guarding the hallway attack
anyone passing through the steel door to the north.

Lead Skeleton (2)　　CR 7

XP 3,200

hp 75 (Tome of Horrors Complete, "Skeleton, Lead")

Combat Tactics: The skeletons charge the northern door from the center of the
hallway as soon as it opens. They attack with single-minded ferocity and run down
any fleeing PCs.

Treasure: Although the skeletons have no gems in their eye sockets, emeralds
make up their teeth and tiny sapphires line their breastbones: 24 tiny emeralds (350
gp each), and 18 tiny sapphires (300 gp each).

The hallway ends before a simple oak door (2 in. thick; Hardness 4; hp 20; Break
DC 15; unlocked) in the west wall. Although unlocked, great age causes the hinges
to stick slightly and create a vast amount of noise when the door opens. The noise
announces the PCs to anyone nearby. Once opened, a small stairway climbing up to
the highest level of the temple (Level **4**, **Area 71**) is revealed.

Chapter 11: Horgrim's Temple Level 4 and Below

Horgrim's Temple — Level 4

The bottom level of the temple itself is a single, very large room inside a pyramid. The walls are 15 feet thick and have strange white marble stripes that rise to the peak of the pyramid. The marble stripes are normal worked stone, but the main part of the walls is the same stone as the rest of the temple. Note that two chambers — accessible through the pit — lie even deeper than this level and are detailed below.

71. Bourafane's Refuge (CR 9)

Strange runic symbols cover almost every surface of the wall. Anyone making a successful DC 18 Knowledge (Arcana) check realizes these runic symbols are actually detailed descriptions of spells and not something left behind by a magic spell, or at least they were before they were defaced. Bourafane, a failed lich shade haunting here, used the very walls as his spellbooks. The eight marble stripes in the room each conceal small storage areas that can be reached only through the use of a *passwall* spell or by breaking through the marble wall (described below).

A single white stone with glowing purple runes stands on a pedestal in the exact center of the room, and a large throne-like chair made of bone set against the southern wall faces north toward the glowing stone. The glowing stone matches the description and sketches of *The White Eye* and the very peak of the temple would appear to be a logical place to store a powerful relic. Unfortunately, the glowing stone, its pedestal, and the floor beneath it are all permanent programmed illusions that are extremely convincing (disbelieved with a DC 30 Will save). The illusions entice greedy raiders to step over a deadly pit trap and plummet 160 feet to a rough stone floor. A passageway at the very bottom of the pit leads to a room storing all the temple's treasures.

The complexity and skill that went into the illusions covering the pit make it very difficult to detect. *Programmed illusions* create a brilliant flash of green light emanating from the false eye along with a booming echo to make it appear that anyone falling though the floor has been disintegrated. Creatures that levitate or fly over the trap do not trigger this illusion. Creatures that attempt to grab the stone see it wink in and out of existence as if avoiding their grasp. Once identified, the pit is easy to avoid. Avoiding the trap also avoids the passageway hidden at its very bottom (**Area 72**).

Lich Shade CR 9
XP 6,400
hp 104 (Tome of Horrors Complete, "Lich Shade")

Tactics: Bourafane was always a bit of a practical joker, something that may be highlighted by the constant loneliness inflicted on him the past few thousand years. Bourafane wants the PCs to get the treasures they seek, but his promises prevent him from openly helping them. When he hears the door (**Level 3, Area 70**) opening, he rises, greets them in a friendly manner, and welcomes them to his small "prison." He waves a hand at the illusionary pedestal and stone and says, "This is what you are seeking. Please take it, but only if you are pure of heart." He uses vague terms to make the PCs believe that the illusionary *White Eye* is actually a good artifact that was stolen and hidden here to prevent others from using it. Bourafane knows about the trap and the true treasure beneath the temple. If the PCs are direct with their questions, Bourafane is forced to give honest answers, but he does his best to use vague terms.

Marble chambers: Only a clever individual realizes the marble stone might conceal storage spaces. The eight marble stripes that reach from floor to ceiling each conceal small niches that can be accessed only through a *passwall* or similar spell or by breaking through the stone (3 ft. thick; Hardness 8; hp 120; Break DC 22). While only three of the hidden chambers contain treasure, these treasures are worth all the effort involved. Bourafane considers all the items listed below his personal possessions. Bourafane attacks anyone attempting to steal his treasures and must be defeated before the chambers can be safely accessed.

Chambers 1–3: Empty.

Chamber 4: A black velvet bag holding 3 perfect emeralds (7000 gp each) and a blue diamond (5500 gp), and a leather bag holding 500 ancient gold coins (worth 1 gp each for gold value or 5 gp each to a collector in a large city).

Chamber 5: A diamond pendant on a platinum chain (*necklace of adaptation*), a *necklace of fireballs (Type V)*, a *hand of glory*, a tattered felt hat (*hat of disguise*), and 5 doses of *restorative ointment*.

Chamber 6–7: Empty.

Chamber 8: Several *figurines of wondrous power*, including a bronze griffin, marble elephant, obsidian steed, and an onyx dog. There is no hint of the command words for these items. Days of study and experimentation are required to learn the command word for each figurine. Additional treasures include *+2 belt of incredible dexterity*, a *gauntlet of rust*, *dust of appearance*, *dust of disappearance*, and *dust of drying*.

Horgrim's Temple — Beneath the Temple

The final level of the temple is actually deep beneath the ground. The short hallway and room here are carved from the granite of the surrounding mountains and subject to all the spells that normally modify or change rough stone. Absolutely no lighting exists in this part of the temple; darkvision or a light source are required to see. These chambers are accessed by the pit.

Note: See the side-view map for the location of these room.

72. Bottom of the Pit

The rough stone floor and walls clearly indicate that the bottom of the pit is deep below the surface. Despite its rough nature, no debris is here, just a thick coat of dust from the surrounding walls. A narrow passageway runs west toward a large room.

73. The Treasure Chamber (CR 11)

Horgrim's faithful used this large room to store vast amounts of money and items to keep it out of the hands of their enemies. Numerous small bags are stacked against the three massive chests, each almost as large as a coffin, which are lined up against the outer walls. A **stone golem** shaped like a statue of Horgrim guards the chamber against all intruders.

Stone Golem CR 11
XP 12,800
hp 107 (Pathfinder Roleplaying Game Bestiary, "Golem, Stone")

Tactics: The golem attacks anyone entering the treasure chamber and continues its attacks until everyone is dead or it is destroyed.

Treasure: Traps do not protect the chests or bags, and all are unlocked. The total treasure trove includes: *The White Eye* (see **Appendix D: New Magic Items**), 23 *amulets of the dark sun*, *+3 longsword*, *+2 shortspear*, *+2 kama*, *+2 studded leather armor*, *+2 bracers of armor*, *+2 amulet of natural armor*, *+2 cloak of resistance*, *cloak of the manta ray*, *monk's robe*, *scabbard of keen edges*, *bage of holding (Type III)*, a *cloak of arachnida*, and 60,000 gp worth of coins and gems.

Concluding the Adventure

After departing the temple, the PCs can give the many evil items they find in the temple to Souref (see **Chapter 7: Arn's Mountain**) who destroys them and rewards the PCs with several items from his treasure trove (GM's option, usually items appropriate to the PCs' character classes). Souref considers the destruction of the eye a great and holy task and rewards the PCs generously if they successfully obtain it. Treasure throughout this portion of the adventure is generally appropriate to the challenges the PCs faced. If the PCs missed some treasure caches, Souref can be used to make up the difference in items and wealth.

While the PCs still need to return to civilization, their new wealth and store of magic items should make travel through the wilderness relatively safe.

Continuing Adventures

The baron and Ander Fierk are still alive and are now running from the king's men with accusations of treason, torture, and murder attached to their names. The PCs might be hired to track down these criminals, or the traitors might begin hunting the PCs to exact revenge.

Londar, once *resurrected*, goes into hiding and slowly rebuilds his power and resources before finally tracking down the PCs and punishing them for their theft of his private papers and spellbooks. Alternatively, Londar might hire the PCs to assist him.

Treasure in Londar's vault and in Horgrim's Temple include treasure maps and papers describing ancient ruins and lost artifacts.

Uvear, after being helped by the PCs, asks them to help him find one of his clan's lost relics.

Major NPCs in Hampton Hill

Statistics and descriptions for **Learah Relight**, **Alfguir K'Eliek**, and **Ander Fierk**, the three individuals most interested in Londar's disappearance, are listed first, followed by statistics for other NPCs in Hampton Hill.

Learah Relight

Learah is a slight, dark-haired woman with a great deal of beauty and presence. Her aquiline features and violet eyes attract a great deal of attention. Her recent marriage to the son of a major shipping magnate has made her wealthy enough to dress in the latest styles. Though she wears a variety of rather expensive jewelry, the disappearance of her uncle has made her partial to the ruby pendant he gave her on her 16th birthday.

Despite some rumors to the contrary, Learah deeply loved her uncle. Londar was one of the few people who could understand the strange changes she went through as she discovered sorcerous powers during adolescence. Londar was also her only remaining family after her parents died in a carriage accident; he cared for her and helped her care for her family's estate. Learah desperately wants to know what happened to her beloved uncle and is willing to hire adventurers to investigate his disappearance. Learah doesn't care about Londar's money, but she does claim ownership of the spells and magic items Londar created, believing she knows what Londar would like her to do with them.

Although she has a key that opens several doors, she has no way past the golems guarding several of Londar's rooms, nor does she know anything about the traps he set throughout his mansion. Learah is disappointed with the sheriff and the town guards, and is actively seeking adventurers willing to help search for her uncle. Learah is satisfied that Londar isn't in any of the regular rooms of his mansion but hopes there might be a clue to his whereabouts hidden either in his office or his tower. She is happy to provide her key to the mansion to anyone willing to investigate Londar's disappearance. Although many doors the key fits have already been opened or broken down, possessing the key allows PCs to demonstrate their right to search the mansion and to be in possession of Londar's things.

Learah and her guards have a suite at The Red House, and she can be found at The White Boar Inn every evening. When she hears of adventurers in town, she sends a message to them asking for a meeting at one of those locations.

GM Note: Learah travels with some expensive jewelry and clothing, so her husband sent three bodyguards with her for protection. Her jewelry is easy to identify and extremely difficult for a thief to safely fence.

Learah Relight   **CR 1**
XP 400
Human sorcerer 2
CN Medium humanoid (human)
Init +2; **Senses** Perception +1
AC 13, touch 13, flat-footed 11 (+1 deflection, +2 Dex)
hp 14 (2d6+7)
Fort +3, **Ref** +2, **Will** +4
Speed 30 ft.
Melee mithral dagger +1 (1d4-1/19-20)
Bloodline Spell-Like Abilities (CL 2nd; concentration +5)
  6/day—touch of destiny (+1)
Sorcerer Spells Known (CL 2nd; concentration +5)
  1st (5/day)—mage armor, magic missile
  0 (at will)—detect magic, light, mending, prestidigitation, read magic
  Bloodline Destined
Str 8, **Dex** 14, **Con** 13, **Int** 10, **Wis** 12, **Cha** 17
Base Atk +1; **CMB** +0; **CMD** 13
Feats Eschew Materials, Great Fortitude, Toughness
Skills Knowledge (arcana) +5, Spellcraft +5, Use Magic Device +8
Languages Common
SQ bloodline arcana (gain luck bonus on saves when casting personal-range spells)
Other Gear mithral dagger, ring of protection +1, gold signet ring (worth 35 gp), ruby pendant on a gold chain (worth 450 gp)
Special Abilities
Bloodline Arcana: Destined (Ex) When you cast a Personal spell, gain a save bonus of its level for 1 round.
Touch of Destiny +1 (6/day) (Sp) As a standard action, touch grants +1 insight bonus to most rolls for 1 rd.

Alfguir K'Eliek

With an average height and weight and nondescript features, Alfguir blends into crowds quite easily when he wants to do so. His short dark hair has begun to gray at the temples, and a few wrinkles have etched their way into his rather bland face. Alfguir's brown eyes always seem to look away from anyone to whom he is speaking, darting around the room nervously as though he is searching for something. Age has slowed and weakened him, but he is still a formidable foe. Not many people know Alfguir very well — he appeared in town shortly after Londar's recent disappearance — but those who have met him in and around town found him to be polite, charming, and cultured.

Alfguir is a senior member of the thieves' guild, and he is the specific thief Londar hired to obtain a number of special items. Londar never paid him for his work, using his reputation and promises of new magic items to obtain "credit." Alfguir has an impeccable reputation and background as an honest merchant and is known to many other merchants and nobles. While his merchant business initially began as a cover story, he runs a true merchant house and does a great deal of legitimate business.

When meeting the PCs or discussing Londar with others, he claims that Londar owes him a great deal of money, and he has excellent forged documents created by a master forger specifically to legalize his claims against Londar. Now that Londar has disappeared, there is no way to prove that these documents are forgeries. Alfguir plays up the act of a wounded merchant who lost a huge amount of money and is searching for someone to help him recover at least some of his losses.

Alfguir claims that his documents allow him to legally send in "representatives" to claim some of Londar's wealth, a claim supported by the local mayor and guards but that Learah contests. Although greedy, Alfguir is content to receive as much money as he can get, offering a "finder's fee" to the PCs to hire them. If the PCs investigate Londar's disappearance on their own or work for someone else, Alfguir attempts to use his forged documents to lay claim to some of their spoils.

Alfguir avoids any risk of exposing his true business. He hired other thieves through the thieves' guild to recover some of the money and items he feels he is owed, but so far, they have either disappeared or failed. Rather than risking more members of the guild and possibly exposing his true business, Alfguir decided to turn to hiring adventurers to do his dirty work. Alfguir does not know that the first group of thieves sent to collect money from Londar fought with him or that Londar died as a result of being poisoned in that battle. This means that he can conceal his involvement in Londar's death even if exposed to truth spells or potions.

Alfguir is staying at The White Boar Inn and can be found dining there every day. He is willing to contact and meet adventurers any place in town and at any time. He keeps his initial contact open, "honest," and aboveboard.

Alfguir K'Eliek   **CR 8**
XP 4,800
Human unchained rogue 9
N Medium humanoid (human)
Init +8; **Senses** Perception +12
AC 22, touch 17, flat-footed 17 (+5 armor, +2 deflection, +4 Dex, +1 dodge)
hp 59 (9d8+18)
Fort +4, **Ref** +10, **Will** +3
Defensive Abilities danger sense +3, evasion, improved uncanny dodge
Speed 30 ft.
Melee +2 rapier +13/+8 (1d6+6/18-20)
Ranged +1 shortbow +11/+6 (1d6/×3)
Special Attacks sneak attack +5d6
Str 8, **Dex** 19, **Con** 12, **Int** 14, **Wis** 10, **Cha** 13
Base Atk +6; **CMB** +5; **CMD** 22
Feats Dodge, Improved Initiative, Manyshot, Point-Blank Shot, Precise Shot, Rapid Shot, Weapon Finesse, Weapon Focus (rapier)
Skills Acrobatics +16, Appraise +14, Bluff +13, Diplomacy +13, Disable Device +20, Intimidate +13, Knowledge (local) +14, Perception +12, Sense Motive +12, Sleight of Hand +16, Stealth +16
Languages Common, Dwarven, Elven
SQ debilitating injury: bewildered, debilitating injury: disoriented, debilitating injury: hampered, rogue talents (black market connections, coax information, esoteric scholar, weapon training), trapfinding +4
Other Gear +2 studded leather, +1 shortbow, +2 rapier, bag of holding i, ring of protection +2
Special Abilities
Debilitating Injury: Bewildered -2/-4 (Ex) Foe who takes sneak attack damage takes AC pen (more vs. striker) for 1 rd.
Debilitating Injury: Disoriented -2/-4 (Ex) Foe who takes sneak attack damage takes attack pen (more vs. striker) for 1 rd.
Debilitating Injury: Hampered (Ex) Foe who takes sneak attack damage has speed halved (and can't 5 ft step) for 1 rd.

Ander Fierk

Ander is a thin, dark-haired gentleman with an extremely pale complexion. His piercing black eyes and unblinking stare make some people nervous, while others find it comforting to know he is focused on what they are saying. Dark clothing highlights his pale skin, giving him an almost ghostly appearance that is enhanced by the magic cloak that billows behind him in perfectly still air. He carries a large travel bag containing spellbooks, spell components, and various other items that he is unwilling to let out of his sight. Ander is really the disavowed son of a major nobleman in a distant country. Ander has long-term plans of returning to his homeland with a small army, slaughtering his family, and carving out his own barony.

Several years ago, Londar and Ander discussed the creation of golems and other creatures out of stone. Letters Londar sent to Ander recently indicated he had found a method to create a stone creature that would be useful in battle. Based on prior agreements, Ander came to town to learn more. Londar's disappearance has triggered Ander's greed. Ander wants the spells he knows Londar created, as well as the methods to create his own army.

When Ander discovers the PCs are planning to investigate Londar's disappearance, he approaches them and offers a great deal of money for the ability to copy some of Londar's spells. He presents himself as a simple wizard in pursuit of knowledge and offers a few potions as a sign of goodwill. Ander's offers of wealth are quite false; he doesn't really have any money to offer the PCs. During his stay in Hampton Hill, he initiates conversations with Baron Kurell and eventually joins the baron, believing that is his best route to power. Ander has rented a small, private cottage to allow him to watch the PCs through scrying and spying to determine whether they have found Londar's spellbooks and papers.

Ander Fierk   **CR 8**
XP 4,800
Male human wizard 9
CE Medium humanoid (human)
Init +1; **Senses** Perception -1
AC 14, touch 12, flat-footed 13 (+2 armor, +1 deflection, +1 Dex)
hp 41 (9d6+9)
Fort +4, **Ref** +5, **Will** +6
Speed 30 ft.
Melee +2 dagger +8 (1d4+4/19-20)
Ranged mwk light crossbow +6 (1d8/19-20)
Special Attacks hand of the apprentice (7/day)
Wizard Spells Prepared (CL 9th; concentration +13)
  5th—dominate person (DC 19)
  4th—black tentacles, summon monster IV, summon monster IV
  3rd—fireball (DC 17), fireball (DC 17), fly, summon monster III
  2nd—fog cloud, invisibility, resist energy, shatter (DC 16), web (DC 16)
  1st—burning hands (DC 15), burning hands (DC 15), disguise self, mage armor, shield
  0 (at will)—daze (DC 14), detect magic, ghost sound (DC 14), read magic
Str 14, **Dex** 13, **Con** 10, **Int** 19, **Wis** 8, **Cha** 12
Base Atk +4; **CMB** +6; **CMD** 18
Feats Brew Potion, Combat Casting, Craft Wand, Craft Wondrous Item, Empower Spell, Maximize Spell, Quicken Spell, Scribe Scroll
Skills Appraise +16, Craft (alchemy) +16, Fly +13, Knowledge (arcana) +16, Knowledge (dungeoneering) +8, Knowledge (engineering) +8, Knowledge (geography) +8, Knowledge (history) +16, Knowledge (local) +8, Knowledge (nature) +8, Knowledge (nobility) +8, Knowledge (planes) +8, Knowledge (religion) +8, Linguistics +8, Spellcraft +16
Languages Abyssal, Celestial, Common, Draconic, Infernal, Sylvan
SQ arcane bond (masterwork light crossbow), metamagic mastery (1/day)
Combat Gear *potion of cat's grace, potion of cure light wounds, potion of invisibility, potion of invisibility, scroll of alter self (CL 9th), greater invisibility (CL 9th), summon monster iv (CL 9th), wand of fireball (CL 9th, 36 charges), wand of maximized magic missile (CL 9th, 18 charges), tanglefoot bag (2)*; **Other Gear** *+2 dagger,* crossbow bolts (20), mwk light crossbow, *bracers of armor +2, cloak of resistance +1, ring of protection +1,* ander fierk's spellbook, 121 gp, 97 sp, 78 cp
Special Abilities
Hand of the Apprentice (7/day) (Su) As a standard action, throw melee weapon (use Int instead of Dex) and instantly returns.
Metamagic Mastery (1/day) (Su) Spend 1 use per spell level increase to apply a known metamagic feat for free.

Baron Kurell

Baron Kurell is a tall, thin man with dark hair and extremely pale skin. He dresses in robes decorated with his coat-of-arms and pretends to be nothing more than a nobleman that has studied wizardry on the side. He keeps his devotion and worship of Orcus a tightly held secret, hoping to someday reveal his true faith. He is a meticulous man, in both his clothing and mannerisms, and is extremely cautious. He keeps his raging tirades and penchant for torture carefully hidden from all but his closest advisors. The baron made an agreement with Londar that he never intended to honor. Unfortunately, Londar's disappearance came a bit earlier than he originally planned. Rather than trying to hire the PCs directly, he throws his support behind Learah Relight's efforts to determine Londar's whereabouts. He mentions that his "dear friend" was researching a few items that some miners discovered near his home and is hoping nothing untoward happened to Londar or the items in his care. Acting as a family friend, despite never having met Learah, the baron encourages her to hire adventurers to search for Londar. The baron believes that adventurers motivated by profit are easier to control and deal with than guardsmen and hopes he can simply pay for or steal back the items he desires.

The baron makes use of *nondetection* spells when he is in public, knowing that he must conceal his true faith. While not terribly charismatic, he is a skilled diplomat and conceals his true motives extremely well. Enraged by recent changes to major trade paths by the young king now on the throne, the baron plans nothing less than a civil war designed to create his own kingdom and reassert his power and wealth through control of several different trade routes. Information received through visions granted him by Orcus helped him begin building a small army powered by several ancient relics. Added powers granted by *Horgrim's Pyramid* and *The White Eye* are all that he needs to tip the scales significantly in his favor.

GM Note: The baron has a suite in The Red House and is traveling with an advisor and three **guards**.

Baron Kurell   CR 11
XP 12,800
Human cleric of Orcus 6/necromancer (undead) 6
CE Medium humanoid (human)
Init +0; **Senses** Perception +4
AC 15, touch 11, flat-footed 15 (+3 armor, +1 deflection, +1 natural)
hp 66 (12 HD; 6d6+6d8+18)
Fort +10, **Ref** +6, **Will** +16
Speed 30 ft.
Melee +1 heavy mace +8/+3 (1d8)
Special Attacks channel negative energy 4/day (DC 14, 3d6)
Domain Spell-Like Abilities (CL 6th; concentration +10)
  7/day—bleeding touch (3 rounds), touch of evil (3 rounds)
Cleric Spells Prepared (CL 6th; concentration +10)
  3rd—animate dead[D], animate dead, bestow curse (DC 17), deeper darkness
  2nd—death knell[D] (DC 16), death knell (DC 16), desecrate, hold person (DC 16), resist energy
  1st—bane (DC 15), cause fear[D] (DC 15), divine favor, entropic shield, hide from undead (DC 15)
  0 (at will)—create water, light, purify food and drink (DC 14), resistance
  D Domain spell; Domains Death, Evil
Necromancer Spells Prepared (CL 6th; concentration +9)
  3rd—lightning bolt (DC 16), nondetection, tongues, vampiric touch
  2nd—detect thoughts (DC 15), ghoul touch (DC 15), invisibility, locate object, see invisibility
  1st—cause fear (DC 14), comprehend languages, hypnotism (DC 14), identify, magic missile
  0 (at will)—detect magic, prestidigitation, read magic, touch of fatigue (DC 13)
  Opposition Schools Conjuration, Transmutation
Str 8, **Dex** 10, **Con** 12, **Int** 16, **Wis** 18, **Cha** 13
Base Atk +7; **CMB** +6; **CMD** 17
Feats Brew Potion, Combat Casting, Craft Wand, Craft Wondrous Item, Leadership, Scribe Scroll, Secret Signs, Spell Mastery, Turn Undead, Weapon Focus (heavy mace)
Skills Appraise +18, Bluff +1 (+5 to pass secret signs), Diplomacy +16, Knowledge (arcana) +18, Knowledge (religion) +18, Sense Motive +19, Spellcraft +18
Languages Abyssal, Common, Infernal, Necronomus
SQ arcane bond (+1 heavy mace), bolster, power over undead
Combat Gear wand of lightning bolt (CL 6th, 20 charges), wand of summon monster iii (CL 6th, 20 charges); **Other Gear** +1 heavy mace, amulet of natural armor +1, bracers of armor +3, cloak of resistance +2, ring of protection +1, wizard spellbook

Special Abilities
Bleeding Touch (3 rounds, 7/day) (Sp) Melee touch attack deals 1d6 bleeding damage.
Bolster (+2, 3 rounds, 6/day) (Sp) As a standard action, touched undead gains desecrate spell benefits for duration.
Spell Mastery (ghoul touch, spectral hand, vampiric touch) You can prepare the chosen spells without a spellbook.
Touch of Evil (3 rounds, 7/day) (Sp) With a melee touch attack, target is sickened and counted as good-aligned for the purpose of [Evil] spells.

Town Officials in Hampton Hill

Strybyorn Arthand

Strybyorn was once a very successful merchant and businessman but he has now taken to being mayor as his only job. He is in good enough physical shape that, despite his gray hair and wrinkles, people usually estimate he is in his low 50s. Strybyorn is actually 67 years old and enjoys his peaceful, quiet life. A quiet, friendly nature and disarming smile have made him such a trusted mayor that any thoughts of replacing him were forgotten years ago. His position as mayor makes him the sole judge for adjudicating disputes and for criminal trials. Although friendly and kind, he strictly interprets the law and does not hesitate to throw anyone, even nobles, into the dungeon if the crime calls for it. He knows that Londar's carriage was found overturned along the Horrik Trade Path and that several other bodies were found with it but turns any further questioning over to **Hamra Ranthas**. Strybyorn has known **Learah Relight** since she was a child and has a very high opinion of her, and he has done completely legitimate business with **Alfguir K'Eliek** in the past. He recommends both people highly. He met **Ander Fierk** one evening and had a long conversation with him. While he doesn't understand why Ander is in town, he found him to be a pleasant enough person. PCs who speak to Strybyorn at length rapidly determine that he does his best to see only the best in people. His advanced age and years of traveling make him open to other people's differences.

Strybyorn Arthand CR 8
XP 4,800
hp 44 (Pathfinder Roleplaying Game GameMastery Guide, "Mayor")

Hamra Ranthas

Townspeople joke that Hamra is a soft-spoken woman with a big axe. Her soft voice is partly due to the large scars traveling down the side of her face and neck. The scars came in a battle with a large troll that invaded nearby forests. Standing well over 6-feet-tall and possessing dark black hair and eyes, she is a rather imposing figure. While she doesn't talk much, most of the townspeople find her presence quite calming.

Hamra and her deputies discovered Londar's overturned carriage and the body of his driver shortly after his disappearance. She is able to tell the PCs where the carriage was found and describe the additional bodies that were found there. Four of the thieves or kidnappers that attacked the carriage were clearly killed by fire or electrical spells of some sort, while a fifth appeared to have been killed by Londar's driver. Hamra originally believed that Londar was kidnapped but now suspects Londar somehow escaped. A week after the discovery, she and several village guards accompanied Learah Relight on a foray to the mansion where they found extensive looting. There was no sign of Londar, but "animated statues" and several deadly traps prevented a more thorough investigation. She finds the lack of a body or ransom note disturbing but believes that it is outside her duty to investigate any further because the accident was outside her territory and the search would reduce defenses for Hampton Hill. Furthermore, she believes further exploration of the tower is beyond the abilities of her guards and doesn't want to risk their life. To cut down on the looting, she has made it clear to all the merchants in town that possessing items taken from Londar's mansion would garner time in the dungeon.

While she actually likes **Learah Relight**, there are bad feelings between the two regarding Hamra's refusal to send guards out to search the mansion again. **Alfguir's** claims about Londar owing him money seem valid and not unreasonable based on the credit she has seen merchants and nobles extend to each other in the past. She knows that Baron Kurell is a baron from the northeast and knows nothing about Ander Fierk.

Hamra Ranthas CR 6
XP 2,400
hp 57 (Pathfinder Roleplaying Game GameMastery Guide, "Watch Captain")
Gear +1 greataxe

The Deputies: Anya, Ria, Mik, and Dane

As a whole, all the deputies are dedicated to their work. They are honest and respected throughout the town. They direct questions about various people in town to **Learah** or **Strybyorn**.

Anya, Ria, Mik, and Dane CR 1
XP 400
hp 16 (Pathfinder Roleplaying Game GameMastery Guide, "Caravan Guard")

Other Important Figures in Hampton Hill

Baeris Blackoak

Baeris is a thin half-elf with delicate features and light brown hair. She wears elegant blue and green silk shirts to highlight the pale green color of her eyes and usually wears black linen pants. Although her soft, musical voice and polite manner make her seem very unthreatening, she is rumored to have killed several men who threatened one of her daughters during a bar brawl. Baeris is extremely protective of her daughters and does her best to keep them away from adventurers and other seedy characters while directing them toward wealthy merchants and nobles. Baeris knows a great deal about the local politics of the area and has numerous stories about Londar and the firework displays Londar put on for the townspeople. Londar was a regular guest in the restaurant and usually had his guests stay in The White Boar Inn, so Baeris has only favorable comments about him. While Baeris knows that Learah Relight is Londar's niece and that Londar cared for her when her parents died, she knows very little else. Baeris has heard that Alfguir K'Eliek is an honest, trustworthy merchant and says this if asked about him. She briefly met Ander Fierk one evening and didn't like him, so any comments she makes about Ander are tainted by her own feelings and aren't based on any real knowledge of the wizard's background.

Baeris Blackoak CR ½
XP 200
hp 9 (Pathfinder Roleplaying Game NPC Codex, "Tavern Singer")

Viarik Kite

Viarik is a tall, heavyset man in his early 40s. Long, graying hair and droopy fat cheeks make him seem like a faithful hound. Brightly colored clothing and a loud voice shake that image, while his polite attitude toward his wealthy customers tends to reinforce it. Viarik loves gossip; in the years since his wife died, he has little else to enjoy. He knows a great deal about local politics, rumors, and gossip. Discussions with Viarik receive a +2 circumstance bonus on Diplomacy checks when gathering information about local affairs. Viarik's opinions and commentaries on anyone in town are easy to obtain, but not always very reliable. He avoids saying anything harmful about any potential clients, but merchants and nobles who own their own homes in the area are always fair game. Viarik is a bit of a coward and doesn't talk about ancient ruins, dungeons, or raiding parties because he is afraid it could bring bad luck.

Viarik Kite CR 1
XP 400
hp 13 (Pathfinder Roleplaying Game GameMastery Guide, "Shopkeep")

Kyrean Lane

Kyrean is a friendly, dark-haired woman that most people find pleasant and easy to deal with. She keeps her dark side well-hidden from those around her; even members of the thieves' guild haven't seen her cold rage. While working in her shop or wandering around town, she wears bright orange or red dresses, only changing into her armor and carrying her bow when she is "working."

Kyrean is the leader of the local thieves' guild but has deferred to Alfguir K'Eliek while he has been in town. Only she and a few members of her guild know Alfguir's true profession and reasons for being here. Kyrean has lost 2 members of her own guild, and 4 members of other guilds were hired to help Alfguir, so she is very hesitant about sending more guild members to Londar's mansion. If asked about Londar, or about Alfguir, she mentions what a fine gentleman Alfguir is and mentions rumors about Alfguir needing someone to help collect some of Londar's debts. Kyrean wisely uses Hampton Hill as a base to study wealthy visitors so they can be robbed later while they are traveling. She tries to keep thefts in and around town to a minimum to avoid frightening wealthy vacationers away.

Alfguir's quest for payment has been putting her, and some of her guild members, at risk of discovery, so she does her best to encourage adventurers to hire on with Alfguir. Any thefts by non-guild members that are carried out in town immediately incur her wrath and planned retaliation.

Kyrean Lane CR 10
XP 9,600
hp 60 (Pathfinder Roleplaying Game GameMastery Guide, "Guild Master")

Mara Lighthand

Mara weaves flowers into her long, pale brown hair as she braids it in a single plait down her back. Her clothing tends toward pale greens and browns contrasting sharply with her pale lavender eyes. A friendly, open nature and her constant ministering to the town's healing needs have made her a well-respected, openly loved member of the community. Mara met Londar several times and was taken in completely by his charming nature; she, like most villagers, believes something horrible has happened to him. She doesn't believe that Londar would ever default on a debt and has problems believing Alfguir K'Eliek's story. The fact that Londar missed Learah Relight's wedding makes her feel all the more sorry for his young niece. PCs known to be helping Learah find her uncle are given special treatment, free healing, and advice. Mara is very suspicious of Ander Fierk; she noticed him traveling toward Londar's mansion several times over the past weeks and believes he is up to no good. If Mara is not found at the shrine to Arn, she is probably wandering the town helping people or at The White Boar Inn for a good meal and some entertainment.

Mara Lighthand   CR 4
XP 1,200
Halfling cleric of Arn 5
NG Small humanoid (halfling)
Init +2; **Senses** Perception +5
AC 14, touch 14, flat-footed 12 (+1 deflection, +2 Dex, +1 size)
hp 38 (5d8+15)
Fort +7, **Ref** +6, **Will** +8; +2 vs. fear
Speed 20 ft.
Melee morningstar +4 (1d6)
Special Attacks channel positive energy 5/day (DC 12, 3d6)
Domain Spell-Like Abilities (CL 5th; concentration +8)
  6/day—rebuke death (1d4+2), touch of good (+2)
Cleric Spells Prepared (CL 5th; concentration +8)
  3rd—create food and water, magic circle against evil[D], remove curse
  2nd—aid, calm emotions (DC 15), cure moderate wounds[D], sound burst (DC 15)
  1st—bless water (DC 14), blessing of the watch, divine favor, protection from evil[D], shield of faith
  0 (at will)—create water, purify food and drink (DC 13), resistance, stabilize
  D Domain spell; Domains Good, Healing
Str 11, **Dex** 14, **Con** 14, **Int** 10, **Wis** 16, **Cha** 10
Base Atk +3; **CMB** +2; **CMD** 15
Feats Extra Channel, Lightning Reflexes, Lucky Halfling
Skills Acrobatics +4 (+0 to jump), Climb +2, Knowledge (religion) +8, Perception +5, Spellcraft +8; Racial Modifiers +2 Acrobatics, +2 Climb, +2 Perception
Languages Common, Halfling
Other Gear morningstar, ring of protection +1, 22 gp, 17 sp, 33 cp
Special Abilities
Lucky Halfling (1/day) Roll a save vs. an attack affecting an ally in 30 ft. They may use either result.
Rebuke Death (6/day) (Sp) As a standard action, touch heals 1d4+2 dam to negative HP target.
Touch of Good +2 (6/day) (Sp) Grant +2 to skill checks, ability checks and saving throws for 1 rd.

KHENDEN BRIGHTSUN

While she openly admits that "Brightsun" is a stage name, she has never given anyone a different name, so she is known throughout town simply as "Bright." Her golden hair, deep blue eyes, and lilting accent suggest she comes from much farther north, but nobody knows for certain. She wears dark blue and purple clothing trimmed in silver while working in the evenings at The White Boar Inn and brighter colors while walking through town during the day. Despite living in Hampton Hill for more than 3 years, she knows far more about the town, and its people, than anyone knows about her. She knows a great deal about local nobles, noble houses, merchants' guilds, and their backgrounds, but doesn't give up such information easily. Her experiences with Londar led her to believe he has a darker nature that he kept hidden from others. She speaks with Learah Relight regularly and thinks highly of her but has a very low opinion of Baron Kurell and is willing to say so. Comments she has overhead lead her to believe Alfguir is somehow involved with the thieves' guild but she doesn't know in what capacity, nor does she easily provide that information for fear of angering the guild.

Khenden Brightsun CR 4
XP 1,200
hp 31 (Pathfinder Roleplaying Game NPC Codex, "Court Poet")

XANTHAQUE

At more than 320 years old, Xanthaque (female elf **archmage**) has witnessed events now considered "history." Her studies carry this knowledge back through hundreds of years. Great age has faded her once golden hair to white but the few wrinkles she does have confine themselves to her hands and arms. Still a very attractive woman, many people in Hampton Hill are fond of her quiet personality and unobtrusive nature. Xanthaque has had bad experiences sharing her spellbooks in the past and is unlikely to be convinced to share them again, unless she has great reason to trust the wizard in question. On the other hand, she loves knowledge and is very focused on historical events and ancient books. Given a few days, she can interpret and analyze any ancient texts the PCs might come across.

Xanthaque did some work for Londar and has had many discussions with him. She suspects his disappearance might be linked to some ancient texts he recently discovered. Londar was very excited about these texts, but Xanthaque never had the opportunity to examine them. Xanthaque is one of the few people familiar with Londar's quest for power, something she is unlikely to mention because she considers it normal for a "young" wizard. If the PCs bring Xanthaque some of Londar's notes and books, she can explain the text dealing with *Horgrim's Pyramid* and informs the PCs that the white metallic sphere required to open it is called *The White Eye*. Her studies allow her to tell the PCs about the forgotten evil god Horgrim, his worshippers, and their destruction by forces dedicated to Arn, a minor god of the sun. She is able to tell the PCs that the only remaining temple to Horgrim is hidden in a hollow mountain known as "Arn's Mountain" after Arn's forces defeated Horgrim's followers. She can give a general location of the mountain, but with Londar's notes and maps she can give the PCs more precise directions. Londar's notes and her own texts describe *The White Eye* as having horrible evil powers, abilities that are enhanced magnified if combined with *Horgrim's Pyramid*.

Xanthaque   **CR 11**
XP 12,800
Female elf loremaster 5/wizard 7
LN Medium humanoid (elf)
Init +2; **Senses** low-light vision; Perception +4
AC 16, touch 14, flat-footed 14 (+2 armor, +2 deflection, +2 Dex)
hp 50 (12d6+8)
Fort +5, **Ref** +8, **Will** +12; +2 vs. enchantments
Immune sleep
Speed 30 ft.
Melee +2 dagger +6 (1d4+1/19-20)
Special Attacks hand of the apprentice (8/day)
Wizard Spells Prepared (CL 12th; concentration +17)
  6th—guards and wards, legend lore
  5th—contact other plane, dismissal (DC 20), dominate person (DC 20), wall of force
  4th—black tentacles, detect scrying, locate creature, scrying (DC 19)
  3rd—fireball (DC 18), shrink item (DC 18), summon monster III, tiny hut, tongues
  2nd—detect thoughts (DC 17), gust of wind (DC 17), locate object, resist energy, see invisibility
  1st—burning hands (DC 16), comprehend languages, grease, hypnotism (DC 16), identify, obscuring mist
  0 (at will)—detect magic, light, mending, read magic
Str 8, **Dex** 14, **Con** 8, **Int** 20, **Wis** 14, **Cha** 13
Base Atk +5; **CMB** +4; **CMD** 18
Feats Brew Potion, Craft Wand, Craft Wondrous Item, Scribe Scroll, Silent Spell, Skill Focus (Knowledge [history]), Still Spell, Toughness
Skills Appraise +12, Knowledge (arcana) +22, Knowledge (dungeoneering) +11, Knowledge (engineering) +11, Knowledge (geography) +11, Knowledge (history) +28, Knowledge (local) +22, Knowledge (nature) +11, Knowledge (nobility) +22, Knowledge (planes) +11, Knowledge (religion) +11, Linguistics +20, Perception +4, Spellcraft +20 (+22 to identify magic item properties), Use Magic Device +16; **Racial Modifiers** +2 Perception, +2 Spellcraft to identify magic item properties
Languages Abyssal, Aklo, Aquan, Auran, Celestial, Common, Draconic, Dwarven, Elder Thing, Elven, Gnome, Goblin, Halfling, Ignan, Infernal, Mi-go, Sylvan, Terran, Undercommon, Yithian
SQ arcane bond (+2 dagger), elven magic, lore, secrets (knowledge of avoidance, lore of true stamina, secrets of inner strength)
Other Gear +2 dagger, bracers of armor +2, ring of protection +2, wizard spellbook
Special Abilities
Hand of the Apprentice (8/day) (Su) As a standard action, throw melee weapon (use Int instead of Dex) and instantly returns.

Appendix B: New Monsters

Copper golem

Created much in the same manner as golems, copper golems are multi-limbed, insect-like guardians. These constructs are often used by temples to protect treasuries, holy sites, and other important locales. They are much more reliable than flesh golems and have the added bonus of adhering closer to many faiths' restrictions on the use of living flesh in magical works. They are also cheaper and easier to make than iron golems, while at the same time providing that certain luster that only a metal golem can.

Copper Golem CR 9
XP 6,400
N Large construct
Init -1; **Senses** darkvision 60 ft., low-light vision; Perception +0
AC 22, touch 8, flat-footed 22 (-1 Dex, +14 natural, -1 size)
hp 96 (12d10+30)
Fort +3 **Ref** +2 **Will** +3
Defensive Abilities DR 10/adamantine; **Immune** construct traits, magic
Speed 20 ft.
Melee 4 slams +17 (2d10+6+1d6 electricity)
Special Attacks Electrical conduction, electrical shock (3d6 electricity, DC16 Reflex for half)
Str 23, **Dex** 8, **Con** -, **Int** -, **Wis** 11, **Cha** 1
Base Atk +12; **CMB** +19; **CMD** 28
Languages none
Special Abilities

Electrical conduction (Su) A copper golem deals 1d6 points of electrical damage with a touch. Creatures attacking a copper golem with unarmed strikes, natural attacks or metal weapons take this same electrical damage each time one of their attacks hits.

Electrical shock (Su) A copper golem can release a bolt of electricity every 4 rounds for 3d6 damage, DC 16 Reflex save for half.
Immunity to magic (Ex) A copper golem is immune to spells or spell-like abilities that allow spell resistance. Certain spells & effects function differently against it as noted below:
A magical attack that deals fire or cold damage slows a copper golem (as the slow spell) for 2d6 rounds, with no saving throw.
A magical attack that deals electrical damage breaks any slow effect on the golem and heals 1 points of damage for each 3 points of damage the attack would otherwise deal. If the amount of dealing would cause the golem to exceed its full normal hit points, it gains any excess as temporary hit points. A copper golem gets no saving throw against attacks that deal electrical damage.

Dragon Statue

These rare constructs are made from the bones and scales of a slain adult or larger dragon. Animated by the same type of magic that creates golems, dragon statues are more of a thematic addition to any mad wizard's tower than a replacement for a more common golem. Calling upon the power and fury of the dragon.

Dragon Statue   CR 9
XP 6,400
N Small construct
Init +4; **Senses** blindsight 60 ft., darkvision 60 ft., low-light vision; Perception +0
AC 25, touch 15, flat-footed 21 (+4 Dex, +10 natural, +1 size)
hp 85 (14d10+10)
Fort +4, **Ref** +8, **Will** +4
DR 10/magic; **Immune** construct traits, acid, cold, fire; **Resist** electricity 30, sonic 30; **SR** 20
Speed 10 ft., fly 90 ft. (good)
Melee bite +27 (1d2+12), 2 claws +27 (1d3+12)
Special Attacks breath weapon 30 ft. cone; 2d6 sonic damage (DC 17 Fortitude negates deafness)
Str 34, **Dex** 18, **Con** —, **Int** —, **Wis** 10, **Cha** 10
Base Atk +14; **CMB** +25; **CMD** 39
Skills Acrobatics +4 (-4 to jump), Fly +10
Special Abilities
Breath Weapon (DC 17) (Su) 30 ft. cone; 2d6 sonic damage (DC 17 Fortitude negates deafness)

Appendix C: New Magic Items

Amulet of the Dark Sun

Aura strong necromancy; **CL** 20th; **Slot** neck; **Price** 2,000 gp

A symbol of those devoted to Horgrim, an ancient evil god of war and magic, these powerful amulets were used to identify the true faithful and often saw use as keys for some temples. Although the process used to create these relics is now lost, they possess enough power that evil wizards and clerics are willing to pay a high price for any functioning amulets due to the bonuses they give mindless undead. The amulets are made of a mysterious dark metal and engraved with symbols representing Horgrim. Raised markings and designs in gold highlight the engraved symbols and focus attention on them. Made in large batches when Horgrim's worshippers were powerful, most of them were lost and destroyed over the past few thousand years. Designed to weed out traitors and enforce loyalty, the evil power contained by one of these amulets varies depending upon who is wearing one. The evil aura is powerful enough to inflict 2d6 points of negative energy damage per round to any good-aligned character wearing one and 1d4 points of negative energy damage per round to any neutral-aligned character. Evil-aligned characters wearing an amulet suffer no penalties or damage, nor do they obtain any bonuses unless they swear fealty to Horgrim while wearing the amulet. Living evil creatures that swear allegiance to Horgrim have permanent *darkvision* while wearing the amulet and can cast *darkness* once per day. Mindless or free-willed undead that swear fealty to Horgrim gain +4 turn resistance while wearing an amulet and evil outsiders that pledge themselves to Horgrim gain a +8 circumstance on saving throws to resist *banishment* or *dismissal*.

Laws in some elven cities still carry a death sentence simply for possessing one of these amulets. The reasons behind those laws are forgotten to all but historians, but the risk of openly displaying such an amulet remains.

Arcanari

Aura -; **CL** -; **Slot** -; **Price** 8,000 gp

These twin books are always found together and are usually bound with heavy gold or silver covers. While not overtly magical, the detailed knowledge within them helps spellcasters of all types. Intensely studying both books, which takes at least one week per book, gives added insight into arcane magic and the art of casting spells. Individuals who take the time to perform such intensive study are rewarded with a+1 untyped bonus to Knowledge (Arcana) and Spellcraft checks. This benefit can be gained only once.

Iliachoam's Beasts and Saddles

Aura -; **CL** -; **Slot** -; **Price** 6,000 gp

Thick parchment pages are bound in a sturdy steel cover for preservation. This lengthy discussion of riding beasts and saddles provides many different hints and techniques for controlling animals while riding them. Unfortunately, the information doesn't mean much to anyone who doesn't already have some riding skill. Individuals who take the time to perform such intensive study who have at least 4 ranks in Ride are rewarded with a +2 circumstance bonus to Ride checks. This benefit can be gained only once.

Iliachoam's Trainer's Guide

Aura -; **CL** -; **Slot** -; **Price** 10,000 gp

Bound in dragon hide and magically preserved, this thick text gives detailed descriptions of various training methods for a wide variety of beasts. Descriptions of the various training techniques presumes a great deal of background knowledge; it is unlikely anyone other than a skilled animal trainer could garner much from this text. Individuals who take the time to perform such intensive study and have 8 ranks in Handle Animal are rewarded with a +2 circumstance bonus to Handle Animal checks. This benefit can be gained only once.

Instruments of the Vearlik

Aura -; **CL** -; **Slot**-; **Price** 7,000 gp

This heavily detailed description of flutes and whistles made by a strange tribe of mountain orcs is interesting only to the most dedicated bard. The book describes the creation of various flutes and how each design creates a different timbre or pitch. Individuals who take the time to perform such intensive study are rewarded with a +1 circumstance bonus to Perform (woodwinds) checks that increases to a +2 if a masterwork or magical flute is used. This benefit can be gained only once.

Jaerel's Jungle Guide

Aura -; **CL** -; **Slot**-; **Price** 7,000 gp

This odd book is bound with, and written on, jungle leaves magically preserved and protected. The detailed descriptions of jungle plants and creatures within might be somewhat outdated, but the information is presented in a straightforward, albeit dry, manner. Individuals who take the time to perform such intensive study and have 4 ranks in Survival are with a +2 circumstance bonus to Survival checks made in jungles. This benefit can be gained only once.

Rainbow Bracers

Aura moderate conjuration; **CL** 7th; **Slot** wrists; **Price** 8,000 gp; **Weight** 1 lb.

Swirls of color move slowly across the surface of these strange silver bracers. The bracers are imbued with enough magic that they glow faintly in the darkness. In addition to granting a +2 armor bonus to AC, the wearer can cast *mage armor* once per day with a duration of 10 hours. Unlike the standard spell, the *mage armor* called forth is visible as a faint, translucent swirl of color surrounding the wearer's body.

CONSTRUCTION REQUIREMENTS

Craft Wondrous Item, *mage armor*; **Cost** 4,000 gp

Rainbow Crossbow

Price 18,335 gp; **Slot** none **CL** 9th **Weight** 9 lbs.; **Aura** strong conjuration

The wooden stock of this light crossbow has been painted with boldly colored stripes that somehow extend to the steel portions of the crossbow. This crossbow functions like a *+2 light crossbow* that fires bolts cloaked in colored light. Regardless of color, the bolts do an additional 1d6 points of damage to all forms of undead. Colored bolts do no additional damage to normal living creatures.

CONSTRUCTION REQUIREMENTS

Cost 9,335 gp; **Feats** Craft Magic Arms and Armor; **Spells** *Heal*

Rainbow Ring

Aura moderate conjuration; **CL** 9th; **Slot** ring; **Price** 12,000 gp; **Weight** —

This special ring is one of Londar Brightrain's special creations. At first glance, the twisted silver ring appears to be tarnished, but a closer inspection reveals that the strange rainbow hues are part of its natural color. Anyone wearing the ring instinctively realizes that they can call into existence a *rainbow staff* as per the spell created by Londar. Summoning the staff requires only the will of the caster and is a free action, but this can be accomplished only three times each day. Once conjured, the staff lasts for 10 minutes before disappearing. Although the wielder must be proficient with a staff, each attack with the staff is made with as a touch attack, and causes 1d6 bludgeoning damage plus additional damage based on the accompanying table.

Caster Level: 9th. *Prerequisites*: Forge Ring, *rainbow staff*. *Market Price*: 12,000 gp.

1d8	Color	Result
1–2	Red	3d4 fire damage
3	Orange	2d8 acid damage
4	Yellow	Target slowed as per the *slow* spell for 2 rounds (DC 15 Will save negates)
5	Green	poisoned; 1d4 Con damage; 1/round for 2 rounds (DC 15 Fort save negates)
6	Blue	3d6 electricity damage
7	Indigo	Target gains the stunned condition for 1d4 rounds (DC 15 Will save negates)
8	Violet	2d8 sonic damage

Note that the wielder cannot determine what type of energy is expended on a particular blow, so creatures with immunities may be unaffected or even healed by some attacks.

Special Items and Relics

The following items are hidden in Londar's Library or the Treasure Chamber of Horgrim's Temple. *Horgrim's Pyramid* and *The White Eye* are evil items that need to be hidden or destroyed before they can be abused by evil creatures.

Decaying Book

This ancient book is bound with worn leather and is so old that the markings on the spine and covers have been almost completely worn off. It is written in an arcane language so ancient that only an avid historian would have a chance of deciphering it with a successful DC 35 Knowledge (History) check. Pictures in the book show clear representations of *Horgrim's Pyramid*, *Korik's Ruby*, and *The White Eye*. If interpreted, the book describes how to activate the pyramid using *The White Eye* and *Korik's Ruby* to create an area of darkness with a one-mile radius that quenches all normal and magical daylight. Pages describing the pyramid's origins and the process used to create it are worn and torn to the point of being incomprehensible.

Horgrim's Pyramid

This strange gold and silver pyramid has several interlocking layers that can be turned around a central axis. Runes along the sides hint at great power, and the pyramid glows with a variety of different magics when studied with *detect magic*, but there is no hint as to what the pyramid actually does. Knowledge gathered from the *Decaying Book* allows one to open the pyramid by placing *The White Eye* in a depression at its base. Once opened, a large, multifaceted ruby must be placed in a precise location inside the pyramid. Once these actions are complete, the pyramid reveals its powers to the person holding it if they are evil or gives them a powerful shock if they are not.

Once activated, the pyramid gives any evil creature holding it the power to create a magical darkness with a radius of 2 miles. Within this area, all *light* spells and light sources are half as effective, and all sunlight and daylight damage effects against undead are nullified. It also grants the possessor the power to use *control undead* on up to 100 HD worth of undead within a 1000-foot radius. In addition to these powers, the wielder can use the following spells 1/day as a 20th-level spellcaster: *animate dead, circle of doom, create undead, create greater undead* and *disintegrate*. Holding or using *The White Eye* at the same time as *Horgrim's Pyramid* doubles the range and power of these effects. Using the pyramid exacts a price: The first day of use results in the loss of body hair and makes the subject sensitive to sunlight (-2 on ability checks, savings throws, attack rolls, and damage rolls in direct sunlight). Continued use ages the subject one day for every hour of use. There is no saving throw against these effects and no way to reverse the aging.

Good characters who attempt to activate the pyramid must succeed at a DC 20 Fort saving throw or suffer 2 negative levels (8d6 negative energy damage on a successful save). Neutral characters who try to activate the pyramid must make the same saving throw or suffer 8d6 negative energy damage (half damage on a successful save).

Korik's Ruby

This large ruby has hundreds of carefully cut facets that focus light shined through the gem into a tight dot several feet away. The ruby is not magical but happens to be the original ruby created for use in *Horgrim's Pyramid*. It was stolen from a popular merchant house in Bard's Gate.

The White Eye

A powerful and deadly relic on its own, *The White Eye* is required to open and activate *Horgrim's Pyramid*. Stored in a hidden temple for thousands of years, there is no exact record of all the powers this item possesses. Made of a strange white metal, it is oblong and the shape and size of a human eye. Glowing runes and strange symbols cover its surface as a mere hint of its evil power. Any good or neutral being within 5 feet of the stone senses its evil emanations without the aid of any magic.

The intelligent item (Int 18, Wis 7, Cha 19; Ego 22; Communication: telepathy; senses: hearing and darkvision out to 120 ft.; AL LE) treats anything that is not evil with disdain, spite, and hatred. Its sole purpose is to destroy good and spread evil, and it considers the creatures that "wield" it simply to be tools to use. Any nonevil creature touching the eye suffers 8d6 negative energy damage with no saving throw allowed.

The eye can be used only by an evil humanoid and has two levels of use. The first level of use is where it is simply held in one's hand. At this level of use, the eye grants the user the ability to cast *animate dead, darkvision, detect good,* or *desecrate* at will. When used at this level, the eye attempts to influence the user (a successful DC 15 Will save to ignore) and convince them to tear out their own eye and use it as a replacement. Anyone bold — or foolish — enough to do so unlocks all the eye's powers and receives the following additional benefits: permanent *darkvision* and *detect good*, and the ability to cast the following spells at will: *detect secret doors, find traps, true seeing,* 2/day; *stoneskin,* 1/day; *haste, globe of invulnerability,* and grants Combat Reflexes and Improved Initiative as bonus feats. Using the eye in this manner results in a constant battle for control (DC 22 Will save each day), with the eye assuming complete control of the creature's body when it finally wins.

Appendix D: New Spells

Etch Stone

School transmutation; **Level** sorcerer/wizard 1

CASTING
Casting Time 1 standard action
Components V, S
EFFECT
Range touch
Target stone or stone object
Duration one hour
Saving Throw no; **Spell Resistance** no

DESCRIPTION

You can magically inscribe messages or text in the target stone using an ordinary quill for one hour after casting this spell. Any type of message, design, or rune created with the quill is permanently inscribed in the stone for anyone to see. Combining additional spells with an *etch stone* spell allows the caster to inscribe hidden or magical messages on simple stone walls. Scrolls or spellbooks can be created in stone if someone were willing to take all the extra time and expense.

Rainbow Spear

School conjuration (creation); **Level** sorcerer/wizard 4

CASTING
Casting Time 1 standard action
Components V, S
EFFECT
Range close
Target one creature
Duration see text
Saving Throw see text; **Spell Resistance** yes

DESCRIPTION

You focus energy to create a spear of a specific color and effect that is thrown as a ranged touch attack. The caster must choose what color to make the spear with each color having a different special effect. The caster can create 1 spear for every 5 caster levels they possess, but can only throw one a turn. Spears must be used within 10 rounds of their creation and can be touched only by the caster. These spears are very useful against targets that have specific weaknesses known by the caster. A successful hit inflicts 1d6 piercing damage plus the following special effects:

Color	Effect
Red	1d4+1/caster level (max 20) fire damage (Reflex save for half)
Orange	1d8+1/2 caster levels (max 10) acid damage
Yellow	Target is slowed as per the *slow* spell (Will save negates)
Green	poisoned; 1d6 Con damage (Fort save negates)
Blue	1d4+1/caster level (max 20) electricity damage (Reflex save for half)
Indigo	Target gains the stunned condition for 1d4 rounds (Will save negates)
Violet	1d8+1/2 caster levels (max 10) sonic damage

Rainbow Staff

School conjuration (creation); **Level** sorcerer/wizard 5

CASTING
Casting Time 1 standard action
Components V, S
EFFECT
Range personal
Target self
Duration 1 min./level
Saving Throw see text; **Spell Resistance** yes

DESCRIPTION

You conjure a shimmering rainbow-colored staff of energy. While the staff does not last long, it is an excellent melee weapon for the wizard unlucky enough to find themselves toe-to-toe with their foes. Although the caster must be proficient with a staff, each attack with the staff is made as a touch attack and does 1d6 bludgeoning damage along with damage based on the following table:

1d8	Color	Result
1–2	Red	3d4 fire damage
3	Orange	2d8 acid damage
4	Yellow	Target slowed as per the *slow* spell for 2 rounds (Will save negates)
5	Green	poisoned; 1d4 Con damage; 1/round for 2 rounds (Fort save negates)
6	Blue	3d6 electricity damage
7	Indigo	Target gains the stunned condition for 1d4 rounds (Will save negates)
8	Violet	2d8 sonic damage

Note that the caster cannot determine what type of energy is expended on a particular blow so creatures with immunities may be unaffected or even healed by some attacks.

Teleport Other

School conjuration (teleportation); **Level** sorcerer/wizard 9

CASTING
Casting Time 1 standard action
Components V, S
EFFECT
Range close
Target creature
Duration instantaneous
Saving Throw Will negates; **Spell Resistance** yes

DESCRIPTION

You direct magical energies at any target size large or smaller within 30 feet to teleport the target to a specific location. The targets must succeed at a Wisdom save or be teleported. The caster must be very familiar with the teleport destination. Any attempt to teleport a target into a solid object, underwater, or a location not firmly known to the caster results in automatic failure. While this spell can't be used to directly injure a target, it can certainly remove a specific victim from battle. Londar Brightrain created the spell to trap a wide variety of creatures for experiments performed in the caverns beneath his mansion.

NECROMANCER
Games™